A Husband for Hire

A Regency Romance

By

Patricia A. Knight

www.trollriverpub.com
A Husband for Hire
The Heirs & Spares Series (Book 1)
Copyright © 2018 Patricia A. Knight
ISBN: 978-1-946454-44-7

Join the fun with Author Patricia A. Knight for giveaways, updates and new release opportunities at: http://eepurl.com/dcJVCn

Other books by Patricia A. Knight:

<u>Verdantia Series</u>

Hers to Command

Hers to Choose

Hers to Cherish

Hers to Claim

Hers to Captivate

<u>Stand Alones</u>
Adam's Christmas Eve

Undertow

Dedication

This one's for you, Mom.
You always wanted me to write a Regency.

Thank you to

A huge *Thank You* to **Marilyn Lakewood** who read every word of this in rough draft about twenty times, brainstormed the ending with me and is the best cheerleader an author could want. Heartfelt thanks to **Elizabeth SaFleur** who rearranged the opening line to the betterment of this story and to **Carol McKibben**, **Kris Michaels** and **Rachel DeLune** who read the first sex scene (and many other scenes for that matter) and gave it a gold star. And finally, kisses, kisses, to **Stephanie McKibben** who hates flashbacks! So there aren't any. Ha! A huge **"Muwah"** to Kira, Diane, and Racheal for being great betas!

Thanks most especially to Georgette Heyer, the Queen of Regency, whose witty banter and charming men captured my fourteen-year-old heart and started a love affair with historical romance that has never left me. I hope you reign in heaven.

Finally, thank you to my wonderful editor, **Josephine Henke**, who rescues me from homonyms, fights the good fight against a plethora of adverbs, keeps the continuity flowing and wrangles all my commas into the right places. I promise I'll get better. You have a thankless job if ever there was one.

Chapter One

London, late February 1814

"These are the best marital prospects you can discover? In *all* of London?"

The Lady Eleanor Constance Russell, sole offspring of The Right Honorable Earl of Rutledge and The Right Honorable Countess of Rutledge slapped the sheet of paper she'd been reading down on top of the mahogany desk and bestowed on her London barrister the look of a woman at her wit's end. Grief for her dying parents and a sense of utter desperation had driven her to actions she considered borderline insanity. If she accepted any of the names on this list, she might as well rent rooms in Bedlam. Eleanor fought the hysteria surging in her breast and tried for a more cajoling tone. "Surely you can come up with more worthy candidates?"

The barrister who had served her family for the last forty years sat immobile in his great chair, hunkered down behind his great desk, his hands steepled in front of his narrow-lipped mouth. "This was no small task you set before me, Lady Russell. We are at war with France. Many of our most eligible men fill our army and navy."

Her troubled gaze swung outward. Outside the windows of Elsington & Elsington, the London hansom cabs clopped past in the traffic-clogged street. Everyone had business to conduct it seemed. With a heavy sigh, she returned to the issue that had torn her away from the bedside of her failing but beloved parents and the celebrated stud farm into which she'd poured twenty-plus years of her life.

Her eyes flicked to the sheet in front of her, and she jabbed at it with an index finger. "Sir Clive Wellery. Fifty-six years of age, just interred his fourth wife, has no property of worth, eleven dependents ranging in age from two months to twenty-two years, known for a propensity to overindulge in spirits and gambling, currently renting a six-bedroom house in Bloomsbury." She shuddered and whispered, "Eleven children." Her eyes rose and gazed at the gentleman across the desk from her then dropped back to the paper.

"Lord Hilary Vance. Sixty-four years of age, of no property or spouse. No dependents, an unfortunate victim of the 'China disease.'" She cleared her throat. "I understand there is no opium den he does not frequent."

The barrister sat motionless in his chair and gave her a disapproving frown. She rolled her eyes. "I am thirty-years-old, sir. I'm not an ignorant debutante."

"I disapprove of your unorthodox education, Ma'am. It did you a great disservice, and so I told your father."

You old fusspot. Eleanor swallowed her retort and returned her gaze to the page on the desk. "And then there is Sir Aubrey Dedham... really, Mr. Elsington? Really?

The fellow lives at the molly houses." She frowned as her barrister stirred awkwardly in his high-backed chair. "Did you think I didn't know the meaning of the term? How am I supposed to persuade a sodomite into marriage with a woman when he is not inclined toward women in the first place?" She scowled. "Though perhaps my possessing no feminine attributes is a recommendation."

"Lady Russell, please…"

Eleanor held up a gloved hand. "Stop. I know what you are going to say. £30,000 will make any man blind. And this last entry." She sighed and relaxed her upright spine for one moment before resuming her erect posture and folding her hands in her lap. "This last marital candidate." She could feel the heat climb her neck into her cheeks at the thought of a man that elegant ever giving *her* a second look and if he did… she'd probably turn and flee.

"The Lord Miles Everleigh, twenty-five, the third of four sons, whose eldest brother is the new Duke of Chelsony. I understand Lord Miles lives on the charity of "friends" in return for his convivial companionship and educated guidance on the purchase of fine bloodstock. What could induce…"

She closed her eyes and fought back the tears that threatened. How had she come to this? Was she going to go through with an action that in her more rational moments caused her to lose the contents of her stomach? In short, yes. The alternative was even more appalling.

One thought of the manor house with its 100,000 acres of attached properties and villages all peopled with men and women who relied on her family for their livelihood... the thought of all this reverting to the Crown because of some quirk in the laws of primogeniture? Accompanying the loss would be the upheaval and complete displacement of the lovely Thoroughbred mares and stallions of impeccable breeding whose pedigrees she could recite to the nth generation and all their offspring, in short, the entire racing stud she'd helped her father make so fabulously successful. Well, it was enough to make anyone cry.

Despite having three torturous seasons on the marriage mart ten years ago, no *eligible* man—there'd been numerous made ineligible by virtue of being unacceptable to her parents or unacceptable to *her*—had stepped forward with an offer to make her his wife. All the wealth and property she would bring with her was insufficient incentive to overcome her plain features, awkward deportment and utter lack of the slightest feminine attribute, so… she'd have to buy a husband—and soon. With no male heir, upon the death of her father, the estate, and all its entailed properties would be subject to the peregrinations of escheat.

"Mr. Elsington…please. What could possibly recommend me to Lord Miles Everleigh? Even rusticating as I have been, I hear the on-dits about the ever-so-handsome and sophisticated Lord Miles Everleigh. There will always be other options for a man like this, much better options than a gawky plank of an ape-leader with shriveled social skills who reeks of the stables and is his senior by five years."

The man across from her cleared his throat. "My lady…if I may be allowed…" He looked over his pince-nez. "The marriage agreement that you have required me to draw up demands a gentleman of a certain …" He shifted uncomfortably. "Ah…"

"Let me assist you. The word you want is desperation. It wants a gentleman who has reached a point of desperation. Well, Mr. Elsington, find more candidates. This week. I'm running out of time."

"Err, yes, Lady Russell. Quite." His eyes softened. "How is your father, my lady?"

Eleanor dropped her eyes and fought for composure until she was sure she could speak without succumbing to tears. "The physicians tell me, '*at most a few months*'. He could go at any time."

"My sincere regrets, ma'am. Lord Rutledge is a fine gentleman."

With a murmur of thanks, she inhaled and rose to her full height. Mr. Elsington was not a short man, but as he stood to escort her out, she topped him by a full head, reminding her yet again of her abysmal lack of any physical feature possessed by an even a moderately desirable woman. She hardened her jaw as she marched out of the law offices to her waiting carriage. There was no point in dwelling on a source of immense hurt that her adoring parents and formidable fortune hadn't protected her from, nor the reasons for her present desperate action. She decided on the instant to go to the one place in all of London where she'd always felt at home regardless of the strictures of polite society and Richard Tattersal's distinct lack of welcome for those of her sex.

"Take me to Tattersalls, John. They have advertised some young breeding stock I want to inspect. We need some outside lines to cross on Dare To Dream."

"Yes, your ladyship." With a tip of his beaver brim, he helped her into the carriage and climbed onto the box. At John Coachman's instruction, the groom stepped away from the leaders, sprang to the back of the carriage and the team of beautifully matched bays stepped smartly away.

The Lord Miles Wrotham Everleigh and his companion, The Right Honorable Reginald Eugene Beechworth, Baron of Stanton, "Reggie" or simply "Stanton" to his close friends, tipped their hats and bowed to two smiling matrons and their wide-eyed daughters who trailed their mamas like ducklings—if ducklings were prone to giggle. At mid-day, shoppers jammed the high street shops of London's Burlington Arcade.

"That Lady Beatrice Alderdice is a lovely item and young enough to be entirely amenable to be shaped to the wishes of a husband." Reggie grinned at Miles. "It's said she's to have £5,000 a year. That sum would keep you in a good supply of fine cattle."

Miles summoned a smile and injected a carefree note in his voice that did not conform to his current inward disposition, but then a penniless gentleman reliant upon the good graces of his friends didn't have the luxury of expressing his true feelings. He must be all things amiable at all times. "Ah, Stanton…you know as well as I, it's not the young ladies I must navigate to acquire a wife…it's their mamas and papas—and no parent worthy of the name would allow me to grace their doorstep—no matter my lineage. Besides, the young lady in question is only fifteen. She's barely out of the schoolroom."

"But if they only knew you, Miles, surely…"

"Ha! That's the thing, you see. They do know me. They know I have nothing to offer their daughters other than the clothes I stand up in."

Both men paused in their stroll to tip their hats at another well-dressed woman of their acquaintance.

"Fiend take it! Miles, you're dashed handsome and well-spoken; you're well-bred, connected to all the right people. Everyone likes you. You're the best friend a man could ask for, and you're—"

"Poor." He laughed. "I haven't a sixpence to scratch with, Stanton, and no expectations. There's no getting over this heavy ground lightly. I'm the third son who lives on his wits and twenty-five pounds a month. No recommendation when setting up a household." He glanced at his friend and chuckled. "Even if *you* think I'm a nonpareil."

His friend sighed. "Well, you have a home with me for as long as you wish it. Mary adores you and...well..." Reggie cleared his throat awkwardly. "You know how I feel about you."

"You're very kind." Miles consulted his pocket watch. "We'd better be off to Tattersalls, or we're going to miss the auction on that hunter you wanted me to look at." At the change of subject, Baron Stanton's face held an expression of relief that Miles found comical though he secretly sympathized. He was no lover of spouting on about his emotions, either.

Eleanor glanced around the courtyard at Tattersalls and noted the auction on heavy hunters had just finished. Her presence at the male bastion of horseflesh drew many disapproving eyes from the gentlemen, but she didn't care. Her groom accompanied her, so propriety was satisfied. She was here on business—not some frivolous passing of time. Her money spent every bit as well as theirs.

The young breeding stock should be up next. Though she was not in the market for a hunter, a particularly prime specimen caught her eye, as did the two handsome men that remained to examine the bay gelding. She wandered over to secure a place in the front of the coming auction, her groom trailing at a discreet distance, and she couldn't help but overhear their conversation.

"Stanton, I'm sure he will be up to your weight and give you many years of good use."

"You're certain he is better than the chestnut, then? Miles, I had my heart set on that fellow."

The other gentlemen chuckled and shook his head. "Reg, the chestnut is a flash horse with his blond mane and tail and those four white stockings, but his legs lack the necessary bone for a hunter carrying a man's weight. He might make a hack for Mary. I promise you…" He leaned over and gave the solid bay horse a fond pat. "This sweet goer will serve you far better though he be dressed in plain clothing. He won't leave you riding shanks mare home from the hunting field."

Eleanor eyed the "plainly dressed" horse in question and thought him not plain at all. While it was true his coloration was of the most common, the animal's build was anything but. He was an example of the best of breeding to purpose. His sturdy, straight, unblemished legs guaranteed whoever rode him out in the morning to hunt would not trudge home on foot in the evening, leading a lame horse. She thought 'Stanton' had received excellent advice, and she watched as a stable boy appeared and led the gelding away. The two men lingered, and she thoughtfully studied what she could see of them. There was something familiar about the taller man, but without a better look, it was difficult to say who he was.

"What do you think, Miles? Shall we stay and see what breeding stock is up next? I wouldn't mind something to send down to the home farm to breed to that old stud Lord Exeter is standing."

"I'm at your disposal, sir. My time is your time."

The elegantly attired gentleman addressed as 'Miles' turned slightly and glanced at her. When she made eye contact with him and nodded, he gave her a quizzical look before a pleasant smile crossed his outrageously handsome face, and he tipped his hat politely. He turned to his friend and must have said something, for the man he was with raised his head and glanced at her, but dismissed her. It was a reaction she was all too familiar with. She was mature, not a beauty and far too tall to appeal to a gentleman's eye. Eleanor drew back, ducking behind another patron. While it was obvious the taller gentleman did not remember her, she did recognize him. *Lord Miles Everleigh.* There were not many men of his height nor breadth of shoulder. Indeed, nature had not scrimped anywhere on Lord Miles. Even she, with her utter disdain for the male sex, had no difficulty whatsoever recalling every detail surrounding her first glimpse of the man.

A conversation of many months ago with a dear childhood friend, now a dashing widow of independent means, came to mind, and color rose in Eleanor's cheeks. Normally she'd find the hours spent selecting and buying a young broodmare a delightful occupation that would consume all her attention, but with the burning issue of finding a suitable marital candidate and the image of the striking Lord Everleigh fresh in her mind, perhaps reconnecting with her old friend was a more… profitable… way to spend her time.

"Eleanor, what a delightful surprise! I had no idea you were in London." The Honorable Lady Florence Lloyd-Smythe entered the elegant parlor of her London residence in a waft of attar of rose and a swish of fine linen and lace.

Eleanor placed her teacup on the saucer in her lap then set both on a low table and rose to meet her friend. "Florence, I've missed you terribly."

"That's your fault, dearest. I've asked you to town often enough." The young widow wrapped Eleanor in a brief hug before she stepped back and motioned to the love seat. "Please sit. We have so much to catch up on." She sank down beside Eleanor. "Oh, fabulous, Cook sent up tea and some of her biscuits and lemon cakes." Florence laughed and patted her stomach. "I must restrict myself to bread and water one of these days, or I won't fit into my new gowns." She grinned at Eleanor and helped herself to a liberal portion of the treats.

Eleanor eyed her with poorly concealed annoyance. "Florence, you look as beautiful as ever. I wish I had some of your curves."

Florence brought her teacup to her lips and sipped as she examined Eleanor from the tips of her toes to the top of her head. "Dear girl, there isn't a thing in the world wrong with you that a good modiste and mantilla maker couldn't cure. You must let me dress you. But I won't belabor the issue. You've heard all my lectures." She smiled. "What brings you to town?" Florence put her teacup and saucer on her lap, her face suddenly serious. "Is it your father?"

Eleanor shook her head. "No, thankfully, not yet... but it is something to do with him, yes." She placed her tea on the low table and fiddled with her gloves. "You remember I told you about the issue with the inheritance?"

"Yes. Last I knew, you and your family's solicitors were beating the bushes for any sort of male relation, no matter how tenuous." She frowned. "I take it you had no success?"

Eleanor slumped and shook her head. "None whatsoever."

"Oh…that's very bad." Florence put her tea on the table and reached for one of Eleanor's hands. "My dear…the Crown will take everything?"

Eleanor nodded miserably. "All but the properties in freehold. I should have to rebuild from the ground up. It will almost certainly mean the selling of many of my horses."

"And there is nothing you can do?"

Eleanor raised her gaze to Florence and held the woman's brown eyes steadily. "I was at *point non plus*, Flo… I instructed our family's barrister to produce a list of marital candidates."

"You are going to get married?"

"Yes. Somewhat married. Temporarily, that is. Well, the marriage will be permanent, just not the husband."

"What?" Florence pulled her hand back and straightened. "You are going to marry and then get rid of your new groom? Eleanor! I believe there are laws that prohibit that sort of thing—much as one might wish there weren't." Florence tapped her upper lip thoughtfully. "Well… I suppose if you didn't get caught."

Eleanor snorted and rolled her eyes. "Not get rid of him as in *killing* him. Just… send him on his way with £30,000 cash and a generous annuity that is dependent upon his never interfering with my administration of

Rutledge. Elsington has a petition drawn up to ask Parliament to allow my first-born male child to inherit the entail. He feels there is an excellent chance the House of Lords will grant it as my father is highly placed, well respected, and his unfortunate circumstances viewed with sympathy." Eleanor squirmed in her seat and examined her shoes. "I know it sounds very disreputable, but my barrister assures me that all the loose ends are tied up in a contract that is unassailable and completely legal. I just need someone desperate enough to sign such a machination... a someone who is acceptable to *me*. The marriage will be announced publically, and I must have cooperation from Father as the petition is in his name..." Eleanor cleared her throat and shifted on the sofa, "...so it must not be a hideous *mésalliance*."

"To risk all on a decision from the House of Lords, my dear? Is that the best solution available?"

"Finding an accommodating male to be my husband and getting an 'Act of Lords' is my only solution, Florence." Eleanor held back from her friend the disclosure of an additional codicil to the marriage agreement that restrained said husband from setting foot on the Rutledge estate unless requested. She also didn't share with Lady Florence that she had decided, over the heated objections of Penwick Elsington, this marriage would be in name only. After the debacle of her coming out many years ago, she couldn't face justifying her present actions to her dearest friend. She didn't have the courage to explain, for it would mean dragging out all those old and profoundly deep hurts and confessing them to Florence. If successful, her current actions would secure Rutledge for her lifetime. That had to be enough.

"And have you broached the subject of such a petition with the Earl?"

Eleanor studied the fleur-de-lis on the wallpaper and wondered at Florence's bravery in decorating with something so French when England was engaged in full-scale war with Napoleon. "When did you put up new wall coverings?"

"They aren't new. You just never noticed before. Don't change the subject, Eleanor."

Eleanor sighed. "Years ago, Father and I discussed such a possibility at some length, but that was before I told him I didn't have the heart to endure another season. He never mentioned it again. I think he and Mother have accepted that I will never marry; the family line will end, and Rutledge will revert to the Crown. I hope my marriage will come as welcome news." Picking up her teacup, she sipped slowly, aware that Florence observed her keenly. "I just need to find a husband for hire…so to speak."

"And have you? Found someone?"

Eleanor's stomach flipped over, and she wished she hadn't had that second piece of lemon cake. "Ah… well… the thing is yes, yes, I've found someone." She swallowed heavily. "I think."

Florence leaned back with a delighted laugh. "Do I know him? Is he well-favored?"

"Oh… Florence." Eleanor slumped further into the sofa and hunched over, supporting her forehead on her hand. "Tell me, did you ever further your acquaintance with Lord Miles Everleigh? I recall you had expressed a desire to do so at one time."

"Lord Miles—? You are considering Lord Miles Everleigh as the potential father for your heir?" Her friend abruptly went silent then her soft chuckle filled the parlor.

"Oh, my very *dear*, Eleanor, I am definitely taking you to a new modiste."

Eleanor simply moaned.

"Lord Miles." Lady Florence savored his name as if it were a delicious confection. "I cannot strike from memory that day in Hyde Park when you asked about his *horse* of all things." She shook her head, her eyes alight with bemusement. "Trust only you, Eleanor, to see the prime 'un with four legs while ignoring the one with two." Florence shook herself as if to expunge her perplexity. "I never furthered my acquaintance with him to the extent I had hoped, however, I'll tell you what I do know." Her chin lowered, and her gaze rested on Eleanor in counterfeit sobriety. "Lord Miles Everleigh is the younger brother to His Grace the Duke of Chelsony. It's a pity about Lord Miles. He's exceedingly handsome, very prettily behaved even if a bit of a rake, and a darling of the Haut Monde. Lord Miles has entrée to the most exclusive establishments; he is received everywhere. On the other hand, His Grace the Duke is generally disliked as being far too high in the instep and a hard-nosed skinflint."

"If Lord Miles is well-behaved, why do you say a rake, Florence?"

The widow flashed Eleanor a mischievous glance. "Immediately upon graduating Oxford, he entered into the tender care of a very 'fast' widow, Lady Margaret Dorchance, and only left her address when she departed for the continent, whereupon he became the live-in 'guest' of The Right Honorable Lady Olivia Norwalk. *She* let it be widely known that Lord Miles was a singularly delightful houseguest." Florence wiggled her eyebrows. "It seemed, unlike Lady Olivia's deceased husband, the young Lord

Miles delighted her well and often." Florence cast Eleanor an arch smile. "She said he was indefatigable."

Eleanor's brain flew in fifty directions. Mental images of how Lord Miles might possibly 'delight' Lady Olivia Norwalk—all of them necessarily vague—flooded her mind, and whatever did Florence mean by "indefatigable"? Embarrassment tied her tongue. She searched for some response that wouldn't reveal her abysmal naiveté.

It truly wasn't fair. Widows and wives had such an advantage. They had entrée into an entire world of experience of which she remained ignorant. Not even her forays into the breeding shed, from which she'd been expelled with humiliating regularity, had offered much insight other than the bald mechanics of "the act." How *that* could be deemed delightful piqued her curiosity mightily.

With a low, affectionate chuckle, her friend took pity on her and continued, "Since then, he's not lacked for open-ended invitations of which he has taken full advantage. Lord Miles stays in his hostesses' good graces by being the best of houseguests—one who knows how to please and when to discreetly *depart.* There's even a standing bet at White's as to which aristocratic widow or bored noble wife will support him when he leaves his current address. At the moment. I believe he is residing with an old school chum, Baron Stanton."

Eleanor eyed her friend with a frown. "Doesn't he have a living of his own? You would think…"

"Yes, you would, wouldn't you? Chelsony is not an impoverished title. However, I suppose with three younger brothers…" Florence shrugged. "As I said, the new Duke of Chelsony is notoriously tightfisted. He's left his two youngest brothers, Lord Miles and Lord Edmund, to live on their wits and the pittance that trickles from his abundant purse. I believe the second brother, Lord Duncan, purchased an officer's commission in the army while the old Duke was still alive.

"You and Lord Miles share a common interest. It's said that he's keen on racing and is quite the authority on Thoroughbred bloodlines. His name was proposed for admittance into the Jockey Club but, alas, he lacks the income to support his passion. So, he uses his expert knowledge to the benefit of his friends. Should I arrange an introduction for you?"

"No. It's not necessary." Eleanor rose and kissed her good friend on the cheek. "I must take my leave of you. You are the best of friends, Florence. For better or worse, I've made a decision, and I must see Mr. Elsington, immediately."

Lady Florence rose and ushered Eleanor to the door. "Regardless of what you have decided, I'm calling on you first thing in the morning to attend to your wardrobe."

Eleanor winced. "Do you really—"

"Expect my carriage at 10:00." Lady Florence gently pushed Eleanor through the front door and closed it firmly behind her, cutting off any more protest.

"Miles, after dinner, I intend to look up Lord John Hadley and Mister Jules Smart at the club. Any interest in joining me for a reconnoiter and a few hands of whist?" Baron Stanton cast Miles a look of inquiry.

"It would be my pleasure, as long as you are kind to my pocketbook," he laughed in reply.

"We will keep the wagering low. I'm determined not to let you get the best of me this time."

Once there, they met up with the two gentlemen known to Miles and Reggie, who agreed to settle into a friendly game of cards at a penny a point. The foursome had been playing for several hours when Reggie commented, "Say, Miles, isn't that your brother, Lord Edmund?" Reggie examined the last card in his hand, scowled and tossed it onto the table. "Your trick, book, and game. Your skill is uncanny," Reggie grumbled. "You win far too often."

Miles smiled and nodded at the pleasant gentleman sitting across from him. "I have an adept partner."

He shot a glance in the direction Reggie had indicated and frowned. Indeed, Ned stood at a dicing board among a group of men, of whom one was well-known to Miles as a thorough scoundrel and card sharp. Miles suppressed a sense of helpless unease. The ill-advised actions of his younger brother featured prominently among the many things over which he had no control.

His attention returned to his partner. "Well played, Lord John. When you ran the trump and returned my opening, you set up my minor suit nicely." He picked up the cards, squared the deck and placed it in the middle of the table. "Gentlemen, if you don't mind, I have an early appointment tomorrow with a certain four-legged arrival. I leave you in the tender clutches of Baron Stanton." He directed a crooked smile at Reggie. "Don't be too cruel."

Reggie slid his chair back and groaned. "I'm coming with you. I promised Mary I'd be early tonight."

The other two gentlemen hooted, and there was much teasing about being tied to apron strings and leg-shackled which the baron took with good grace.

"Just you wait, you hooligans. Your turn will come." As they stopped in the foyer and summoned a footman to gather their greatcoats, gloves, hats and walking sticks, Reggie lowered his voice, "Did you see who Lord Edmund was gambling with? That man has a reputation as a Captain Sharp, and the on-dit is he runs a gang of murderers and thieves. I would warn your brother off at the first opportunity."

"Yes. I'm only too aware. I have already spoken to Ned on several occasions about the unsavory company he keeps and advised him to seek other associates." Miles looked at Reggie as they walked out of the club and flagged a cab. "He's twenty-one. Remember yourself at that age? I can't tell him anything. I'm afraid he's already in the clutches of the cent-per-centers, but he keeps reassuring me that he'll come about."

"What are you going to do?"

Mile's face tightened, and his full mouth became a thin line. "As with everything else in my life, there is damn little I can do but watch as the ship breaks apart on the rocks and then show up the next day to salvage the wreckage."

The second-floor chamber maid drew back the curtains to let in the morning sun and lit the coal fire that had been laid in the hearth the evening before. "Morning, my lord. I've left hot water for you on the dressing table and placed your clean linen in the wardrobe. Your morning coffee will be up shortly, and breakfast will be in the small dining room at 10:30." She dropped Miles a brief curtsey and left the room.

Mile scrubbed at his eyes and shoved himself into a sitting position in the luxurious bed of the well-appointed guest chamber in Baron Stanton's London townhome—a bed in which he was the sole occupant, thank heaven. Due to Reggie's kind invitation, he'd had a hiatus from the nocturnal activities that accompanied that of being a kept man. Not that he held the lovely ladies who had sheltered him in dislike... nothing could be further from the truth— delicious bits of femininity all of them, and he was very grateful. It was just rather hard on a man's ego to forge an existence based solely on being an agreeable companion with skill in the bedroom arts. He hoped he had more substantial talents.

As an aristocrat, working in any profession but law or the Church would result in social ostracism. He would not be received anywhere. He found the law excruciatingly dull and was by temperament, entirely unsuited for the clergy. As long as his half-brother held the purse strings in a stranglehold, his only option was to surrender his independence and live at the ducal residence under his brother's thumb, or offer his services as "gentleman friend, escort and companion at large" in exchange for room and board—very hard on a man with any pride, a character trait he'd discovered he had in excess.

He sighed and swung his legs over the edge of the bed. His Grace was forever berating him as a ciscisbeo, a Casanova, a man-whore... but then, his half-brother, the Duke, had the solution within his grasp. As Miles reminded him on occasion, all he need do was stake Miles to a small farm and a few well-chosen broodmares, and Miles would change his living circumstances forthwith. In furtherance of provoking His Grace to that end, Miles made no effort to curtail his notorious exploits with the fairer sex.

He viewed Reggie's invitation as a temporary reprieve. *Ah well, time to face another day of being a useful houseguest.* He brightened. Reggie's new hunter would arrive today. They could have a ride in the park and test the horse's paces. He rang the bell to summon the young footman who was doing double duty as his valet. Appearance was vital when it was your calling card.

Washed, shaved and dressed impeccably, he sauntered into the small dining room.

Reggie's wife Mary, the sole occupant, looked up from the remains of her breakfast and smiled. "Good morning, Lord Miles. You're looking very dashing, as usual. Stanton has gone to the stables to see after his latest purchase. He said he'd wait for you there as you'd no doubt want to try him out first thing." She waved at the buffet laid on a nearby sideboard. "Please make yourself free with whatever is left."

He chuckled as he placed some toast, slices of cheese and ham on his plate and crossed to his usual chair. "Yes, I'd intended to go straight to the stables, but I'm reluctant to rush off when I've such beautiful and charming company."

"Flatterer." She cast him a laughing glance. "You can make up the loss of your cordial presence by accompanying me on my shopping excursion this afternoon. I'm to have some new riding habits made up, and as you're fast friends with the always smartly attired Lady Norwalk, you can give me an educated male opinion." She frowned slightly. "Stanton complains I'm too staid." She raised her hot chocolate to her mouth and took a small sip. "Oh, and something's come for you in the post."

A thick white packet sat on the table by his usual setting. "Hmm…it's from a barrister." He frowned. "I can't imagine." Putting it aside to read later, he faced Mary with a smile and all evidence of genuine interest. "Now, tell me, what dressmaker will have your patronage, and what styles are you contemplating?"

Thankfully, Mary wasn't one of those women who rattled on about fripperies until a man's head whirled, and it wasn't too long until he was the sole occupant of the dining room.

He eyed the thick white packet, strongly tempted to ignore it. In his experience, legal professionals rarely sent good news. But there was nothing to be gained by putting off the inevitable. If by some chance he was being sued for say, alienation of affection or worse, paternity—always a possibility though he'd been careful—the sooner known, the sooner dealt with. He opened the envelope, smoothed the thick folded sheets flat on the table and began reading as he swallowed his coffee. He stopped mid-sip, his cup suspended in mid-air. A frown developed between his brows, and when he left the table an hour later, his destination was not the stables.

Chapter Two

At the law offices of Elsington & Elsington, Miles handed his greatcoat, top hat, gloves, and cane to a clerk and was shown into a large office in which a mahogany desk piled with neatly organized paperwork occupied the center of the room. Floor-to-ceiling bookcases crammed with leather-bound books and scrolls of papers made up the walls that surrounded it. An elderly, emaciated man with full, mutton-chop sideburns just as gray as the sparse hair on his head, rose from behind the monstrous piece of furniture. His thin lips twitched in a skeleton of a smile, and he bowed. "I assume I have the pleasure of addressing Lord Miles Wrotham Everleigh?"

Miles returned his bow. "I am the same."

"Penwick Elsington, Esquire. I serve as barrister to the Earl of Rutledge and by extension, his daughter, Lady Eleanor Russell. I gather from your presence that you received and read my missive?"

"Yes."

The man motioned to a pair of wing chairs situated in front of a bay window. "If you would join me, please. We might as well make ourselves comfortable. I suspect you have a number of questions for me."

"That's something of an understatement." Miles arranged the tails of his black morning coat and relaxed into the upholstered chair, crossing one top-booted leg over the other.

"Quite," the barrister said. "Irregular, this whole business." He caught Miles with a direct gaze. "Where would you like me to begin, my lord?"

"You might start with why Lady Russell came to feel she needed to marry under such peculiar terms and how she determined I would suit her needs. After that, perhaps you can detail exactly what is expected of me if I go through with this. What does she expect her money to buy her?" He softened his voice at the last to remove some of the prickle from his blunt words.

The gentleman across from him closed his eyes and sighed. "Indeed. Allow me to start at the beginning." He lifted a crystal carafe of deep amber liquid. "Brandy?"

"Please."

Several hours and a carafe of French brandy later, Penwick Elsington cleared his throat and confirmed, "So you agree, my lord, to honor the lady's wishes and go through with this?" Elsington looked away with an expression of distaste on his face. "Including her wish that the marriage be in name only?"

"Yes." Miles marveled with inner bemusement at the strange turns his life took. "You realize a hasty wedding will give rise to the worst sort of gossip. If you wish to lessen the scandal, mind— I said lessen, there is no way to avoid some due to the discrepancy in our ages—it would be in Lady Russell's best interests if I were seen to pay my address in the customary ways. Riding in the park. Attendance at social events." He shrugged. "The normal way a man goes about trying to attach a lady's affection." Miles studied the older gentleman as a half-smile twisted the corners of his mouth. "I would put myself between Lady Russell and the worst of the scandal if she will allow it. Her reputation will still suffer, but it could be put about that I compromised her." Miles found a spot on the far wall to study. "I won't deny it. The 'ton', those high-flying social elite, will find it all too easy to believe, and hopefully, cast me as the villain."

"You would prefer your good name rather than hers be tarnished?"

Miles shrugged. "What little there is left of my good name. I've no doubt my half-brother, the Duke, will express his extreme displeasure at my 'misconduct,' but life, in general, will be easier for her if she is seen as the victim."

"Society is rarely that kind to a woman, but we might as well try. What of yourself, sir?"

"I cannot care what society says of me. I'm not in a position to care." Miles held Elsington's gaze without apology until the man looked away with an uncomfortable clearing of his throat. In truth, Miles did care; he cared deeply that he was perceived only as 'ornamentation' but there was little to be done if he wished to continue to associate with those of the aristocratic class he'd been born into. In order to survive, he'd had to bury his pride under a landslide of practicality. He'd been offered little choice.

Elsington pursed his lips and studied his brandy glass. "I have advised Lady Russell that tongues will wag in a most uncomplimentary fashion; she may no longer be received in the first circles, but she is fixed on this course of action. Indeed, I can see little else for her to do if she is to hold Rutledge intact." He stood and offered his hand to Miles. "I've always thought myself a reasonably good judge of character. After speaking with you these past few hours, I must tell you, my lord, I believe Lady Russell chose wisely when she decided upon you."

"We shall see, won't we?" Miles laughed without humor. "I cannot conceive that it says anything good about a man's character when he's willing to be bought, but then I've sold myself for far less substance than what Lady Russell offers." He shrugged, adjusting the fit of his coat and flicked an imaginary hair from his lapels before engaging Elsington again with a flat smile. "I will present myself at these offices the day after next to sign your papers."

Eleanor arrived at Elsington & Elsington early and cursed herself for doing so. Over an hour remained before she signed her life away as she knew it. Each chime of the quarter hour from the clock in her barrister's office sounded like an announcement of doom. She adjusted the pleats in the skirt of her smart morning gown for the twentieth time, straightened the braided frog closures on the front of her navy redingote, tucked her kid half-boots underneath herself and narrowly refrained from scratching at her veil. The single layer of embellished white tiffany fell in a charming manner from the brim of the fashionable result of a hat maker's art. Florence insisted the hat went perfectly with her new gown, but the confounded fluff tickled her nose. She squirmed, trying to find a comfortable position in her tightly-laced new stays.

Drat Florence, anyway. With brutal efficiency and remorseless badgering, she'd cowed Eleanor and the French modiste into submission. The result of said bullying was a complete overhaul of Eleanor's wardrobe right down to her nightdresses and stays. While she'd never confess it to Florence, she'd loved the entire experience.

For the first time in her life, she felt womanly. Her new undergarments gave her body a shape she'd never suspected was possible. She had breasts for heaven's sake. The sheer, white, muslin shifts with their delicate embroidery were scandalous in their transparency and so soft against her skin. Donning silk stockings with satin ribbon garters was an exercise in sensuality when one was used to nothing but knitted wool or cotton. But it was the gowns that transformed her into a woman of fashion unrecognizable to herself. The deep jewel colors and sumptuous fabrics brought out features Eleanor wasn't aware she possessed. She'd always felt her hair color resembled nothing more than a dead rodent, but the hues that Florence dressed her in brought out shades of platinum and gold and her new layered cut had coaxed waves and curls from previously limp hanks. Suddenly she noticed that her eyes were the color of autumn leaves, gold and brown with specks of green, and her face, while still angular, had fleshed out. She would no longer agree with the description of herself as a "horse-faced maypole"—an unkind remark she'd had to misfortune to overhear at her very first ball. In short, she felt remade.

But what was the point of all this new plumage when she planned on leaving town in a fortnight? This legal arrangement she was purchasing was not a real marriage.

She slumped until a busk delivered a sharp poke in the sternum and reminded her to straighten. *Lord Miles Everleigh is the point, Elle,* she scolded. *You do want to make a good impression.* She rolled her eyes. *Have you already forgotten you are paying him to go away and stay away?* She slumped only to straighten with a slight yelp at another sharp poke to her breastbone. Grumbling, she reached under her veil and rubbed her itchy nose vigorously. A moan of gratification slipped from her—just as the door opened and Lord Miles Everleigh and her barrister entered. She slammed her hand back into her lap and bolted upright from her chair, but the damage had been done. She'd been caught scratching and moaning in public, most unladylike and reprehensible actions. Laughter lurked in the gray eyes that met hers.

"Lady Eleanor Constance Russell, may I present to you, Lord Miles Wrotham Everleigh,"

She shot her gloved hand in Everleigh's direction.

He caught the tips of her fingers and gently lowered her hand to waist high, over which, unlike her clumsy gesture, he made an elegant bow. "I am charmed." A smile played on the masculine features of her future husband, and his gray eyes warmed. "You are the woman from Tattersalls."

With a nod, she dipped in a slight curtsey as he relinquished her hand. Her heart raced in her chest, and her breathing deepened. A rush of novel emotion filled her. She felt… petite. Dainty. She hadn't realized, but Miles Everleigh was every bit her height. No, taller. She had to look up to catch his eyes. She was used to being the tallest person in a room with few exceptions, but with his broad shoulders and well-muscled frame, Lord Miles dwarfed her …and he was dreadfully handsome. Ridiculously attractive, actually. First things first, however. Beyond all else, Eleanor wanted a good beginning with the gentleman she would forevermore call her husband.

"Lord Miles, before we start with the binding signatures, I wish to express my thanks to you for agreeing to what must seem a most ill-conceived series of actions." Eleanor strove to soften her strident tone. If only she weren't so nervous! "By giving me the protection of your name, you are allowing me to preserve a life and a property that is very dear to me, and I will be forever grateful."

"I believe gratitude is in order all the way around," he said. "The benefit to me in this transaction cannot be ignored. I deeply appreciate having the wherewithal to conduct my life in a manner of my own choosing." He held Eleanor's gaze with a startling directness.

Was he not happy? Had he not chosen the direction of his life? The question just now occurred to her, and she felt ashamed she hadn't thought of it sooner. She knew well the sort of desperate imperative that must compel anyone who agreed to her proposition. She studied him through lowered lashes, and he met her perusal with steadiness and a slight twist to his mouth suggestive of self-deprecation. He possessed an air of dignity, a quiet assurance, and equanimity of manner that would normally indicate an ease of spirit. If she understood his words, his inner emotions did not conform to his outward appearance. It could not be easy for him to be dependent upon the whim of host or hostess. A flurry of sympathetic emotions—mixed with a good dose of pure physical attraction—distracted her for a moment. Flustered by the alien feeling, she studied her gloves. "I'm pleased you view our arrangement as beneficial."

"Lady Russell, Lord Miles, if you would be so kind…" Mr. Elsington indicated four chairs arranged around a large round table at one end of his office. At each chair were pen, ink and a leather blotter.

Lord Miles seated her before taking his chair. At some hidden signal, a clerk entered bearing a stack of papers a foot high and placed them on the table, separating them into three stacks of equal height and then sat in the fourth chair.

"Lord Miles, you have read a copy of this agreement in its entirety. Do you have any questions before making your final commitment?"

"None. I found it quite straightforward. Upon my marriage to Lady Russell, £30,000 will be credited to my London account, of which you have the particulars. I will receive a yearly annuity of £2,500 thereafter until my death." He smiled faintly. "The annuity being dependent entirely upon my lack of interference in the business affairs of The Lady Miles Everleigh—nee Lady Eleanor Russell, as determined solely by her ladyship and her barrister, Elsington & Elsington. Immediately after the wedding, I will remove my presence and agree to keep my person from the estate of Rutledge and the vicinity of my wife unless or until Lady Miles requests my attendance."

As he murmured the last qualification in arid tones, Eleanor felt the weight of his regard and occupied herself with ensuring her ink pen had a proper point.

"Exactly." Elsington nodded at the clerk. "Mr. Benjamin will be our other witness. Shall we begin?" Elsington's gaze swept her and Miles in question. At their nods, he began to feed them paper with a brief explanation, and she signed until her hand cramped into a claw.

"Very good. That's the end of it." Elsington cast a disapproving gaze at the clerk who had just stifled a yawn.

"You are dismissed, Mr. Benjamin." When the door closed behind the man, he turned to Eleanor and Miles. "I will place the announcement of your pending marriage in the papers. I have already taken the precaution of securing a special license from the Bishop of Canterbury. The marriage, itself, will take place in the side chapel of All Hallows by the Tower in two weeks time. I will arrange for a clergyman to preside. The attendance of one or two members of your family and a few close friends is certainly understandable; however, bear in mind the limits of space." His thin lips pressed together in a smile. "I believe a quiet ceremony with few flourishes is in order."

Eleanor nodded and looked at Miles.

"Whatever Lady Russell wishes is acceptable to me. I never expected to wed and have given a ceremony little consideration."

Unwilling to meet his eyes, she looked away. "I, too, gave only passing thought to a ceremony I never thought to experience. Quiet and simple suits me very well."

"My lady…" Miles low voice returned her gaze to his. "On a different note, I believe it would lessen gossip were you and I to be seen together in public behaving in an amicable fashion."

She stirred awkwardly in her chair. "What did you have in mind?"

"I suggest riding or driving in the park several mornings. I would like you to attend Lord and Lady Willingham's ball with me on Tuesday next, and whatever else you might find a pleasant way to pass the time. Shopping?" He raised an eyebrow and gave her a winning smile.

"I would be delighted to ride or drive with you, Lord Miles, but as to the ball and shopping…" She grimaced.

"Are you the rare female who doesn't like to shop or dance?" he teased.

"I'm not social, so my dancing skills lack polish. I don't shop because I have deplorable taste. If I'm well turned out today, it is due to my childhood friend Lady Florence Lloyd-Smythe." She straightened her posture and lifted her chin. "You will find I don't possess many feminine qualities, Lord Miles." A subtle defensiveness filtered into her voice.

"I see." His gaze dwelled on her with the same acuteness he'd used sizing up the bay at Tattersalls.

She was very afraid he *did* see, and the thought sent her spirits crashing, though why his good opinion of her mattered she'd have been hard-pressed to explain.

He pushed out of his chair and rose. "I will call on you tomorrow for a ride in Hyde Park, say, 1:00? May I provide you with a suitable mount?"

She pushed her chair away from the table with his assistance and stood to face him. "I do not require you to furnish me with a horse. I maintain my own stable, thank you. As to 1:00? If you make it 6:30 a.m. there's a chance we could get in a good gallop."

His smile started small then broadened into a charming grin of approval that left her struggling to maintain her composure and not blush like a debutante. "No staid canter in the park for you? Well done. 6:30 a.m. and a good gallop it is."

If she was smart, she would never allow him to see how he affected her. He could name any term or condition, and she would comply simply to have him look at her like that.

Chapter Three

Windblown and out of breath, Eleanor pulled up near Lord Miles' gelding and attempted to school her mount into a respectful canter, laughing as her gray mare leaped and cavorted, tossing her head in a general protest at the curtailment of her early morning gallop. "I concede! You won! You wouldn't have had such an easy win were I astride, sir!" she called. "In a less public venue, I would have bested you."

Lord Miles laughed in return. "I don't doubt it. You must ride at least five stone lighter. We will put it to the test if an opportunity presents, m'lady." In easy increments, he dropped his bay down to a walk, and Eleanor finally cajoled the minx she rode into more decorous behavior and moved to walk alongside him.

When he'd arrived at the mews behind her townhome at 6:30 sharp, riding the seventeen-hand bay hunter she'd seen his friend purchase at Tattersalls, she'd been waiting, walking the yard, mounted on her Arabian mare. If she'd had a small chance at resisting his appeal in her barrister's office, seeing the elegant figure he cut on horseback finished her. After a nod of his head and a comment about it being a fine, clear morning though a trifle nippy, they'd ridden in congenial silence through the gates of Hyde Park. She'd studied him covertly as they covered the short distance from her Mayfair home to the park. The man had a beautiful seat and light hands, and his horse, which she knew to be an unfamiliar mount, moved forward with a loose, swinging gait and a happy bob of his head, completely at ease with the man on his back. More than most, Eleanor appreciated a kind and skilled rider—and it was hard not to appreciate such a handsome one.

Other than grooms exercising their masters' and mistresses' horses, the bridle paths were deserted, and they had no more entered the park and the beginning of Rotten Row when Lord Miles had turned to her. "Are you familiar with the small pavilion toward the end of this path?"

"Yes."

"Shall we gallop?"

"Oh, yes!"

He put a gentle spur to the bay's side and picked up a slow canter, which lengthened into a ground-eating gallop. Eleanor easily kept pace, and when she'd laughed and tapped her mare lightly with her crop to put her gray nose in front of the bay's, he'd answered with the same, and their gallop became an all-out, hell-bent, race to the pavilion. She couldn't remember when she'd last laughed so hard. As they pulled up to a walk and turned for home, their horses blowing and prancing beneath them, an all-encompassing feeling of contentment settled in. Her mind turned to their conversation of the previous day, and she wondered at something he'd said. Later, she blamed her sense of joyous freedom for her lack of restraint and loss of all decorum.

"Yesterday, at my barrister's… you said you were grateful for the wherewithal to live your life as you chose… or something to that effect. Have you been very unhappy, Lord Miles?" From the stiffening of his posture and his suddenly shuttered expression, she realized she'd erred as soon as she'd asked, but she couldn't take it back.

He flashed her a tight smile. "As an affianced couple, I give you leave to dispense with formality. You may address me as Miles."

The silence lengthened and with growing unease, she wondered if he would answer at all. She glanced at him from time to time as they walked. She'd been too direct. It was her biggest fault. She winced and drew a breath to apologize, but her words stilled on her lips when he captured her in a deliberate gaze.

"I wouldn't say I was unhappy… more I had a general feeling of futility, of simply marking time, of not living the life I'd hoped for myself."

She considered his response and wanted to ask him further questions but lacked the courage. "Thank you for answering. You needn't have, and I beg your pardon. My question was horribly intrusive. I've ever been taken to task for my bluntness. It's one of my many flaws of character that men find unattractive." She cleared her throat. "I don't know how to flirt or dissemble."

He shrugged as if to make light of her lack of tact.

Ah well, might as well be in for a pound as a penny. "What will you do with your £30,000?" She braced herself for a polite set down.

This time, he responded without hesitation. "I'm going to purchase a modest farm in Newmarket and set up a

Thoroughbred stud. I've had my eye on the property for several years and have already spoken to the landowner. I want to breed and train racehorses." He gave her a much more amiable glance. "I believe you know something about that. The Rutledge stud is well known for its bloodstock and their successes on the race course."

Her mare chose that particular moment to take exception to some leaves that blew across the path and swirled up into her face, and it was several minutes before Eleanor could respond. "Yes, we've been very fortunate."

"I suppose luck plays a part in any success, but in the case of the Rutledge stud, I'd put it down rather to knowledgeable management. Are you much involved in the day-to-day operations?"

"I am—more and more so since Father fell ill. I will miss him terribly when the day comes, but the truth is I've been directing the entire Rutledge estate for several years." She threw a quick glance at him. "Does that horrify you? The thought that a woman manages one of the larger estates and Thoroughbred studs in England?"

Miles glanced at her with raised eyebrows, followed immediately by a wry smile. "I put no limits on what an intelligent female is capable of. From my personal experience, a woman is every bit a male's equal in dealing with the minutiae of running a large property. Probably more capable than some men, if truth be known, so … no, Lady Russell." He shrugged. "Not horrified."

"Eleanor, please, if you are to be Miles. As you said, we are to be wed."

"Yes, we are." He laughed, not without a little humor, and inclined his head. "Eleanor."

"I do hope we won't always be awkward with each other," she blurted. She could only trust he recognized the sincerity in her bumbling pronouncement.

"No. We needn't be awkward," he answered with such an easy grin and agreeable manner that she understood all the more why he never lacked for a roof over his head. "And Eleanor, I will never take you to task for straightforward speech. I far prefer it."

Her pleasure at his comment left her tongue-tied. When Miles initiated an inquiry into the bloodlines of her mare, she leaped on the subject with immense gratitude. It was a topic she could converse upon at length.

When they rode into the carriage yard of her townhome, he dismounted and then helped her down. His body felt hard as she slipped briefly against him before he settled her firmly on the ground and the strong hands that clasped her waist released her. It was the closest nonfamilial contact she'd had in years and an inappropriate handling of her body had he not been her "intended"—at least that was the reason she gave herself for being so breathless. It couldn't have been the proximity of an attractive male. She was immune to that sort of thing.

Turning her mare over to her groom, she reached behind and gathered up the trailing skirts of her riding habit by slipping the loop sewn into the hem for just that purpose around her wrist. Freed to walk without tripping, she stepped back and squinted up at him from under the brim of her feminized chapeau bas. He was intolerably attractive, not brash or bold or top lofty—simply charming of manner and possessed of an overwhelming masculine allure. Perhaps she wasn't as immune to men as she'd thought. "Thank you for a delightful morning. I've enjoyed it tremendously."

"It was my pleasure. Shall we do this again tomorrow? 6:30?"

She offered him a warm smile. "Please."

"Have your groom check your offside billets. One of the buckles on your girth has torn through the leather. I noticed as we were walking home." He bowed and mounted his horse. With a touch of the silver handle of his whip to his hat brim and an, "Until tomorrow, Lady Russell," he turned his mount and rode out, never looking back.

With a heartfelt sigh, like the rawest girl, Eleanor watched his upright figure until he disappeared around the corner of the yard and then chided herself for being an absolute ninny. Turning, she went into the stables to find her groom and inspect her saddle. Lord Miles was correct. One of the three leather straps that affixed her girth to her saddle had torn. She or Barnaby, her groom, would have found it the next morning, as she always inspected her tack before mounting, but the novel experience of a male not in her employ being attentive to her welfare felt... nice.

"What do you mean you're to be married in a fortnight?" Reggie blinked owlishly and thunked the brandy decanter down on the sideboard with less than his usual aplomb. "Miles!" He shook his head as if to settle his brains. "Of course I'll stand up with you, but 'pon rep, sir. Who is the lady?"

Miles leaned against the mantelpiece in Reggie's study, one booted foot crossed over the other, and gazed at the blue lick of flames in the fireplace. He raised his brandy and tossed half the glass back before answering. "The Lady Eleanor Constance Russell, the only child of The Right Honorable Earl of Rutledge. The announcement is in this morning's Times."

"The devil you say! The Earl of Rutledge as in the Rutledge Stud? Won the St. Ledger Stakes and Epsom Derby last year?"

"The same."

"I didn't know he even had a daughter. What, is she still in leading strings?"

Miles laughed without humor. "No, quite the opposite. I believe we were still at Oxford when she first came out." Mile shook his head at the consternation on his good friend's face. "I think you will like her, Stanton. She has a lively mind and a forthright, nonsensical way about her." A wry smile curled one side of his mouth. "Very forthright."

"Is she very much your senior?"

"I'd guess at five or six years."

"Egad, Miles!" Reggie cleared his throat after a pause and offered hopefully, "Good rider?"

"Bruising. Her personal mount is a glorious Araby mare, but as difficult and tricksy an animal as I've ever seen. I couldn't recommend such a mount for half the men I know and certainly not for *any* woman. Lady Russell dealt with her splendidly."

"A beauty?"

"No, but not an antidote. She has…countenance."

"Countenance?" The disappointment in the baron's voice was comical.

Miles grinned. "And a fine pair of hazel eyes, a womanly figure even if slender… and is very nearly my match in height. You glimpsed her. She was the woman I asked about at Tattersalls."

"Good gad…a veritable Amazon then. Not an affair of the heart, I take it?"

"Reg." Miles leveled a look of reproach at his good friend.

"Well…?"

"We have an agreement. I'm not at liberty to expound."

"Like that, is it?" Reggie groaned. "Are you that pressed for blunt, Miles? I could give you…" He held out his hands as if fumbling for words, and when Miles frowned and shook his head, Reg dropped them, only to scratch at the back of his neck with a grimace. "'pologies…but it's not right. Your brother's swimming in lard and you've pockets to let."

Miles leveled another disapproving gaze at his friend.

"Can't imagine you leg-shackled—not to a bracket-faced, long Meg. Always thought if you did marry, it would be to some pretty, well-inlaid widow. Someone jolly and full of fun."

Miles snorted quietly. "The terms were advantageous." He sipped at the remaining brandy in his glass, nursing it, swirling it around as he gazed unseeing at the golden liquid. "Be happy for me, Stanton," he murmured.

His best friend grinned half-heartedly and shrugged. "Of course I'm glad for you if this is what you want." The casement clock ticked quietly in the silence for many seconds. "Err…what do I tell Mary?"

"Ah…" Miles sighed deeply. "Tell her I met Lady Russell through a friend, thought we'd suit, made her an offer. She accepted. All very April and May." He pointed a finger at Reg. "Not a whisper that I'm not taken with the lady. Mary would be disappointed in me. She's quite the romantic."

"Yes. I mean, no, no, I won't tell her the particulars."

Miles and Baron Stanton looked at each other in silence for several long beats, and then the baron raised his glass with a tenuous smile. "To the parson's noose. I wish you all happiness."

"Eleanor! You abominable tease! How dare you keep me in such suspense!" Eleanor's butler had no more gotten out, "Your ladyship, the Lady Flo..." than Florence had burst into the front parlor where Eleanor had been going through her correspondence.

She stood to greet her friend who enveloped her in a cloud of rose scent and a crushing hug.

Florence straightened and regarded her friend with impatient expectation. "So, tell me... did he sign it? Did he agree?"

With a helpless laugh, Eleanor motioned to the settee. "Please, sit. Tea?"

Florence rolled her eyes. "Thank you, but *no*. I didn't come for tea! I've been on tenterhooks since the day before yesterday and not a word from you, you horrid, abominable woman."

Eleanor shot her friend a wary glance. "Yes. He signed. We are to be married in the small chapel at All Hallows by the Tower in two weeks. Well, two weeks less two days by now. I've meant to ask if you'd act as my attendant."

"Of course, you goose. I wouldn't dream of missing it." Her expression became abstract. "I'll put you in the silver lama with the sprigged white sarsenet overdress, satin ribbon trim and matching slippers. We will dress your hair simply, a la Aphrodite, with pearls and ribbons, and give your cheeks the slightest kiss of rouge." Florence gave a happy shiver and returned her gaze to Eleanor's. "You will look like an angel."

Eleanor chuckled helplessly. "I'd settle for clean and neat."

"What nonsense. We can do much better than that." Florence inhaled with suppressed excitement. "So … what did you think of the oh-so-elegant and oh-so-handsome Lord Miles Everleigh?"

"I thought him kind."

Florence wore an expression of hopeful expectation, but after several long moments passed and Eleanor didn't elaborate on her four-word statement, Florence gave harrumph of disgust. "You met with him for several hours yesterday afternoon and came away with, 'He's kind'?"

"Well… I also rode with him in the park at 6:30 this morning. He thought we should be seen together."

Florence pursed her lips and glared at Eleanor. "At 6:30 a.m. no one of any import is awake."

"I don't know what else to say," Eleanor moaned. "He was everything a gentleman should be. He's a positive Corinthian in the saddle and is much too well-favored for my peace of mind. I like him tremendously—far more than I should on such short acquaintance." Her eyes fell to her lap, and her voice dropped to a murmur. "I'm afraid, Florence."

"Darling, whatever for?"

"I could never engage the affections of such a man."

"Do you want to?"

She nodded slowly, still unwilling to raise her eyes. "But I know how hopeless it is. I'm far too plain and far too firmly on the shelf to interest such as he."

"Ballocks."

"Florence!" Eleanor straightened abruptly, and her gaze flew to her friend. Both women pulled long faces and then burst into laughter. Florence recovered first.

"Don't even pretend you are shocked, and it's true, dearest. You sadly underrate yourself. While you are far removed from sixteen, unlike most women, your looks have improved with each passing year. Your face has nary a wrinkle, and while you've remained slender as a willow, you've developed those curves you were missing at sixteen. Were our friendship not of such long standing, I think I could hate you. Besides, where men are concerned, the proverb, 'When all candles be out, all cats be grey,' holds truth."

"Scant comfort." Eleanor shot her friend a sideways glance.

"I'm simply telling you that in matters of the boudoir, men are not always exacting as to the physical aspects of their partner, and if Lord Miles is someone you think you want... well..." The dark-haired widow shrugged negligently.

"But do I? Is the... marital duty... worth all the fuss and bother?"

"Yes," said Florence baldly. "Done properly, it is wondrous, and if you wish to affix his softer emotions, I would suggest it is a requirement; otherwise, Lord Miles will turn elsewhere and be lost to you. Besides, how else are you to beget an heir? Now, tell me, however did you come to be riding at 6:30 in the morning?"

Eleanor gave an inward sigh of relief about the change of subject and chatted happily with her dear friend for the better part of the afternoon before the widow rose and announced that she had plans for dinner with a gentleman friend and would call on Eleanor in a day or two.

As Miles rode into Eleanor's yard in the dim light of an early February morning, he found she awaited him mounted on her mare and walking a wide circle in the courtyard. He was less startled at the sight of her this time. He'd expected Eleanor to be like every other female of his acquaintance and give promptness only a passing curtsy. He'd been surprised and heartened when he'd been spared a long wait the previous morning. But then, she'd been waiting for him at Elsington & Elsington, too.

Like the previous morning, Eleanor was beautifully attired. She wore a form-fitted riding habit of deep olive camlet, the jacket a la Hussar and richly ornamented on the sleeves and lapels with black soutache braid in the French passementerie style. A snowy cravat of lace cascaded down her breast from a stand-up collar of pristine white muslin. A version of his top hat, though not so high in the crown and with a broader brim, sat on her head. A few tendrils of ash blonde hair escaped to soften the nape of her neck. She rode up to him with a smile, her expression open and alight with pleasure. The chill in the air had pinked her cheeks. She made a fetching package indeed. While he'd not describe her as a beauty, there was still something about her that arrested the eye. She was a fine-looking woman who showed to particularly good effect on horseback.

"Good morning, Lord Miles. I trust I find you well?" She must have seen the admiration in his gaze for she colored in a most becoming manner and her direct eye contact turned tentative.

"I am well, Lady Russell." He motioned in the direction of the park. "Shall we?"

She nodded, and they turned the heads of their horses and rode out. The outing went much the same as the day before, with neither of them engaging in much idle conversation on the short traverse to the park. Riding between the stone pillars marking the entrance, their gazes intersected and she returned Miles' smile.

"What happened to your bay?"

"His owner requisitioned him for later today, so I decided to let this fellow stretch his legs." He reached down and patted the neck of his neat chestnut hack. "I'm afraid, if you give your mare her head, you are going to get the better of me this morning. In his prime, this old gentleman would have given her a proper challenge, but he has some age and old injuries. I don't want to ask much of him."

"I understand. We certainly don't have to be neck-and-nothing like yesterday," she agreed. "I'll be content with a simple gallop."

"Then lead the way, Lady Russell."

"Eleanor," she called over her shoulder as she opened her hand and allowed her mare to pick up the pace.

Mile was satisfied to follow at a somewhat reduced speed, and though the senior gentleman beneath him pulled at the reins and asked for the freedom of his head, Miles held him to a strict, steady pace. The well-mannered gelding conceded and settled into a rhythmic gallop. Only

Miles felt the slight hitch and lack of drive in what used to be a free-flowing, powerful stride. Eleanor was waiting for him when he pulled up at the pavilion.

"What a lovely, well-mannered fellow. He does show some age to him. How old is he?"

"Badger is twenty-five. He and I share the same day of birth. I should have pensioned him off years ago, but I can't bring myself to do it. I would worry about him under another's care." He shrugged and chuckled. "It's difficult enough to walk by him in the stables. Badger always looks so hopeful as I approach and so offended when I ride out on another mount."

"It's hard to say goodbye to old and faithful friends." She gave him a soft look of sympathy. "I cried for days when Father declared my first pony no longer fit."

"Should we take the long way home through the park, Eleanor? We'll have more chance to talk."

"Yes, let's." She smiled in agreement.

"Tell me, is Rutledge developing any enticing prospects for this year's Derby?"

At that question, Eleanor fell into an animated description of the upcoming three-year-olds that would carry the silks of the Rutledge Stud. As all things racing were near and dear to Miles' heart, the next two hours passed without notice, and they rode into the carriage yard, laughing and conversing as if they were boon companions of many years. As he once again helped Eleanor down from her horse, her attractive face glowing with high spirits, a thought struck him, stunning in its clarity—he could develop a very comfortable marriage to this woman, a real marriage—if he received the barest hint from her that she desired such a thing.

The request to appear at Elsington & Elsington at 3:00 that afternoon came as a surprise to Miles. Upon arrival, he was shown into the senior partner's office. Across his vast desk, Penwick Elsington held Miles in a steady, foreboding stare.

"I received an agent from the Prince of Wales in my office this morning. He advised me that the announcement of your nuptials drew the personal notice of the Prince Regent. It is not often that a racing stud of such note as Rutledge becomes potentially available to the Crown. The Prince Regent is loath to relinquish it. Apparently, our Regent is curious about the circumstances surrounding what he considers 'precipitous actions' that will result in the loss of a property of interest to His Royal Highness. The substance of the agent's speech was clothed in innuendo and vagueries. However, the conclusion left no room for equivocation. I have been put on notice that the validity of your pending marriage will be held up to close scrutiny.

"Upon your marriage, I will, of course, submit a claim to the Crown asking that Lady Russell's first-born male child be allowed to inherit. While that will be of no consequence to you, it will add to the appearance that your marriage is entered into for the begetting of an heir."

Miles crossed his legs and drummed his fingers on the arm of the upholstered chair. "What can they do?"

"Until the Earl of Rutledge dies, nothing. After he dies, when his will is probated, as long as there is no hint of fraud, the marriage stands, and the Petition for Inheritance that I will file will be considered. A decision may take years. While there is no legal precedent for nullifying a marriage under these particular circumstances, we are dealing with His Royal Highness the Prince Regent. Parliament and the Church of England will give him a hearing no matter how outrageous his claims. Lady Russell will be ruined regardless of the outcome. Your union must be legally unassailable to forestall any action His Royal Highness may choose to take. It is possible agents will question Lady Russell's staff. I'm certain her servants are loyal, but it would be best if they had nothing to lie about." Elsington held Miles in a direct, unblinking stare. "To avoid any appearance of deceit, the marriage should be consummated."

Miles drew himself even more upright in his chair. "What you are suggesting is medieval. The lady made it clear this is to be marriage in name only. I believe I signed something to that effect. Furthermore, after the ceremony, I am expected to absent myself immediately from her proximity and her affairs of business or risk revocation of the annuity."

"I prefer to leave nothing to chance. An immense estate and Lady Russell's future and reputation, are at stake. I will advise her of the present situation and suggest a remedy. Lady Russell is an eminently practical woman. She will do what is necessary." Elsington tapped his fingers on his desk and examined Miles with a calculating expression. "Failing that, seduce her. Your reputation is that of a gentleman of certain...experience."

The man's cold, outrageous proposition gave rise to an immediate feeling of repugnance for both the suggestion and the barrister. Miles closed his eyes and ground his teeth at even the thought of introducing such a delicate issue into the nascent friendship between him and Lady Russell. Unless handled with the utmost tact, she was bound to bow her back, and he would hardly blame her. "I will broach the subject with Lady Russell." He rose to his feet, ready to be quit of Penwick Elsington. "It is her decision." He struggled to keep disgust from his voice. "Your other…proposal…I reject out of hand."

Chapter Four

As Eleanor dressed for Lord and Lady Willingham's ball she viewed with some alarm the rapid passage of time. The last ten days had advanced seamlessly, each day filled with pleasant diversions and public outings sponsored by Lord Miles Everleigh. There were drives and promenades in Hyde Park at more public hours, attendance at Astley's to watch the famous equestrienne ballet and a convivial afternoon spent walking Somerset House's exhibition of fine paintings. If she were in the habit of filling her mind with false hopes and illusions, she could easily convince herself that Lord Miles's attentions sprang from a growing regard for her, but she drew rein short of that mark. It was much more likely he was simply a beautiful gentleman of equally beautiful manners who was making the best of an awkward situation. Still… however unfounded, a part of her longed for a different interpretation as she found herself becoming more and more enamored with the handsome lord who seemed to draw out the best in her. She liked the woman who emerged when in his company, and he had a congenial circle of friends who readily accepted her into their midst. Only one issue overset her peace of mind.

Dwelling like a burr under her saddle was the correspondence from her barrister—the terse description of the prince regent's acute interest in their marriage and Elsington's final notation that she should take care to provide *every evidence* of conjugal union. A sick feeling disturbed her attempt at calm composure every time she reviewed the words Mr. Elsington had written. She'd been over and over his correspondence, hoping with each reading to discover some alternative meaning to be taken from his message—with no success. She dithered as to whether to mention it to Miles, for what should she say? She could not bring herself to be so forward about such a delicate subject as copulation with a virile male she'd known less than a fortnight. Every time she considered doing so a hot blush suffused her features and her mouth went dry, so she said nothing at all.

As her hairdresser put the finishing touches on her coiffure, the door to her dressing room opened and Mr. Clay, her butler, announced, "M'lady, Lord Miles Everleigh is here. I've put him in the small parlor."

Eleanor nodded in response. "Please tell Lord Miles I will be down immediately."

She wore a high-waisted, gold-embroidered Mazurine blue satin underdress with cap sleeves and a low, scooped neckline topped by a blonde lace overdress with a scalloped hemline—floral figures picked out in metallic gold beads covered the entirety of the overdress. A single clasp of sapphires and diamonds held the overdress closed in the middle of her ribcage, allowing the beaded lace to fall open in the front and reveal the heavily embroidered and beaded design on the front of the Mazurine blue satin. Her matching slippers peeked from the richly beaded hemlines. Off-white over-the-elbow kid gloves covered her arms, and long dangle earrings of sapphires and diamonds fell from her ears to tickle the tops of her bare shoulders. The clasp on the front of her overdress matched the circular hair ornament that affixed an ostrich plume onto a narrow band of lace set around her simple coiffure of soft curls.

After a touch to rearrange a wandering strand, her hairdresser stepped back. With a muted smile in the mirror, Eleanor rose, draped a fringed silk wrap on her arm, and followed her butler down the stairs. For once, she could find no fault with her appearance.

When she entered the small parlor and Miles rose to greet her, the look on his face was everything she could have hoped for, and happiness soared within her.

Miles took her shawl and arranged it on her shoulders before offering his arm and escorting her out to the waiting carriage. "You are in exceptionally fine looks this evening, Eleanor."

"Thank you, and I daresay with you as an escort, I will be the envy of every woman in attendance." She spoke only the truth. Lord Miles was a handsome man under any circumstances. In black and white evening dress, she considered him without equal.

He climbed into the carriage after her and gave her a smile that would melt a heart more heavily armored than hers. "Yours is the only opinion that matters."

That she believed him sincere only drew her further under his spell. Over the past week and a half, she'd observed that when Lord Miles escorted a woman, he was *with* that woman despite the flirtatious provocations offered by every female over the age of puberty. Miles bestowed 100% of his attention on Eleanor; heady stuff for a woman inured to being overlooked or addressed only because of the requirements of polite society. Most shocking of all, Eleanor held the strong suspicion that he *enjoyed* her company.

He frowned briefly. "I believe my half-brother, the Duke, will be attending this evening with his wife. As head of our family, it would be remarked upon if I do not make you known to him."

Eleanor eyed him as the team of match bays moved forward. The interior carriage lamp gave the enclosed space a soft golden glow. "Why the frown?"

"He is a disagreeable man puffed up with his own consequence."

"I see. Should I expect to be publicly cut?"

Miles replied in a manner devoid of emotion. "A gentleman would never cut a lady in public whatever the cause, but then, I have never considered Edgar a gentleman. Whatever his actions, they will be more directed at me than you."

She shrugged her shoulders. "He cannot say or do anything more brutal than others before him."

Miles eyed her with a softening of his expression and reached for one of her gloved hands. Before he could claim her hand, however, she forestalled any unwanted expression of sympathy he might have offered.

"Who else should I expect to see tonight? Will I know anyone there?" She listened with half an ear as Miles began to enumerate the number of his friends that she might expect to see that evening. The other half of her attention assembled the haughty, impersonal persona she assumed anytime she was forced to socialize with the ton.

She'd waltzed before—but *never* like this. The glittering ballroom faded into her periphery, overwhelmed by Miles' strong arms holding her close, his confident lead sweeping her into the crowd of couples and maneuvering her in twirls and dips until she felt she was flying. Her awareness shrank until only the music and the virile male who bent her body effortlessly to his will remained. As the strains of the violins faded and they came to a stop, Miles still holding her in his arms, Eleanor raised a face glowing with elation to him—another precedent, as for the first time in her memory, she didn't tower over her partner. "Oh... may we do that again?"

His grey eyes sparkled. "Absolutely." And he swept her off into another heady whirl of steps.

She'd lost count of time when he drew her off the dance floor and led her by her hand toward a cluster of gentlemen and ladies grouped by an open French door. He paused and turned just before reaching them. "I'm going to introduce you to my brother and his wife. After this, you need never set eyes upon them again. I apologize in advance for his boorish behavior."

Miles stopped in front of a gentleman of medium height and saturnine features, unremarkable other than for the heavy black eyebrow that crossed his forehead in a uniform, unbroken line. His lower jaw was somewhat undershot and resulted in prematurely forming folds under his chin, and his nose would have made a good bowsprit on any ship of the line.

"Your Grace, Madam, I would like to make known to you my bride-to-be, Lady Eleanor Constance Russell, only daughter of the Earl of Rutledge. Lady Russell, His Grace, the Duke of Chelsony and Her Grace, the Duchess of Chelsony."

Eleanor curtseyed to the Duke and his Duchess as he made a stiff bow and then raised his quizzing glass, tipped back his head and examined her as if she were some entomological specimen pinned to a felt board. His actions failed to intimidate as his head reached only her shoulders, and from her vantage point, she could count the long black hairs that curled out of his prominent nostrils. It was a somewhat leveling observation. His wife, though not overtly welcoming, was far less stilted but even more plain and diminutive—to the point where when she dipped in a shallow curtsy, the extravagant, three-foot-long, peacock feathers of her headdress threatened to whack Eleanor in the face.

"Lady Russell, your servant," the Duke drawled flatly. "I cannot imagine what idiocy possessed you to tie yourself to my brother. I can only pray you do not live the rest of your days in regret." Having rendered Eleanor speechless, he announced with bombastic pomposity, "We will not be attending the ceremony. I see little need to bestow the distinction of my presence on such an ill-advised union." He held his arm out to his wife. "I promised Lord Gardener I would listen to some investment scheme of his involving a railroad. Now would be a propitious time." The Duke nodded at Eleanor. "Lady Russell..." His mouth tightened until his lips disappeared. "Lord Miles. Tell Lord Edmund I meant what I said. Not a farthing. Not a pence. Not a tanner. Good evening."

As she and Miles watched the couple amble away, he snorted and muttered, "That went well, don't you think?"

Eleanor dropped her gaze to the toes of her shoes, bit her lip ferociously and fought to keep a hysterical giggle contained. She couldn't conceal her predicament from the ever-observant Miles who stuck a spoke in her wheel by chuckling.

"Go ahead and laugh. He's ridiculous. By the way, the 'Lord Edmund' he referred to is my younger brother, Ned. Are you at all thirsty? Hungry? Should we partake of some refreshment?"

"You are a horrid man!" she gurgled and raised her face to his, her eyes sparkling with hilarity. "You *know* I cannot be seen laughing," she hissed, still struggling against mirth. "How unseemly! Everyone will understand why and it would certainly reach his ears." She closed her eyes and took several steadying breaths. "I would love some punch."

Having collected their punch, a footman bearing several small plates that they had loaded with tasty comestibles followed Miles as he escorted her to one of several tall tables arranged around the room for those who didn't wish to juggle their plates and cups as they ate and drank.

"You look nothing like His Grace, and he is significantly older than you." A faint smile tipped her lips. She reached for a tiny finger sandwich and nibbled. "You are certain you are blood relations?"

"Fomenting a scandal, Lady Russell?" Miles replied in a voice of humorous reproach. "I believe I have been served enough of that dish already."

When she made an incoherent noise of distress, he shook his head and smiled. "I took no offense. His Grace and I have different mothers. Edgar is the eldest from my father's first wife—the marriage by all accounts beset with difficulties from the outset. She died in her early thirties of an inflammation of the lungs. My mother was father's second wife. He adored her despite the fact she was French and thirty years his junior. Edgar never forgave my younger brother nor me for the blatant favoritism father displayed toward us." Miles lifted a negligent shoulder. "And who should blame him? It must have been difficult to grow up discounted by one's own mother and unloved by one's sire."

"Truly? I have always thought that to be loved, it helps to be loveable."

Miles coughed into his closed hand in what Eleanor suspected was an aborted laugh.

"Whatever would your father have said about His Grace's lack of familial care for his younger brothers?"

"Hmmm. It is an interesting question that shall forever remain unanswered. Father died intestate and very suddenly—a failure of his heart. Edgar seized possession of the title with a tight-fisted clutch that hasn't loosened in the last four years. My sweet-tempered, vibrant mother had her jointure as Dowager Duchess, but Edgar has the administration of it and has bullied and browbeaten her into such a state she is almost a nonentity." Miles offered her a tight smile. "Unfortunately, I lack the wherewithal to help her."

Eleanor took a small sip of her punch. "Surely, that is about to change?"

His lips thinned. "As you say." His words came out clipped, then he drew the curtain of his effortless charm over any true emotion and smiled. "They have announced another waltz. Will you do me the honor of this dance?"

She placed her cup on the table, pasted on a return smile and dropped a slight curtsy. "With pleasure, sir." What she wished to say was he needn't dissemble; he needn't hide his feelings from her. However, with a sense of loss, she realized Lord Miles owed her no further insight into his intimate thoughts and emotions, and she had no right to ask. Though shortly to be his wife, she had no true standing in his life.

They danced until she pleaded exhaustion and begged to be taken home.

Miles settled Eleanor into the carriage and thumped on the roof with his cane to signal the coachman. He was struck by how attractive she looked when flushed with color and glowing with pleasure. In a mere two days, they would be wed, after which it was more than probable he would see her rarely, if at all. The thought produced a melancholy downturn of his spirits. He genuinely liked Eleanor and conjectured that, with additional time, he would more than merely like her. There remained an unpalatable issue that must be broached, however, and with only two days to the wedding, it must be done soon.

"Eleanor?"

"Ummm?"

"How legally unassailable do you want this marriage?"

She straightened and flashed him an apprehensive glance. "Completely."

"Penwick Elsington contacted me to advise that Prinny's lawyers are sniffing around. It seems the Prince Regent is not willing to see such a valuable property slip out of his hands at the last hour. Any suggestion of something havey-cavey and there will be an inquiry and possible invalidation of the marriage."

"I'm aware. Elsington has sent correspondence to that effect."

"Good. Then the subject I'm about to discuss is not foreign to you."

Eleanor fiddled with the folds of her dress and frowned. "I've thought of little else this week."

"Indeed? You've given no sign of it."

She glanced at him with visible wariness. "Perhaps some of your elegant composure is rubbing off on me."

For the last week, he had hashed a variety of approaches to this subject through his mind and concluded he had no experience with skittish virgins and lacked the slightest notion as to how to go on. He had decided an appeal to her practical side was the safest course.

"I'm afraid I'm going to fly in the face of your express wishes and make things awkward between us," he teased lightly.

"And we've been rubbing along so well," she responded in the same tone. An apprehensive smile flashed across her face. "Just say what you need to say."

"It is unlikely that the government and Church would act on any such petition to nullify a marriage, even one initiated by His Royal Highness. It would be costly, time-consuming and unprecedented, but should they do so, your good name will be ruined. Of course, of greatest significance is that it would nullify the petition to change the line of inheritance. You would lose Rutledge." He disregarded a frisson of aversion and braced himself for her reaction to his next words. "So... could you see your way forward to consummating this marriage?" He cleared his throat and watched Eleanor's face color as scarlet as a cavalry man's coat. "It is medieval, and so I told Penwick

Elsington, but he seems to think it will add credibility to our union."

"Yes," she croaked and then cleared her throat and stated more clearly. "He thinks it will help. I agree… ah… to all of it."

Miles lifted his chin to loosen a cravat grown suddenly tight, smoothed his cuffs and offered her an apologetic smile. "I did warn you about the awkwardness."

She waved him off with a limp hand and appeared to make every attempt to disappear into the upholstery of the carriage. Her overwhelming discomfort destroyed his customary aplomb and drove every safe topic of conversation from Miles' head. For the remainder of the trip home, only the sounds of the activities in the street and the clop of the horses' hooves disturbed the silence while he berated himself inwardly for being a heavy-handed clod. She looked anywhere but upon him, until he'd seen her safely to her door.

She turned to him and finally met his gaze with a brittle smile.

"Thank you for a lovely evening. I cannot remember another its like. Our wedding is scheduled for 3:00 in the afternoon day after next. I have a number of arrangements that will occupy all of my time until then. I look forward to seeing you at All Hallows for the ceremony and afterward I would like to come here for … ah… for… " She cleared her throat.

Miles' heart went out to her for her gallant attempt at insouciance. It hurt him to see his self-possessed Eleanor so undone. It didn't pass beneath his notice that he already considered her "his." When he took one of her hands in his, he detected a slight tremor.

"I will treat you with every consideration, Eleanor," he murmured with a reassuring smile. "I give you my promise."

"Of course you will." Her head jerked north and south, but her eyes refused to meet his. "Of course."

"As it happens, I, too, will be fully occupied. I'm riding to Newmarket to finalize the purchase of the property I mentioned to you. I expect to be back in ample time for our nuptials."

"Then I wish you a swift journey and a safe return." She drew her hand from his and offered a brisk, "Good night."

Lingering for a moment on the wide front steps, he waited until the butler had secured the door before he departed.

He had offered to make their union as legitimate as possible in an effort to secure her future and her good name—to protect her. He had the purest of motives—well, mostly pure; a portion of him warmed at the idea of possessing her, of her being uniquely *his*. He had little doubt he would enjoy making love to Eleanor—if she could be brought to enjoy it also. How to accomplish that had exercised his mind these last few days. The fact remained. Contemplation of their wedding night engendered a degree of concern, and he felt like the worst sort of scoundrel for looking forward to it, regardless.

Ned was waiting for him when the carriage pulled into the mews at Reggie's townhouse.

"Finally! I thought you were going to dance all night."

"Hello, Ned." Miles took in his brother's dishabille, from his limply tied and stained cravat to his wilting shirt points, unshaven chin and muddied top boots. As his eyes traveled down, everything about his brother proclaimed a man fagged to death. "What have you been up to, little brother? You look like the devil."

Ned laughed. "You know how it is. Just getting about on the town. I saw the announcement of your wedding in the *Times* and came to wish you happy. You always did have devilish good luck. Lady Eleanor Russell, eh? No counting ha'pence for you anymore."

"The announcement was twelve days ago, Ned."

His brother had the grace to wince and look away.

Miles took a slow, steadying breath. "I saw His Grace this evening. He said to remind you, you'd not get a farthing from him."

Ned turned the air blue with his curses. "If our father had not acknowledged him, I'd swear him no blood of ours."

Miles studied his far-too-handsome-for-his-own-good younger sibling and sighed. "How much, Ned?"

"Oh, it's nothing like that, Miles. I promise. I simply wanted to offer you my—"

"Cut line, Edmund. What are your losses?"

"… I was so sure I could win it back. Luck that bad couldn't continue, so I borrowed… but I didn't, you see— win it back. I lost what I'd borrowed and more and now…" His brother's voice trailed off miserably. "I don't know how it got to be so much, Miles." He raked his hands through his hair in a gesture of desperation. "I don't know what I'm doing here. You don't deserve to have my irresponsibility laid at your feet. You've enough on your plate." He turned to face Miles and offered him a shadow of his boyish grin. "I'll come about, never fear. I wish you happy, brother. If anyone deserves it, you do."

Miles grabbed him into a ferocious hug. "Neddy, as if I wouldn't help you." He set him away at arm's length and shook him gently. "I warned you, did I not? You cannot run with that set." He searched his brother's face. "You *cannot*, Ned." He dropped his arms. "Now, what do you owe?"

"You are the best of brothers, Miles. The best. I promise I'll be more careful."

Miles sighed and gave Ned a stern look of inquiry.

"£5,000."

"Say again?"

His brother swallowed heavily and cleared his throat. "£5,000."

"£5,000…by all that's holy!" Miles pinched the bridge of his nose and said goodbye to plans for French drains to improve the drainage in the farm's eastern fields, a new foaling barn and modernizing the bathrooms in the main house to include indoor plumbing. "I'll be gone from London for the next day or so. I'm riding to Newmarket to finalize the purchase of that property I told you about. I'll be back in the morning the day after tomorrow. Before I depart, I will write you a draft and enclose instructions to my bank directing them to extend credit against my expectations, but Ned…" He looked up and held his brother with a stern gaze. "This must be the end of it. My arrangement with Lady Russell is such that my funds are not unlimited. After the purchase of this property, I simply won't have the ready."

"No more gaming. You have my promise."

He wished he could take his brother at his word, but he'd been disappointed once too often to lend his avowal any credence and tried one more time to lure Ned from an environment that he couldn't help but feel would damage his brother beyond salvation. "Think about making your home with me, Ned—you and Mother. You've always been a magician with young stock. The living will be spartan at first, I grant you, but we'll have a life out from under His Grace." He held Ned in a steady gaze, hoping to see agreement. He was disappointed. "At least tell me you'll think about it?"

"Of course, Miles. Just a few more weeks to kick up my heels—no gaming—then I'll gladly get into harness with you."

Miles sighed. No exhortation from him would alter his brother's behavior. He had to hope that sooner or later Ned would come to his senses. "Stop by in the morning. I'll have a draft waiting for you to cover your debt and living expenses for the next quarter."

"Thank you, brother. Safe travels." Ned backed away, smiling his thanks before he turned with a wave and disappeared into the night.

Chapter Five

Miles closed his eyes, groaned softly and then walked after the carriage toward the mews. When he entered the soft golden light of the stable block, he sought out the head groom. "Gordon, please saddle the new bay hunter. I'm off to Newmarket as soon as I pack a few things."

"Burning the candle at both ends, Lord Miles?" the short man replied with a laugh. "You have a long ride ahead of you, my lord."

Miles smiled. "Yes. I've set myself up for two wearisome days. But, it can't be helped. I've much ground to cover and little time to do it in. I can sleep anytime."

The dark mass of London fell behind him as he rode toward Newmarket at a clipping trot. Maintaining a steady pace and stopping only briefly to have a hot drink at one of the posting-houses, he arrived at "The Sturdy Plowman" as morning light was beginning to streak the horizon with soft lances of pink and gold. He handed his bay off to the staff and inquired about hiring a fresh mount. Coming to an agreeable arrangement, he made his way to the common taproom for a light breakfast before he continued to the Woodward farm. He'd been up a full twenty-four hours straight. He'd stayed up until dawn many a night entertaining one of his patronesses, so long hours of physical exertion were nothing new. He figured he could catch a short nap later that evening before riding back to London. If pressed, he'd do without sleep entirely.

From The Sturdy Plowman, he found the private lane that meandered through a large wood of full-grown oaks and elms before opening onto a broad swath of cleared land, neatly fenced into paddocks of thick emerald grass where a dozen or more mares and colts grazed. The manor house and stable block occupied the horizon.

Yew and perfectly trimmed hedgerows lined a circular drive, and a fountain gurgled in the center lawn, its splashing water like crystals in the morning sun. Smooth rock walls, a subtle mix of gray and gold, formed the exterior of the two-story manor replete with mullioned windows looking out on the world. Spirals of smoke wafted from tall chimneys, and songbirds warbled, competing with the cluck of chickens and the honks of geese waddling near the stable block behind and to the east of the manor house. It was an eminently rural scene.

His gaze roved admiringly over the stone and timber perfection that housed the four-footed residents. Through open double-doors, an immaculately clean interior could be seen. Tan
bricks paved a long, wide, central aisle flanked by dark-stained, wood-paneled stalls with polished brass grills from which heads of inquisitive horses appeared, their attention captured by the activity in the stable yard.

As he rode toward the house, the sole occupant in the paddock on his right raised her sculptured chestnut head from grazing and pricked her dainty ears at him. A soft whicker preceded her all-out sprint to the fence line where she breasted the railing not more than six feet from him, wheeled and blew back across the paddock in a dazzling display of speed and infectious high spirits. She raced around the fence line and whirled to a stop facing him, bouncing on stiff legs and fracturing the morning air with explosive snorts. As he watched, a smile grew, and when his own mount blew in retort and pranced sideways with a waggle of his head, despite his physical fatigue, Miles laughed aloud at the antics of the young mare and the response she provoked from his sedate hired hack.

*This…this…*he thought to himself. *I covet this life*—a life removed from the artificialities of society that prescribed his every move. A life free of his suffocating, oppressive older brother. He pulled up and sat on his horse in the middle of the lane, surveying the natural beauty that surrounded him with abiding satisfaction and an unfamiliar sense of optimism. *This will be mine.*

"Lord Miles!" A rider approached from the direction of the stables and hailed him, and Miles raised his hand in greeting.

"Good morning, Mr. Weldon. I hope the notice of my impending visit reached you before I did."

The farm manager chuckled and closed the distance between them with a pleasant smile. "Yes. We got word of your coming, though I didn't expect you at dawn. The paperwork is in order and waiting for your signature. I'm just on my rounds to inspect the broodmares and babies and watch the morning workouts. Will you join me, my lord?

You'll get another look at the stock you've purchased along with the farm."

"I'd like nothing better. Lead on."

As they rode toward the crest of a nearby hill, Weldon indicated the young chestnut that had put on such a display of good spirits. "You are very fortunate in the timing of your purchase, Lord Miles. We have great hopes for that filly. She's entered in the 1,000 Guineas for three-year-old fillies this spring. Very serendipitous how we came to have her. Lord Marlburl bought what we thought was an open broodmare from the Earl of Rutledge to cross on our old stallion." Weldon grinned at Miles. "That season, we never got to breed her to our stud. Ten months and fourteen days after we purchased her, the mare dropped that lovely filly. The Earl of Rutledge has been trying to buy her back from Lord Marlburl ever since. Now it seems he will have her after all, even if by indirect means." The farm manager looked at Miles, curiosity evident in his tone and expression. "I heard of your impending marriage to the Earl's daughter. Congratulations, sir. Will you be adding this estate to the Rutledge holdings?"

"Thank you. No, this property will operate independently of the Rutledge stud." He had little desire to expound on the details though Weldon was clearly leaving an opening to do so. Miles straightened in the saddle. "Rutledge didn't know the mare was bred when he sold her to you?"

Weldon shook his head with a grin. "Rutledge has a young, unproven, five-year-old stallion, Dare To Dream. That filly's momma was one of three test mares exposed to him when he was a two-year-old. The breeding manager slipped up and included this filly's momma in a group of older mares that were sold. Needless to say, he is no longer in the Earl's employ. Day Dreamer, that's the filly, will be the first of Dare To Dream's get to race. Lord Marlburl nominated her to the Newmarket 1,000 Guineas Stakes and the Epsom Oaks this year."

"The 1,000 Guineas and the Oaks? She's that good?"

Weldon smiled and nodded, then shot Miles a rueful glance. "Barring injury or other mishap, you will have the pleasure of seeing her run carrying your silks."

Miles studied the chestnut filly with a horseman's appreciation of her clean lines. It was hard to find fault with her.

Miles extracted every iota of knowledge he could from the wealth stored between Mr. Weldon's ears about management of the physical property, the horses, and the breeding programs, the training routines—in short everything about which his lively brain had questions. Early morning stretched into late afternoon before he returned to the manor house to sign the documentation necessary for the transfer of property and chattel into his name. The housekeeper showed him into a small but beautifully furnished library where Lord Marlburl's man of business waited.

"Lord Miles."

"Mr. Anderson."

The two men nodded at each other and Miles seated himself where Anderson indicated.

"I trust you enjoyed your day with Mr. Weldon?"

"Very much. I'm more determined than ever to finalize this purchase."

Anderson's lips twitched in a slight smile. "If you will sign here, here and here…" He pushed papers toward Miles and watched as he scrawled his name where indicated.

"Very good, my lord. And if you will also sign these here and here."

Miles repeated his signature twice more and sat back.

Anderson scanned the documents one more time. "I believe all we need now is the exchange of monies."

"To that end, here is my draft for the full amount agreed upon, written on my London bank." Miles reached into his inner lapel, pulled out a long envelope and handed almost the entirety of his wedding settlement, less the monies he'd promised Ned, to Lord Marlburl's agent.

The man opened the envelope and looked in. "Yes, this seems in order." Anderson rose and walked around the desk where the signings had occurred and offered Miles his hand. "Congratulations on your purchase, my lord. Lord Marlburl wished me to convey his apologies that his health prevented him from being here in person, and he offered his thanks that you have chosen to retain the current staff. Some of them have been in his service for over forty years."

"I can see no reason to interfere with management clearly doing an exceptional job."

"Yes. Quite. I believe Mrs. Brody has set up the small dining room for us. Shall we continue our discussion over dinner?"

His sense of exuberance kept him going until he rode into Reggie's yard in London as yet another morning dawned, marking forty-eight hours that he'd been without sleep. When Miles slid from his horse and handed off the reins to a stable lad, his head felt as if someone had stuffed it full of cotton wool and it took all the energy he could summon to drag himself up the steps and into the house. He called for the footman who did double duty as his valet, handed off his dirt-splattered coat and hat, and instructed him, "Under no circumstances allow me to sleep for more than three hours. I'm to be married this afternoon at 3:00 and I'll need to be made presentable."

He staggered up the stairs to his room and fully clothed, right down to his muddy boots, fell face-first onto his bed. Sleep claimed him immediately.

Chapter Six

“ **I** believe I'm going to be sick.” Eleanor stared straight ahead and tried not to react to the sway of the carriage. After a rainy morning spent in the clutches of Florence and her maids, she'd set off to the church as the afternoon exploded into a celebration of brilliant sunshine and freshening air. A dreary day of London's sulfurous fog and pelting ice would have better suited her mood. Had she swapped her luxurious carriage for a three-sided tumbril, the setting would have completely appropriate.

Lady Florence smiled at her reassuringly. “You're never sick, and I cannot ever remember you in better looks. You're simply ethereal. Besides, it's normal for a bride to have some nervous jitters.” She gazed at Eleanor with a sly pursing of the lips. “Particularly if the groom is such as Lord Miles Everleigh.” She chuckled softly and stared out the window at the passing traffic with a dreamy expression. “Would that *I'd* had such a stallion to look forward to on *my* wedding night …” Florence breathed a long sigh.

Eleanor shuddered. "I can't do it," she whispered.

Her friend rolled her eyes. "Balderdash. Your tragic airs have no place here, dearest. I'm becoming quite cross with you. Now cease and desist."

Eleanor slumped into the corner of the coach. "Fine," she snapped. "But I don't know what to do other than spread my legs and allow him to have his way with me. I'm not a passive sort of female, Florence."

Florence snorted. "Eleanor, you don't have to *do* anything, at least not the first time. Your husband will guide you. Simply accommodate yourself to—"

"What do you mean, the first time!" Eleanor straightened in her seat and eyed Florence with alarm. "You never mentioned *multiple* times."

Florence closed her eyes and braced her fingertips on her forehead, her expression one of strained patience.

"Florence, you don't understand." Eleanor gazed at her hands clutched in her lap. "In truth, I'd feel better if Lord Miles weren't such a nonpareil. I'm convinced I cannot but fail to measure up to even the lowest of his expectations. I heartily wish I didn't like him so much for it will make his distaste for me when he … ah, when he… " she swallowed heavily, "… consummates our union all the more humiliating."

Florence regarded her steadily. "Has he ever said or done anything to indicate he holds you in distaste either bodily or in conduct of person?"

"No, but—"

"Did he not willingly and without coercion enter into this marital agreement?

"Yes, but—"

"Did you or did you not tell me that you and he have practically lived in each other's pockets these last two weeks; that you conversed and laughed together on a range of subjects; that he has introduced you to his closest friends and danced you into blissful exhaustion?

"Well, yes, but—"

"Wasn't it he who broached the subject of consummation to protect your interests?"

"Yes, but—"

"I'm disgusted with you, Eleanor. I never took you for such a craven ninny. Lord Miles Everleigh's every action for the last fortnight indicates he holds you in genuine regard. Now, stop being so doltish and calm your fears."

Eleanor glared at her friend who glared right back. Tense silence held sway for a long moment until the absurd situation in which she found herself in struck Eleanor as humorous. The corner of her mouth twisted and Florence snorted and swallowed a laugh.

"A craven ninny? Really?" She regarded her friend blandly. "That's what you think of me?"

Florence tipped up her chin and fought down a smile. "A *doltish*, craven ninny."

Eleanor arched an eyebrow.

"All right." Flo sniffed. "I'll be generous. A beautiful, gloriously gowned, doltish, craven ninny, who will have every man at All Hallows congratulating Lord Miles on his vast good fortune."

The wedding passed in a blur. Eleanor could remember nothing of it. She must have made the appropriate responses at the appropriate times, but she moved in a fugue state until awakening with a start at the statement by the clergyman, "I now pronounce you man and wife. You may kiss your bride, my lord."

Miles smiled down at her and in a graceful gesture in keeping with the elegance of the man, tipped her chin up and pressed his mouth gently on hers before straightening and moving them down the aisle to sign the register at the back of the chapel. He hadn't lingered in the kiss, and while she had nothing to compare it to, she wouldn't describe it as chaste. Never in her entire thirty-odd years had three seconds moved her so profoundly. She'd expected to feel awkward at being kissed. Instead, Miles had made the intimacy seem the most natural thing in the world. Despite Florence's repeated assurances, she'd expected to feel some distaste at such personal contact but instead found herself swamped with confusion at her strong desire for him *to kiss her again.*

Per their agreement, they left immediately post-ceremony for her townhouse to partake of a light dinner and… and… her mind rebelled at thinking further. As soon as he'd entered the carriage after her, Miles settled on the opposite bench. His sheer male presence seemed to occupy the entirety of the coach, but perhaps she was just hyper-aware of him. He removed his top hat and placing it on the seat beside him, leaned his head back with a muffled groan and closed his eyes. Freed of the need to be circumspect, Eleanor studied her new husband's masculine face and elegant form with what she could only term as avarice.

"Do I pass muster, Lady Miles Everleigh?" His low silky voice teased her.

She didn't know how she'd betrayed herself. "You must be aware your features send every normal female's heart aflutter."

His head lolled from side to side with the sway of the carriage. He'd still not opened his eyes. He gave all the appearance of a man fagged to death—was he truly exhausted, or did he so regret the upcoming consummation that he couldn't bear to look at her? The "craven ninny" in her sounded a call to arms.

He gave a low chuckle and opened languid eyes to regard her briefly before closing them again. His body remained relaxed against the velvet squabs. "I would never describe you as a normal female," he murmured.

"No." Eleanor shielded her tender feelings behind a curt response. "I believe you share that opinion with the majority of the ton."

His eyes remained closed, but his lips curled in a slow smile. "If asked, I would describe you as an uncommonly handsome woman of impeccable comportment, great sensibility, and unusual intellect."

"Oh."

At that one, uncomfortable syllable, he opened his eyes again and captured her in a steady gray gaze alive with amusement before, once again, his lids descended, and his loose body swayed to the motion of the carriage. An incipient smile lingered at the corners of his mouth.

They accomplished the remainder of the ride to her townhome in silence. His sincerely uttered compliments had reduced her tenuous composure to shambles, though it seemed he didn't share her turmoil of spirit. To her intense irritation, Miles appeared to sleep.

"The footmen have removed three of your untouched plates in the last hour, Eleanor. Would you like to dispense with the dessert course entirely and retire to your chambers?"

The picture of self-possessed relaxation, Miles sprawled in his chair at the intimate table her staff had set for them in her library and regarded her steadily through sleepy eyes. He drew idle circles on the white Damascus tablecloth with an indolent index finger and occasionally sipped from his second, or was it the third, glass of champagne. While he'd eaten with a hearty appetite, he'd been surprisingly abstemious, refusing the red and white wines offered with the meat and fish courses and only sipping at his champagne.

But then he would be composed, wouldn't he? He'd probably been the chief orchestrator of scenes like this with great regularity whereas she was afflicted with a nervous desire to have this night over with and no interest whatsoever in food or drink. Well... timidity had never featured strongly in her character, no matter Florence's accusations. She placed her napkin on the table. She removed her gloves from where they lay in her lap and arranged them beside the napkin.

Miles straightened immediately and stood to assist her from her chair. "I take it that's a yes." He turned her to face him and held her hands in a light clasp.

She nodded and dropped her attention to their joined hands. His were wonderfully warm. The unfamiliar contact of flesh on flesh provoked...feelings...in her.

"Eleanor..."

"Mmm?"

"Look at me, please."

She raised her face to his and met his gaze boldly. "What?"

"Ah, there you are. I worried some imposter had stolen the place of the self-assured woman I've come to greatly admire." He smiled, and she couldn't help but answer with a roll of her eyes and the trace of a return smile. "I understand you are nervous, but I assure you, there is every chance you will enjoy what we do tonight."

She twisted her face into a wry grimace. "But will you?" His throaty chuckle was unexpected and did astounding things to her insides.

"Without a doubt. Men are the easiest of creatures to please."

She examined him closely, but he stood before her with an easy honesty that she couldn't bring herself to question, just as there was no questioning the intensity of her attraction to him. He was too handsome, too vital, *too male*. Miles could add one more besotted female to what she was certain was a lengthy list. A strong sense of possessiveness swept through her when she considered he was *her* husband. For the rest of his life, Miles Wrotham Everleigh was legally bound to *her*, and at least for tonight, he would be her husband in truth. That had to count for something. She straightened. "I should like it very much if you would kiss me again."

His eyes lost some of their sleepy look and his expression sobered. He dropped her hands and brought one of his to wrap the nape of her neck with his thumb under her chin, while the other hand slipped around her waist and drew her toward him. He lowered his lips to hers and brushed her mouth lightly, interspersed with gentle nibbles, coaxing and seducing her into yearning for more. When he pulled back slightly only to re-engage by wickedly tracing the seam of her mouth with the tip of his tongue, she gasped. With a low murmur of approval, he deepened his kiss into her open mouth with a firm pressure of warm lips and an invading tongue. *By all the saints above!* She fisted her hands in the superfine of his lapels and pulled, insisting he intensify the unprecedented sensations that swept her from head to toe, sensations she was feeling for the first time in her life, sensations that demanded a further exploration.

He seemed to understand her silent command and responded with a firm mastery that unraveled her. Parts of her body to which she had never given thought heretofore were behaving in unfamiliar and intriguing ways. A flush of languid warmth built in her, leaving her relaxed and energized—all at the same time. Eleanor closed her eyes and lost herself so thoroughly in Miles' spell that it took her a moment to comprehend what had happened when he straightened and with hands on her hips, held her away from him.

"Go upstairs, Eleanor. I'll give you some time to prepare, and then I'll join you." His voice sounded hoarse.

Dropping her arms off his shoulders, she opened her eyes and blinked to bring him into focus. "My chamber is the second door on the right at the top of the stairs." She stepped back; his arms dropped away. With a brief curtsey, she maintained a dignified pace until clearing the door of the library, whereupon she abandoned all dignity. Hiking up her skirts, she pelted up the stairs and into her bedroom where she immediately crossed to the bell pull and gave it a vigorous yank. An eternity elapsed, though her clock read only five minutes, as she paced and then sat and then rose—only to pace again before a knock on the door sent her flying to answer.

"Finally! Sally, help me out of this gown and have Edith prepare a hot bath for me. I'll have the lavender bath salts, please. Two generous spoonfuls. Lay out my new negligee, and I'll need help taking down my hair. Oh, and have someone retrieve my gloves from the library. I seem to have left them behind." She strained behind her to reach the tiny buttons fastening her sheer overdress.

"Yes, Ma'am. Oh! Be careful, my lady, you'll tear it in your hurry, and it's such a gorgeous gown. I'm sure you'll wish to wear it again."

Eleanor stood and quivered in impatience as her maid summoned the chambermaid, repeated her instructions and then began to methodically remove Eleanor's wedding attire. Finally, her attendant wrapped her in a voluminous oriental robe, and Eleanor slipped into her bathing chamber.

"Sally, I don't need your assistance with my bath, but please stay and help me with my hair."

"Yes, madam."

Sinking into the warm, fragrant water, Eleanor finally allowed herself a shiver of pure excitement. Yes, she was nervous. She found it impossible to believe that Miles could desire her—no one ever had before—but down the home stretch, curious anticipation had overtaken fear of physical embarrassment by a nose and looked to be the winner of this race. Finally, she would be initiated into the mysteries that most of her sex had known for years, and if the rest of what Miles would show her matched the kisses he'd bestowed on her in the library? *Oh, my.* She bit her lower lip and sank up to her shoulders in the scented water with a most un-Eleanor-like giggle.

From the warm response of his bride to his kisses, their wedding night was going to be a memorable experience. Eleanor had swanned out of the library in a composed and dignified manner, but he had very good hearing, and it told him she galloped up the stairs. He chuckled to himself, pleased beyond all reason at her eagerness. He couldn't think of anything he'd dislike more than initiating such intimacies with someone who lay frozen and merely endured. He enjoyed physical pleasures as often as the next man—perhaps more so should the testimony of his paramours be truth and not flattery, but even at his most inexperienced, he'd striven to give as much delight as he took. Fortunately, the lovely older women who'd taken him under their wings had been supremely good instructors, and he had every confidence in his ability to satisfy Eleanor if she would be a willing participant.

Beyond the simple courtesies owed any woman on her wedding night, he felt something for Eleanor, something beyond admiration, something deeper than simple liking—a strong affection, perhaps. He didn't know. None of his previous "hostesses" had evoked the feelings he possessed for his new wife. Whatever the emotion was, it had grown steadily since he'd first met her, and the idea that he'd see her rarely after tonight brought a sense of gloom unusual to him. *Bah...more than likely temporary mopishness brought on by exhaustion.*

The clock read 8:00. The water pipes had been banging for several minutes so she'd obviously decided on a bath. He'd allow her until 9:30 and then go up. Hopefully, that would be enough time. He doubted he could keep his eyes open much past that. He picked up the Madeira bottle sitting on a small table, crossed the library to a likely looking velvet sofa, poured himself a short glass and sat. Placed facing the fireplace, the seating was just as comfortable as it looked. He stared into the flames, sipping pensively, and fed his lustful thoughts about exactly what he'd like to do to Lady Eleanor Everleigh. Replete from an excellent dinner, enveloped in the embrace of down cushions and warmed by a glowing fire, sleep crept toward him with insidious stealth and ambushed him unawares. Not even the glass rolling from his fingers and dousing his trouser leg with Madeira was sufficient to wake him.

"There you go, my lady." Sally drew a hairbrush through Eleanor's waist-length hair and pronounced, "A woman's glory, to be sure, Ma'am. I've put all your jeweled hairpins in the cloisonné dish. Edith has turned down your bed and swept it with a warming pan. A decanter of port and cold collation is set out on the small table in your sitting room should you or Lord Miles wish a late-night nosh. Is there anything else you need before you retire?" Sally's reflection smiled at her in the mirror.

"No, thank you very much. You and Edith are dismissed for the evening."

Sally dipped in a curtsey and in the mirror, Eleanor watched them leave, the two young women's heads together whispering and giggling. For the last two weeks, she'd have had to be blind and deaf to miss the excitement and pleased approval all her staff exuded at the announcement of her marriage to Lord Miles. Eleanor studied herself in the mirror. With her abundant hair loose and free-flowing she looked a decade younger. She felt a decade younger. A sense of girlish excitement suffused her, and for once in her life, she allowed it—with a cautionary reminder that it was only for tonight.

Eleanor lifted her sheer nightdress and slipped between the pristine white sheets. Florence had assured her that this sort of transparent nothingness would drive any man wild with desire. Was it possible she could engender such passion in that magnificent man? With a sense of restrained hopefulness and much fiddling with the sheets, her hair, her negligee, she arranged herself in what she hoped was a seductive position and waited for her groom to appear.

After thirty minutes of staring at the door, she flipped back the covers, slipped her feet into her slippers and tiptoed to the door. Opening it a crack, she listened intently. Quiet shrouded the house. She frowned and pursed her lips. *Patience. Don't rush your fences, girl.* It's only been…she glanced at the mantle clock…two hours since dinner. *He's being a gentleman and allowing you time.* Somewhat mollified, Eleanor moved to her floor to ceiling windows and pulled back a drape to look out onto her small garden. The stars were barely visible in the hazy London sky, but the moon was bright enough that she could chart its course. The pale yellow orb hung just above the treetops. With a huff, she picked up the book she'd been reading on the history of the Byerley Turk, one of the foundation race sires in England, and settled back into her bed to read.

An hour later she couldn't ignore the ugly whispers in the back of her mind—whispers that reminded her how unattractive men had always found her; how not even a fortune could make her desirable. *But he'd wanted me in the library!* she argued back. *He seemed eager.* It's one thing to give a woman kisses and quite another to do the deed, said the whispers. Perhaps he cannot bring himself quite up to the mark after all. *No…no…Everleigh will come.*

Another hour passed.

And another.

In a state of numbness, Eleanor found her dressing gown and slippers and padded softly down the hall past the sleeping footman—she wanted no witnesses to her night of ignominy—and descended the stairs to the first floor. She slipped into the library and summed up the pathetic situation in one sweeping glance. From the strong smell of the sweet Madeira wine and the gentle snores emanating from the sofa, Lord Everleigh had succumbed to drink. The whispers in her mind suggested he'd been in need of Dutch courage to face bedding her. Whatever the reason, his presence on the sofa instead of in her bed failed to flatter. She couldn't have been more stunned if she'd fallen off a galloping horse. Indeed, she felt the same inability to draw breath and the same shocking physical hurt.

Eleanor fled to her bedroom and rang for her dresser.

"Yes, my lady?" Sally rubbed sleepy eyes and surveyed Eleanor's bedchamber, straightening when she realized the bed was almost undisturbed and she stood alone with her mistress. Eleanor gave her credit for concealing any reaction she had almost immediately.

"Prepare a traveling bag for yourself and me—just the necessities. We are returning to Rutledge. Send a footman to John Coachman and tell him to put the grays to my post-chaise. I wish to leave within the hour."

"Yes, ma'am, but..." Sally opened her mouth, closed it, and opened it again.

"Speak up, Sally."

"But what about Lord Miles?"

"What about him?"

Sally shrugged helplessly, her arms making vague gestures.

"My fervent prayer is that I will not set eyes upon Lord Miles Everleigh for the remainder of my life."

Chapter Seven

M iles opened his eyes to a fire gone cold and some sort of commotion in the hall outside. He shoved himself upright and blinked— then leaped up and strode to the library door turning the air blue with curses. Too many servants for this hour of night bustled back and forth in the hall.

"You there." He grabbed the arm of a passing footman. "Get me Lady Eleanor's maid. On the instant."

The young man drew up stiffly. "Terribly sorry, my lord, but that is not possible. Miss Conway is no longer in residence."

"What! For heaven's sake man, where can she have gone at this hour?"

"She left with Lady Russ—Miles, sir."

"Left?"

"Yes, my lord."

"Where the hell did they go?"

"I believe my lady's destination was Rutledge Manor, my lord."

"The devil you say! How long ago did they leave?"

The footman sniffed and eyed Miles' pants with disdain. Miles ignored his impertinence as he well understood its source. The red Madeira stain on his fawn inexpressibles could not be missed, and he stank like a winery. "When did Lady Miles leave?"

"The Lady Miles Everleigh departed thirty minutes ago with instructions to close the townhouse immediately, put the furniture under Holland covers and pull the knocker from the door. You will need somewhere else to reside the night, my lord."

Horrified disbelief drove Miles to ascend the stairs two at a time and storm into the bedchamber Eleanor had said was hers. He stopped in the center of the room and turned in a complete circle. The wardrobe doors hung open with the inner contents in disarray. Stockings and gloves draped the open drawers of a chest of drawers. Everywhere his gaze landed, signs of a hasty departure greeted him. He moved to the bed. A transparent wisp of a nightgown had been thrown carelessly across it. A long rip marred the delicate bodice—torn as if its wearer couldn't shed it fast enough. A faint waft of Eleanor's clean scent reached his nose, and he groaned. "Eleanor...what you must have thought." His shoulders slumped, and he closed his eyes. "I'm so very sorry."

His pace when he left was vastly more subdued than when he'd entered. One thought and one thought only occupied his mind. He must make this right.

A hansom cab dropped him off at Baron Stanton's, and he went to his bedchamber and rang for a servant. In these aristocratic households, someone was always available even in the dead of night.

"Lord Miles? We weren't expecting you back tonight, my lord. How may I help you?" The baron's somewhat baffled housekeeper blinked sleepily.

"Yes, my plans took a sudden change. Sorry to roust you from your bed at this hour, Mrs. Batmin, but I need to speak with Baron Stanton."

She dropped a polite curtsey and murmured, "I'll send someone for him, my lord."

Miles stripped off his wedding finery and dressed in serviceable riding clothes. A short search under the bed revealed a small portmanteau into which he packed several changes of linen and his toiletries. Reggie surprised him by appearing in less than an hour with his bony feet tucked into red velvet slippers. A long tasseled nightcap covered his head and hung down over his left shoulder onto a figured oriental banyan in Coquelicot red. "This better be good, Miles. I love you like a brother, but it's half-past four in the morning…besides, I thought you'd be with your new bride."

"May I borrow a horse, Reg? I'll change mounts at the first available posting house and send him back. I need to leave town for a bit, and I can't take Badger. He won't be up to the hard pace."

A frown wrinkled his friend's brow. "This is very unlike you—to leave in such a harum-scarum way, but of course, you may have the pick of my cattle."

Miles closed and latched his bag. "You are the best of men, Stanton. I've been extraordinarily careless and have inflicted immeasurable hurt on Lady Miles. I believe she is on her way to Rutledge Manor as we speak. I must see what I can do to correct the wrong I've done her, and I must do it quickly. The longer she believes that …" Miles shook his head. "I won't go into particulars, but this must be remedied quickly."

Reggie's eyebrows flew up, and his posture became haughtily erect. "Disappointed in you, my lord. Very unlike you to inflict injury on a virginal female. I thought you possessed of greater finesse."

Miles gave a bark of forced laughter. "By all that's holy, Stanton, not physically. She's quite—intact. The injury was emotional."

Miles' friend blinked like an owl and then relaxed. "Oh…well, then. I want the whole story when you return, or I shall expire of curiosity."

"I'll give you what I'm at liberty to share. Though… I may go on to my farm in Newmarket. I might not return to town."

"If so, then Mary and I shall descend upon you like a plague of locusts." His friend paused. "We shouldn't have to sleep in the straw, would we? I doubt Mary would enjoy rusticating that much."

Miles crushed his friend in a bracing hug and then stepped back. "I have very adequate guest rooms, never fear. I cannot delay. Give my love to Mary, and Stanton…" He winced. "Could you keep an eye on Ned?"

"Be off with you, Everleigh, and yes, I'll keep an eye on your pesky brother."

Despite his late departure from London, he dogged Eleanor's heels the entire eight-hour journey to Rutledge Manor. He'd thought he'd catch her, but a combination of her coachman's superb driving and the prime bits of blood and bone that comprised her teams—and she'd changed them twice at posting houses along the way—had frustrated him. When he'd stopped at those same posting houses to acquire a fresh mount, he'd been told, "Just missed her, my lord. She changed horses and was off—in a powerful hurry, too."

He'd been within sight of her carriage; on narrow bits of road he'd heard the coach horn blown in warning, but at the spanking pace she'd set, he never caught up with her. Her pace had only increased as daylight broke. His admiration for John Coachman grew with every mile that passed under his horse's galloping hooves. The rate of speed with which Eleanor traveled pounded into his brain with every step of his laboring horse, the degree of her fury and hurt. His mouth grew tight as he urged the slug he rode to a better effort.

To say the lands comprising the Rutledge estate impressed Miles would be a vast understatement. He'd grown up on a big estate and was no stranger to grand properties but nevertheless, the acreage and surrounding towns that were attached to Rutledge—from the thousands of acres in pastures and tillage to the prosperous villages he rode through—spoke of monied attention. Vast sums had been spent not only on the home estate but on the tenant farmers and merchant villages that surrounded Rutledge Manor. It was no stretch of the mind to understand why Eleanor was so desperate to hold Rutledge together and Prinny so anxious to acquire it. But to Miles, none of it began to address the true jewels of her inheritance—the splendid racehorses whose slender legs pranced onto England's racetracks, and more often than not, bore Rutledge's blue and gold colors into the winner's circle.

Eleanor's team had been unhooked from the traces and was being led off when he rode into the central courtyard at Rutledge Manor, dismounted and handed his job horse off to a groom with instructions to return it to the last posting house in the morning. He mounted the wide port cochere steps to the fifteen-foot, double oaken doors and with a deep breath and a straightening of his shoulders lifted the lion's head knocker and rapped loudly.

The door opened, and Miles stepped through, handed a doorman his whip, stripped his hands of his gloves and shrugged out of his great coat. He draped his coat, top hat, and gloves across the stunned man's still outstretched arm. "Good afternoon. I'm Lord Miles Everleigh. I'm here to see my wife."

Miles gave a jerk to the skirts of his closely fitted riding coat, stretched his neck and checked his appearance in the entry hall mirror. His cravat was somewhat disheveled, his hair was more than a little tousled, and he could stand a shave, but under the circumstances, it would have to do. Nothing could be done about his mud-spattered top boots. However, he doubted he could get any further into Eleanor's bad graces than he'd already done.

"Your w-w-wife, my lord?" the man stuttered.

"Yes. The Lady Miles Everleigh. Formerly, The Lady Eleanor Russell." He bestowed his most winning smile on the doorman. "She arrived somewhat ahead of me. Where may I find her?"

The footman was rescued by the appearance of a dignified gentleman that Miles assumed was the butler.

"Baines, see to Lord Miles's apparel. I'll escort him to Lady…" the presumed butler bestowed a steady look of impervious calm on Miles, "…Miles Everleigh." With a small bow, the man continued, "I am Walters, butler to The Earl of Rutledge. I apologize for my failure to greet you at the door. If you will follow me, my lord."

With an unhurried, deliberate pace, the butler led Miles down a wide marble hallway of twenty-foot ceilings, one side of which was comprised entirely of floor-to-ceiling windows and lining the opposite side, open doors gave glimpses into opulent chambers. Walters stopped at one that remained partially opened, and Miles could hear Eleanor respond defensively to a gravelly male bark.

"…married, yes, that's what I said."

A raspy female voice, trembling with age responded, "Oh, my darling girl! How wonderful, but wherever is your groom? We must be introduced."

"Mother, there is a slight irregularity. You see, I ah… ah… Here's the thing… ah…"

Through the door, Miles could see Eleanor's hands floundering awkwardly. He cleared his throat. "Walters, I'll announce myself. Thank you."

The man bowed. "Certainly, my lord."

Miles thought the man muttered, "Good luck," as he withdrew, but he might have misheard. With a bracing breath for courage, Miles strode boldly into the room to confront his runaway bride and two fragile persons of extremely advanced age, both wrapped in warm blankets and seated in front of a ripping fire—none other than The Earl of Rutledge and his Countess. He'd never set eyes on them before, but it couldn't be anyone else. Eleanor's father must have been a lion of a man, for even in advanced age he made an imposing figure with iron-gray hair and piercing blue eyes. Her mother was an unusually handsome woman whose face of classic bone structure was wreathed in a cloud of pure white hair.

"Lady Miles, how did you get so far in front of me? My dear, had I known you would set such a frantic pace, I'd have elected to ride with you in the carriage." He strode forward and kissed a wooden Eleanor lightly on the cheek and, turning to her parents, made an elegant leg, first to Lady Rutledge and then to the Earl. "Lady Rutledge, Lord Rutledge, Lord Miles Wrotham Everleigh at your service. I am the third youngest to His Grace the sixth Duke of Chelsony, and as your lovely daughter was just informing you, I have the blessed good fortune to be her husband." Miles gave Eleanor a warm look. "A mutual acquaintance made us known to each other, and three days later we agreed to be married. Isn't that right, Eleanor?" Miles gave her a steady look that dared her to disagree.

"We did?" She blinked and shook herself. "Ah…yes, yes, we did. Three days later."

"I apologize for what must seem precipitous actions and for not seeking your approval, my lord, but events quite swept us off our feet. I simply couldn't wait to make her mine."

"Oh…a love match. Oh, Eleanor, my sweet child, I'm so very, very happy for you." Lady Rutledge brightened, held her hand to her breast and gave a heartfelt sigh of joy. "Such a pretty speech from such a handsome man." She beamed at her daughter. "I knew someday someone would have the good sense to appreciate the treasure that you are."

The Earl's hawk-like gaze settled on Miles skeptically, as if he knew exactly how close to an outright lie Miles had sailed, but his lips quirked in amusement. "The Duke of Chelsony, eh? I knew the old Duke, your sire…knew him quite well. Good man. Can't say as I care for the present Duke." The old gentleman paused to catch his breath. "My daughter has a level head on her shoulders. I have no objection if you've won Eleanor's acceptance. Eleanor…?" His gaze shot to his daughter and he narrowed his eyes. Eleanor appeared to be in another world, and it wasn't until Miles nudged her gently that she returned to the present.

"Ah…yes, Father?"

Miles never knew what Eleanor's response might have been as the Earl was afflicted by a spate of heavy coughing and struggled for breath. For the first time, Miles noticed a nurse who'd been sitting quietly in the corner of the room. She crossed to attend the Earl.

"Here you are, my lord." She unstoppered a bottle, poured a strong-smelling syrup onto a spoon and offered it to the Earl, who swallowed it without complaint.

Lady Rutledge warbled, "Show your husband to your apartments, dear. Get out of your dirt, and we'll see you again at dinner. I know I speak for Rutledge when I say we are delighted to have you as a new son-in-law, Lord Miles. Such a godsend."

Miles bowed again, and Lady Rutledge offered a shaky hand, which he took, gently kissing the age-spotted skin.

"Lady Miles?" Miles offered his arm. With a face devoid of expression, she took it, and he led her out of the room.

When they had cleared the door, Eleanor shook off his arm and without inflection stated, "Follow me." She picked up her skirts in both hands and proceeded to quick march— there could be no other way to describe her martial gait— down the wide hall to a grand staircase, whereupon she slapped one hand on the handrail and head down, attacked the stairs, never looking to see if he accompanied her. On the second floor, Miles strode after her down a densely carpeted hallway and into a suite of elegant rooms.

"Close the door, please," she directed quietly. When he'd done so, she drew herself erect and hissed, "Just what do you think you're about?"

"Eleanor, I could not allow you to leave London thinking what you must have been thinking. Will you please let me explain my failure to—"

"Your failure to come to my bed?" she snapped. "I believe I put two and two together and arrived at four. I saw you in the library, foxed, stinking of wine and dead to the world hours after … after." She clenched her fists and tightened her jaw. Her eyes appeared suspiciously moist. "You need not humiliate me any further, my lord."

He closed his eyes and gathered his patience. "I deserve your animosity, and I am not here to humiliate you. The boot is quite on the other foot. It is I who am mortified. I greatly regret the events of last night, and I'm here to explain… if you will please hear me out?"

"I have no desire to hear anything you have to say, my lord. Your actions have spoken quite clearly, and I wish most heartily that you will leave here and never cross my path again."

The vehemence of her statement was disheartening. There was little he could do if she'd closed her mind to him and he had enough male pride that he would not beg her to listen. That she was wrong about him did cause a ripple of irritation—particularly since he'd gone to some effort to disabuse her of her erroneous assumption and set the matter right, but what caused him the most disquiet was that she held a mistaken belief about herself—a belief confirmed in her mind by his inaction. He stood and regarded her with some empathy as she glared back at him, oozing hostility born from hurt and shame for which he held himself responsible. Regret was a bitter fruit, and he had partaken of it thoroughly in the last few hours. "I don't suppose there is anything I can say that will make you hear me out or believe my sincerity should I force you to listen?"

She turned her back to him. "Nothing."

He studied her erect back for a long moment and said gently, "Eleanor, I highly recommend that you don't live the rest of your life clutching wounded pride to your breast. From personal experience, I can testify that it makes for a cold existence."

"How would you know? I should think you devoid of pride, as you openly live off the charity of lonely women like some bloodsucking leech."

He stiffened and inhaled deeply at the insult—and tried not to allow her words to wound, a more or less unsuccessful effort. He reminded himself that she felt he'd rejected her and was striking out in hurt more than anything else, but the verity in her statement could not be denied Regardless of the mitigating circumstances, despite the truth of her accusation, he did retain enough self-respect to deny her the opportunity to abuse him further.

He reached into his riding coat, pulled out a slim silver card case and extracted a thick embossed card. Holding the card between his fore and middle fingers, he placed it on a small table by the door. "Should you ever require anything from me, this is my direction. I am not returning to London." He bowed. "I will take my leave of you, my lady. I wish you only the best. Please offer my regrets to your parents that I will be unable to join them for dinner."

She never once turned around as he left.

As soon as the door closed behind Miles, Eleanor fell on her bed, hugged her pillow to her breasts and dissolved into a deluge of sobbing. The emptiness of being unwanted as a woman was a pain she didn't think she would ever overcome—which made her even angrier, as she never, never, never did anything so missish as shed tears over a man. She didn't indulge for long. With shuddering gasps and many swipes at her eyes and cheeks, she shoved herself off the bed and jerked the pull for Sally. She would *not* be unraveled by the events of the past two days.

When all was said and done, she had accomplished what she could to secure Rutledge and hopefully, her days would continue as they had for the last ten years. She had a good life, surrounded by people who cared for her, and the supreme satisfaction of watching horses she had bred and trained perform most credibly on the race courses of England. So what if an elegant younger man with sparkling grey eyes who had made her feel young and vital and desirable for two memorable weeks had proved to be just as faithless as the rest of his misbegotten gender.

A knock sounded at her door. "Ma'am, do you wish help dressing for dinner?"

"Enter, Sally. Yes, help me out of this carriage dress and ring below for some hot water."

"Um…my lady?"

"Yes?"

"Was that Lord Miles I saw departing the house?"

"I don't wish to speak of it, Sally, and you are never to mention his name to me again."

"Sorry, ma'am," she muttered. "T'is a dreadful shame. He seemed ever so nice a gentleman, and I thought perhaps you liked him, too.

"Not one word more, Sally. I allow you far too much liberty, and you overstep."

"Yes, ma'am. Sorry, ma'am."

Tears threatened, and she blinked them back rapidly as something bleak twisted in the region of her heart. Sally was right. She had liked Miles—more than liked him—but after such an affront, such a humiliation … well, the hurt was out of all proportion to the act.

"Please put out my rose damask with the French lace overdress, and I'll have the rose quartz ear drops and matching necklace."

Now she must give some thought as to what to say to her parents about the sudden absence of her handsome husband. Her father would look at her with his wise eyes and know she was bamming them, but perhaps she could come up with some reason that would soothe the tender heart of her mother. As much as Eleanor had suffered during her failed debut, her dearest Mamma had suffered more, and Eleanor would do almost anything to spare her additional disappointment.

She'd been a late-in-life child, a miracle born long after her parents had given up hoping and upon her birth, her mother's world had revolved around Eleanor. Her father had treated her in equal portions like the son he'd never have and a cherished daughter to be protected and cosseted. He'd educated Eleanor in the management of Rutledge, in its horse farms and breeding barns, in the rotation of crops for best yield and what surfaces made the best roads in the villages surrounding the great estate house—the benefits of thatch versus slate for roofing—in short, in all the minutiae attendant with the excellent management of a great estate.

The transition of power from the Earl to his daughter had been one of seamless efficiency, and more and more often, it was Eleanor that the agents and managers and tradesmen sought out for decisions. It was her word that shaped policy on the vast estate and in the villages surrounding Rutledge.

As she made her way down the grand staircase to the family dining room, not the opulent room where fifty guests could be fed at one time, but the intimate room that seated eight, Walters stopped her.

"My lady, the excitement of your joyous news overcame the Earl and Lady Rutledge, and they have ordered supper in their rooms. They convey their apologies and hope you'll understand if they wish you and Lord Miles a good night."

"Of course. Please tell Cook to send a tray to my room as well."

"Yes, your ladyship. I'll have two trays sent up."

She cleared her throat. "No. Just one. Lord Miles has been called away." She smoothed the front of her gown. "I don't expect his return in the foreseeable future."

Walters' visage remained expressionless. "Yes, my lady. I will tell Cook to prepare a single tray."

He bowed and walked off in his unperturbed, purposeful manner, and Eleanor let out a breath she hadn't realized she'd held. God bless Walters. She wondered if even the second coming of Christ would provoke the man into some display of emotion. She turned and retreated to her room with a huff of amusement at the mental image of Walters' flat tones announcing, "My Lords and Ladies, Our Lord Jesus Christ, The Only Son of God."

Her amusement was short-lived, washed away by a sense of immense sadness and regret. In hindsight, she wished she hadn't acted so impulsively and had at least heard what Lord Miles had to say in his defense—even if it had been utter nonsense. She beat back another attack of tears and muttered an admonition to herself about becoming a watering pot.

Chapter Eight

The next morning, she rose at her usual hour of 5:00 a.m. and consumed the hot chocolate and toast left on the small table just inside the door to her apartments. Lord Miles' calling card, still where he left it from the evening before, caught her eye.

M. W. Everleigh
The Fairwood Stud
Wodditton Road, Newmarket

She paused for a moment, made a quick decision, and threw the card into the top drawer of her dressing table.

She completed a brief toilette and pulled on a man's linen shirt, navy wool waistcoat, buckskin breeches, and a tall pair of black and tan riding boots. She twisted her hair up under a tweed pork-pie cap and donned a knee-length riding coat and tan gloves. Suitably dressed for a day in the fields—as a man, she trooped downstairs to the front entrance.

"Lady Eleanor." The night doorman closed his book and sprang up from his chair to open the front door for her.

"Morning, Jeffers, and it's Lady Miles now. I have married. What are you reading?"

"Yes, ma'am. Sorry, ma'am. *Lady of the Lake*, your ladyship."

"And is it a good book?"

"Not as much as *Ivanhoe*, ma'am. It's poetry… but it passes the time."

She smiled at his mournful face. "Well, please tell Walters to advise Mamma I'll see her and Father at dinner. I've only been away three weeks, but I'm chafing to make the rounds with Mr. Bitters. I'll stop for a meal at the Spotted Hare in Stelton."

"Yes, my lady. Nice to have you back, your ladyship, and felicitations on your marriage."

"Oh…yes. Thank you." She nodded at the young man and hustled across the dark cobblestone courtyard to the stable block and the office of the manager of the stud, Mr. Bitters. A golden glow spilled from the window. Well versed in her habits, he'd anticipated her.

She inhaled deeply when entering the immaculate stables where, through the brass grills of the loose boxes, the gaslight revealed shapes of tall equines in their warm rugs. The sound of contented munching and the sweet smell of hay and horse met her senses and the weight of the world—or at least the events of the last couple of weeks—slipped from her shoulders. She stood motionless, closed her eyes and simply drank in the beloved sounds and smells of home.

"Toby's saddling Mouse for you, madam. Thought we'd start with the broodmares and foals just as soon as it gets light enough; meanwhile, we can have a look at the stallions. We will join Fedder when the mob gets ready to go to morning workouts."

She turned with a brilliant smile. "Mr. Bitters." The fifty-something gentleman had been with Rutledge since boyhood, first as an exercise boy, then when he grew too heavy for the young horses, as an under groom, then a groom, and now as the manager of the stud. It was under his tutelage, as much as that of her father, that Eleanor had gained her love and knowledge of the Thoroughbred horse. Give Bitters the name of any notable animal, home-bred or not, and he could recite back sire and dam for several generations with all their wins and losses, and even the tracks where they had raced. The "mob" to which he referred were the two and three-year-olds in race training, and "Fedder" was Rutledge's long-suffering resident trainer—long-suffering because he patiently endured Eleanor's frequent and opinionated disruptions of his carefully plotted development of their young prospects.

"That will be lovely. How's Dare? How's my boy?"

Laughter greeted her question. "As full of himself as ever. He's at grass in the southwest paddock with the Oldham mare and Red Molly for company." Her manager cleared his throat and looked elsewhere. "Thought it best to have him separated from the older gents as they went about their business." A bright flush of red painted his cheeks.

"Of course. Very sensible." It never failed to delight her that Bitters blushed scarlet every time he had to discuss with her an issue involving breeding and stallion management.

As they walked down the stable row, Eleanor looking into the stalls that housed the two senior stallions of Rutledge, she and Bitters chatted about the happenings while she'd been in London. Exercise boys slipped quietly down the stairs from their quarters above the stables, and with soft murmurs to their charges, began preparing their assigned mounts for the morning's first workouts. At the clip-clop of shod hooves on the brick aisle and a light clearing of a male's throat, Eleanor turned. The head groom, a man in his late fifties, stood holding both her horse, a tall, flea-bitten grey, and Bitters' rangy brown.

"My lady." The older man bobbed his head in a gesture of respect.

"Thanks, Toby." With a smile, she led her gelding into the yard, tossed the reins over his head and with Toby holding her offside stirrup, slipped her foot into the irons and swung up. She sighed in contentment as she settled her seat into the saddle. Turning to Bitters, she complained, "It was such an inconvenience to be restricted to riding sidesaddle. Every time I am in London, I swear it will be my last, but I always seem to return."

Turmoil roiled her belly. Eleanor would give anything to never again speak of her marriage, but if anyone deserved to hear of it from her own mouth, it was Julian Bitters. She spent the majority of her days with him in the normal course of affairs, and over the years, in addition to his professional management, Bitters had become her friend and closest confidant. He knew things about her she could never share with her parents.

It was the stables that she'd run to when any storm upset her childhood world, and it seemed she always wound up in Bitters' office, tucked into his worn couch, drinking a hot cup of tea and munching on a digestive biscuit, while pouring out her sorrows. He'd listen patiently, dry her tears, offer a bracing comment and the perfect distraction of a new puppy or kitten or foal. In later years when she'd returned, beaten down and sore of heart from her seasons in London, he'd greet her with a gentle hug and an offer to let her breeze their latest promising colt. How could one stay in the doldrums on the back of a glorious Thoroughbred as they stretched out in flight across the turf? No woman on earth had ever gone faster. She was sure of it. Plus, she trusted Julian Bitters' discretion. She hemmed and hawed and finally blurted. "I got married in London."

Silence settled in while they set their horses to a walk and pointed their noses down the main carriage drive.

"Yes, your ladyship. I'd heard."

She slid a glance at him. His gaze remained fixed between his horse's ears without any discernible expression.

"His Grace the Duke of Chelsony's second brother, Lord Miles Everleigh. He's not going to be living here… I mean, he won't interfere… I mean there will be no change…" She collapsed a little in exasperation. "I don't know what I mean." The clop of hooves competed with the early morning birdsong for a long moment. "Bitters, I *paid* him to marry me—and then go away and stay away."

"I understand, ma'am."

"You do?"

"Yes, ma'am." Bitters offered her a faint smile. "You did what was necessary to protect yourself. I'll not sit in judgment."

"Father and Mamma think it's a love match, for Lord Miles told them as much last night. I don't know what to say—how to explain his absence. Surely they will think it peculiar."

Bitters coughed into his hand. "Your father's a downy one, my lady. If I were you, I'd just go along as you've been doing."

"Do you really think that will serve? Simply say nothing and just…carry on?"

"I should think so, my lady." Bitters picked up a trot, and that was the last of their conversation until they reached the far pastures of the home farm where she spent two joyful hours among her broodmares and their latest creations.

"I believe I see Fedder waving at us, ma'am. We can join him on the crest of the hill and watch the workouts from there."

Eleanor stroked the satin coat of a protective mother and laughed at the antics of her young foal as it peeked at her from under its mother's round belly. "Yes, I'm very interested to see the progress Cinsyr has made since I've been gone."

"He's going to be a prime 'un, ma'am, for a fact. Not many two-year-old colts as I know can give him a run. Shame he's not a year older. We'd have the Newmarket 2,000 Guineas winner for certain.

"And our three-year-olds? Anyone showing promise?" She frowned as she remounted and they turned toward a substantial rise beyond which lay the flat swaths of manicured grass where the young racers were trained. "I was crushed when you wrote about Henley's bowed tendon. I held such strong hopes for her in the Epsom Oaks and perhaps the St. Leger."

"A heartbreaker for sure, ma'am. It was a bad bow. She's on stall rest for the next six months, and then I think we should consider breeding her. She'll not race again." Bitters shook his head. "Cerki's not up to any distance much past six furlongs. She's strictly a sprinter. Adornica has shown us nothing. I'm afraid she's best sent to Fred Hastener to be trained up as a lady's mount. She should do well in that job as she's quiet and very pretty." He shrugged. That's the fillies." His expression lightened. "I do have one bit of news you'll enjoy."

She eyed him in inquiry.

"Remember that Old Codger mare that a certain dolt of a broodmare manager sold off in ignorance? One of the first we exposed to Dare?"

"Yes! Lord Marlburl never would sell her filly back to us—the provoking man."

"Well, I do have news of her. Seems 'Day Dreamer,' for that is how she is registered in The General Stud, broke her maiden in a spectacular style. She won the 1,000 Guineas Stakes at Newmarket by a length and a half and pulling away at that. Effortless speed. I was told she wasn't even tested." Bitters grinned broadly and chuckled when he saw Eleanor's reaction.

Her jaw dropped in open-mouthed joy, and she danced in the saddle. Her steady gelding ignored the off-balanced bouncing occurring on his back and stoically walked along. "Truly? How fabulous. I must drop Lord Marlburl a line to congratulate him and offer him a re-breeding on Dare."

Bitters voice sobered. "The farm's been sold, you know—house, lands and racing stock."

"No... I didn't know. Who bought it? Perhaps we could renew our offer to buy the filly, though with her recent win, why would they sell? With a new owner though, perhaps?" Eleanor bit her lip to contain her excitement. "What if the new owners aren't keen on racing?" She laughed. "Maybe they raise sheep! Oh, Bitters... what do you think? Is there a possibility?"

Their horses crested the top of the hill, and they both waved at Fedder who turned his own mount to join them.

"I couldn't say, ma'am." Bitters response was subdued. "You'd have to write and make inquiry."

"I will, as soon as I return to the house." She all but clapped her hands. "To whom shall I direct my correspondence? Who is the new owner?"

Bitters' voice turned flat. "The owner of the newly renamed Fairwood Stud is The Lord Miles Wrotham Everleigh."

Chapter Nine

Miles had no more ridden into the courtyard of Fairwood when his new employees, women, and men, poured out of the manor house and outbuildings, led by Mr. Weldon, voicing cheers and congratulations. A champagne cork made a loud popping and foam poured out of the mouth of the green bottle handed to him before Miles had even dismounted. He held the frothing bottle away from him with a laugh.

A ring of well-wishers surrounded Miles and added to the feeling of celebration with a chorus of, "Huzzah! Huzzah!" and "Welcome home, my lord!"

"Day Dreamer's won the 1,000 Guineas, sir! By a length and a half. Nothing was going to touch her. Remarkable performance!" Weldon grinned at him. "Her groom is spoiling her rotten as I speak. I did as you ordered, my lord; all the horses from Fairwood that Lord Marlburl scheduled to go off at Newmarket, started. We had other good showings but nothing to compare with Dreamer. She's the queen of the farm, today."

He looked about the sea of upturned smiling faces, somewhat dazed by Weldon's jubilant news. "Of all things… fancy that! Day Dreamer took the 1,000 Guineas." Another unified cheer interrupted him. "I'm devastated to have missed it. I believe champagne should be broken out all around. This victory is far more yours than mine. Mrs. Brody, will you take care of it please."

At that, the volume and number of cheers redoubled, and Miles handed off his bottle to a stable hand and dismounted, putting the reins of his horse into the hands of a waiting groom. "See that the gelding gets returned to the coaching house at Six Mile Bottom. Now," he turned to Mr. Weldon, "I need to see Fairwood's newest star."

"Yes, sir." Weldon grinned and shouted good-naturedly to the crowd surrounding him. "Be off with you. Enjoy the bubbly. Dreamer doesn't need the lot of you descending on her. The lady needs her rest. Remember, you've still got your chores to attend to so don't get bosky."

With much teasing and laughter, the crowd dispersed in search of the promised champagne and Miles walked to the stables with his steward. Entering the brick building, it wasn't difficult to locate the star attraction's stall. A refined chestnut head hung over the half door and lipped treats of carrots and apples from her groom's hands as he stroked her head and crooned words of lavish praise.

Miles stepped forward and ran his palm up the filly's satin neck, his eyes inspecting what he could see of her. "You are her groom, then. Your name? Were you at the track today? Did you see her run?"

The young man, his excitement barely contained, responded with a tug at his cap, "Jemmy Struthers, at your service, m'lord. Ah yes. I seen her. Ever so swift, she was. The jock held her at the back until I was *that* scared she'd not get her chance, but then, he swung her clear and let her run." The groom's face filled with joy. "And like a streak o'light she was. Our girl showed them others her heels—as if they wasn't even trying, sir! Even that Deluth—her wot's supposed to be such a terror." Jemmy grinned. "Won a whole ten shillings from Deluth's groom and wasn't he fair put out!"

Miles laughed and slapped the young groom on his shoulder. "Good for you, Jemmy. Get her out for me, will you? Walk her up and down a bit? I'd like to see her again."

"With pleasure, sir."

Miles could hardly credit the passage of time. Almost two months had come and gone since he'd arrived at his new property and the days had been filled with strenuous, manual work. Not above getting his hands dirty and lacking the funds to pay for additional help, he'd pitched in everywhere practical, digging drainage ditches in the eastern paddocks, driving one of the teams that plowed the spring fields, rebuilding the old rock walls that divided the pastures. At night, half-asleep from physical exhaustion, he went over the books with Weldon and mired himself in the daily accounts of running Fairwood. The wherewithal to make much-needed improvements was an ever-present worry. The prize money from Day Dreamer's win was a godsend.

In short, there was no part of life at Fairwood that he didn't throw himself into with abandon, intent on learning every aspect. Always, there was the matchless joy of watching *his* horses, be it the mares gently cropping grass as their youngsters fought mock battles with others their age, or his racers thundering across the flat verge, muscles straining, nostrils flared as they obeyed their inherited imperative to *run*.

He'd also taken the better part of ten days to remove his mother from the untenable position she endured at Chelsony Hall. He'd felt a profound sense of satisfaction after installing her in her own apartment of rooms at Fairwood and turning over the management of his house to her. By acting as his hostess and in putting to right the neglected gardens that surrounded the manor house—or whatever else she wished to turn her hand to—he was hopeful that she would rediscover, as she put it, her *gaieté de coeur*—her gaiety of spirit and her *joie de vivre*—her joy in life.

As comfortable as he was with his new employees and as much as he enjoyed seeing his mother starting to bloom hand-in-hand with the gardens, in the odd moments when he wasn't staggering into bed at night or growing bleary-eyed trying to balance tally sheets, his thoughts turned to a particular woman. This woman shared his passion for the Thoroughbred horse, and with her, the exchange of new theories and proven methods had flowed without restraint. It was a route his thoughts retraced with greater frequency as days passed. He missed her dry wit and insightful comments. He missed her sensible attitude and ruefully admitted to himself that he could certainly use her experience. The healthy animal within that had rarely gone without a regular outlet for his male urges reminded him of her passionate response to his kisses and chided him for his cold bed.

When he added together the number of times she'd intruded into his thoughts, he realized he'd given frequent thought to the whole of her—the woman who had provided his avenue to this heaven on earth—and his conscience simply would not allow him rest. He came to a most reluctant decision—one he'd only become reconciled to after weeks of self-reproach—and decided he'd make one more peace offering in an effort to put right the damage he'd wrought to their association. The offering would be painful to him and Fairwood—he could well imagine Weldon's howls of outrage—but if it mended Eleanor's hurt, he'd count the cost justified.

His interview with his farm manager went as he'd expected.

"Have you taken complete leave of your senses, my lord? This is the action of a mad man!" Weldon's voice rose in hostility and volume until with a sense of mild curiosity, Miles wondered if the man would lunge over his desk and physically assault him. Weldon seemed to recall his position, however, and drew rein just short of physical attack, snarling, "I strongly object to this…this…lunacy!" Without taking his leave, the man abruptly stormed out of Miles' library, slamming the door so hard that it failed to catch and rebounded open with a quiver.

Closing his eyes, Miles inhaled a steadying breath, released it slowly, and then rose and crossed the room to a window which looked out on the intimate garden his mother was returning to vibrancy. He crossed his arms on his chest and tried to find some calm within, but the thoughts and emotions running through him were as disorderly as the water that tumbled willy-nilly down the irregularities in the rock wall that formed part of the garden's water feature.

"I was coming to see you and overheard what you told Mr. Weldon." His mother regarded him from the open door with gentle knowing eyes, a soft smile giving her beautiful face a beatific countenance.

"*Maman.* Come in, dearest." His gaze returned to the garden scene. "Then, you also heard his response. My steward declares I've gone mad. I think I'm in agreement with him."

A soft swoosh of gown and footsteps ended at his side, and his mother took his arm, laying her head against his shoulder, and joined him in gazing out the window.

"What do you think?" he murmured.

"Hmmm… that it was a lovely thing to do, and that I'm very much looking forward to meeting your Eleanor."

He raised his eyebrows and drawing back, gave his mother a look of inquiry. "Why do you call her *my* Eleanor? I've told you how I came to marry her. This is strictly a business arrangement."

His mother held him in a playful gaze, a mysterious smile flirting with her mouth. "Miles, my darling boy," she chided gently. "You would never have given that lovely filly to a business associate."

Eleanor snuggled into Julian Bitters' old sofa, sipped her tea and stared into the flames of the fireplace, her muddy boots propped on the fire-irons. Heavy rain had interfered with the afternoon rounds, and both she and her stud manager had retreated to dryer spaces. "I need to give this sofa a new covering, Bitters."

A low chuckle greeted her in response. "Aye, my lady. It could do with some refurbishing, but then would you feel so free to put your muddy self upon it?"

Her eyes smiled at him over her pottery mug as she took another sip of hot liquid. "It's difficult to decide what's more dirty—me or the sofa. But, I understand your point. The sofa will stay as is." She sighed. "It's going to be a quiet spring for Rutledge with Cinsyr our only hopeful."

"Yes, that it is. But you know how it goes. Feast or famine. You run three of your own against each other, or you run none." Bitters shrugged. "'Tis the way of it." He paused thoughtfully. "Have you sent an inquiry to Fairwood about purchasing Day Dreamer, the Old Codger mare's filly?"

She threw an admonishing glance at him. "No, and I'm not going to."

"It would be nice to see the get of Rutledge's newest stallion winning under Rutledge colors."

"Agreed."

"It would be nice to have the management of an enormously exciting home-bred back in our hands. Not to take anything away from Fairwood—they've done a decent job with her—but we've been at this game a little longer."

"Agreed."

Bitters held her gaze steadily. "So...?"

"So, I've not made inquiry, nor do I intend to do so—and that's the end of it."

Bitters grunted. After a lull during which only the snapping of the fireplace and the muffled thuds of the occupants in their stalls could be heard, her stud manager asked, "Any improvement in the Earl?"

She stretched forward and set her mug on the floor, then settled into the sofa and allowed her head to loll backward. "Thank you, Bitters. You are such a ray of sunshine."

A snort answered her flat complaint. "I do my best, ma'am."

With a heavy sigh, she closed her eyes. "Since my return from London, he's taken to his bed. Mamma won't leave him, so I've instructed her bed to be moved in beside him as she is too feeble to endure so many hours in a chair." Tears creased her cheeks, and her voice thickened. "I'm losing them, Bitters. They'll go together. I'm certain. He of a multitude of ailments and she of a broken heart."

She felt Bitters place a warm hand on her shoulder and press a linen handkerchief into her hand. "The house will feel like an empty cavern when they are gone." She sniffed. "It already echoes."

"At least they will go knowing that you have done your best to secure Rutledge, my lady."

Yes, she'd done her best to secure Rutledge, and it had only cost one small piece of her soul. She wiped her tears, blew her nose and sat up. "Well, I suppose I should take advantage of this foul weather to catch up on my correspondence. Lady Florence Lloyd-Smyth wants to visit, and I should respond to her letter, and there is something from my barrister in London." She rose. "I'll see you in the morning."

He nodded as she turned to leave and she knew he watched her from the window of his office as, through the deluge, she sprinted across the courtyard to the front entrance of the main house.

The doorman swung the door open for her and she didn't pause, but pounded up the grand staircase, down the hall and into her apartments. She rang for her maid and began stripping herself of her sodden garments. Two hours later, bathed and dressed once more as "Lady Miles Everleigh," she checked in on her parents.

"How are they, Laura?" she murmured. The nurse looked up from her reading and crossed the chamber to stand beside Eleanor as she looked down at two dear faces, both asleep in their beds.

Laura replied in a low voice, "The Earl had a difficult night, my lady, but her ladyship slept peacefully. The dears were up for several hours this morning and have just fallen asleep again. Should I ring you when they wake?"

"Yes, if you would please." She smiled at the nurse. "I'll be in Father's study."

The nurse dipped into a curtsy. "Yes, my lady."

Exiting quietly, Eleanor made her way to the first floor and into the masculine room that served as the hub of operations for Rutledge. She sat in the Earl's huge leather chair and sorted through the mail piled on a silver tray in the middle of her father's immense desk. The missive from Elsington & Elsington bearing four shiny red seals demanded her attention first. She scanned through the opening address with its predictable courtesies and got straight to the pertinent message:

> .... *after determining Elsington & Elsington had been the victim of a burglary, we searched the interior of my office most thoroughly. I regret to inform you the only papers we discovered missing from my files were that of your premarital contract with Lord Miles Everleigh and some of the addendums thereto.*
>
> *I can only speculate as to the purpose of this egregious theft; however, I feel duty-bound to remind you of HRH's pernicious interest in your recent marriage and to put you on notice that should you receive a personal visit from one of his representatives, which I feel is only*

a matter of time, it would be advisable to appear ensnared in conjugal bliss.

I am devastated at our failure to protect your most private papers and ...

The communication from her barrister ended with all the usual prostrations of apologetic blather. She thoughtfully folded the letter and put it in the top right drawer of the desk. Who could possibly desire a copy of her prenuptial agreement other than the Prince Regent? It was worrisome in the extreme, and a feeling of foreboding apprehension overwhelmed her momentarily. She disciplined herself to long, slow breaths and lectured herself, "rational mind over raw emotion". There was little point in getting ahead of events. If or when an agent for Prinny appeared at Rutledge, she'd deal with him. Until then, she had other immediate issues more pressing.

As the unpredictable spring weather was prone to do, it went from drenching rain to brilliant sun by evening, and when Eleanor paused the next day to take lunch with her parents in their bedroom, the sun still shone brightly in milky blue skies. She'd no more gotten a piece of roast beef to her mouth while listening to her father give sought-after advice on what to plant at the Balisters' tenant farm, than a knock at the door sounded. Laura answered. The footman's voice carried into the bedroom.

"Mr. Bitters requests her ladyship's presence as soon as may be convenient. Not an emergency, he said, but something of great interest to her ladyship."

"I heard him, Laura." Eleanor stood and put her napkin on the table. Leaning over she kissed her father and mother on the cheek. "I'll see you at dinner, my dears. Please mind

Laura, Father. She tells me you've been difficult about taking your medicines."

He grumped some indistinguishable answer and waved her off with a gnarled hand, and her mother smiled up at her. "Tell Bitters to come visit. We miss him."

"I will, Mamma. The sun has come out, and it looks like it's decided to stay. Would you like me to have Walters send some footmen to take you out to the garden? You and Father might enjoy some sun."

"Oh, that would be grand, wouldn't it, darling?"

Her father smiled at his wife. "If you would like it, my dear."

Eleanor turned to Laura. "Bundle them warmly, and I'll send up some footmen with the wheeled chairs."

She relayed her instructions to Walters and then sought out Bitters to discover what it was that "was of great interest" to her.

"Ah, my lady." Bitters opened his arm and directed her into the stable aisle where a young groom, unfamiliar to her—she knew all her stable workers on sight and by name—stood holding the lead line of an elegant chestnut mare.

"Oh! Bitters…" Her voice oozed admiration as she walked slowly to the attentive horse and ran a caressing hand down her long neck and up to scratch at the mare's withers, a universally "itchy" spot for any horse. Stepping back to admire the animal further, she glanced at the young man. "Hello. I'm Lady Miles and who might you be? Furthermore, who is this lovely lady?"

The young man pulled at his cap. "Jemmy Struthers of the Fairwood Stud, my lady, and this be Day Dreamer, the filly wot won the Newmarket 1,000 Guineas." He reached into his jacket and pulled out a formerly cream envelope, creased and much marked with dirty fingerprints, and handed it to her. "My master, Lord Miles, says if you'd be so good as to read this and I'm to…" The young groom broke off his explanation with an impassioned plea. "Please don't send me back, ma'am. Lord Miles said I can stay with Dreamer if you agree. He'd pay me wages n'all. Don't send me back, ma'am. My girl needs me. Cause ain't nobody else—"

Eleanor held up a hand to stop his outpouring. "Mister Struthers, silence. Allow me to read what Lord Miles wrote?" She smiled. "Please?"

Jemmy nodded nervously, and Eleanor, with a wide-eyed glance at Bitters that conveyed her amazement and consternation, broke the seal on the letter from her husband and read.

Dear Lady Miles,

> *I cannot let another day pass without addressing the harm my inappropriate action or lack of action caused you on the evening of our marriage. While I understand how you could arrive at the conclusion that you did, I feel I must set the record straight—less to make you see me in a better light, though I should hope that you might—but more that you might see yourself in a better light.*
>
> *To facilitate my explanation, please allow me to reconstruct the events leading up to that certain evening.*
>
> *I'm sure you will recall the Willinghams' ball and my escorting you home. Upon leaving you at your door, I proceeded to Baron*

Stanton's residence, borrowed a hack and rode ten hours to Newmarket where I spent the day riding the property of the Woodward farm. Since it came into my possession, I have renamed the property Fairwood Stud. It is this farm that I spoke to you about purchasing that day in Hyde Park. Completing my tour, I dined with the seller's agent and finalized the purchase of the farm whereupon; I hacked another ten hours back to London to arrive late morning on the day of our wedding.

I slept briefly, rose and appeared at All Hallows to be married. I thought you a vision of loveliness and congratulated myself on my good fortune. I do not wish to be vulgar, but I anticipated our night together with some eagerness. I say this only so you may understand my state of mind. At the time of our post-wedding dinner, I had been awake and physically engaged in some fashion or other for the better part of sixty hours with precious little sleep.

When you left for your bedchamber, I collected a glass of Madeira and settled on the sofa in front of the fireplace with the intention of giving you an hour and one-half to make ready. At which point, Eleanor, I fell soundly asleep, not waking even when the glass of Madeira slipped from my hand and saturated my clothing.

Let me restate this so that there can be no misunderstanding. My failure to appear in your bedchamber on the night of our wedding *was not a result of a lack of desire, nor was I drunk. It was a result of sheer fatigue. Had I to do it again, I assure you, I would arrange events far differently.*

Which leads me to a certain four-legged beauty that I assume is now standing in your stables accompanied by her devoted groom.

It is custom for a new husband to bestow a bride gift on his wife. Due to our peculiar circumstances, there was little that I felt I could offer you that would have any meaning, for whatever I gave you would have been bought with your own coin; until by the greatest of happenstance I discovered that the purchase of the old Woodward farm also included a promising young filly out of your unproven stallion, Dare To Dream. I arrived at Fairwood Stud to take permanent possession shortly after she won the 1,000 Guineas Stakes at Newmarket. You can imagine my great joy as it has ever been my ambition to be successful on the track. It was an auspicious start to my new life. This was a horse that could make prominent the name of Fairwood Stud.

After much consideration, and contrary to the strong adjurations of my farm manager, I would like to give this lovely filly to you as your bride gift—accompanied by her groom, whom I pray you will retain as it would break his young heart to be parted from her—with my fervent request to forgive me and think better of yourself. I hope the gift of Day Dreamer will convince you, as I was unable to do in person,

*that I continue to hold you in the highest
regard.*

*I remain
Your Most Obedient Servant,*

M. Everleigh

The letter shook in hands she couldn't hold steady, and
the muscles in her face—most particularly those of her
chin—quivered uncontrollably. Never in her life had she
striven so fiercely for composure as she did at that moment.
In addition to Miles' letter, she unfolded a formal transfer
of ownership, filed with The General Stud. Clutching
Miles' correspondence in one hand, she shoved the
accompanying registration papers toward her stud manager
and then stuffed her betraying hands and his letter into her
pockets.

Bitters hadn't ceased his scrutiny of her since she'd
opened the letter and she forced out raspy words of
explanation. "Lord Miles has given me the filly as a bride
gift. Please see that she and Mr. Struthers are housed and
find the lad some Rutledge livery."

She whirled around and strode out of the stables,
pulling deep breaths that turned into helpless sobs before
she reached the doors to the great house. *Damn that man.*
He'd reduced her to tears over him *again.* Pausing briefly
on the threshold, she wiped her face on her sleeve and
jerked open both doors, surprising the doorman.
Wordlessly, she swept by him, up the stairs and into her
room whereupon she threw herself face down on her bed
and wept without restraint into a pillow to muffle her
unchecked cries. This time she didn't censor herself, and

she sobbed until she had no more tears to cry. With a final shudder, she rolled onto her back and stared at the ceiling through swollen lids.

What was worse? Thinking Lord Miles Everleigh had succumbed to drink because he found her unattractive, or knowing that she'd misread the situation thoroughly and had driven him away with words purposefully chosen to wound and belittle—words he did not deserve. She pulled out his letter and reread a portion.

"….*I feel I must set the record straight—less to make you see me in a better light, though I should hope that you might—but more that you might see yourself in a better light….*"

For him to be so generous and forgiving when she'd been so hasty and judgmental… She felt unwell and very forlorn. Once again, her stupid, stupid pride had tripped her up. She stifled another sob, rose from the bed and rang for her maid.

The past couldn't be undone, and no matter how gloomy and despondent she felt, she needed to dress for tea with Mamma and present a happy front. "I could have gone on stage," she muttered to herself. "I've practiced enough pretense."

"….*but more that you might see yourself in a better light….*" She hung her head. Her husband's insight into her character was uncomfortably astute.

Chapter Ten

"**M**iles! How's life as a new husband? And where is Eleanor? You didn't bring her with you to London?" Baron Stanton's wife, Mary, almost skipped into the small parlor where Miles sat conferring with his closest friend over what to do with Ned who lay upstairs in one of Reggie's guest rooms beaten almost unto death. He rose to his feet and clasped her outstretched hands.

"Mary, you are a vision of loveliness this evening. I suppose married life suits me as well as the next man." He grinned and winked when she made a face. "Now, Mary… it wouldn't do to seem too enthusiastic."

"You men." She reclaimed her hands and shook her head at his wry response, then sobered. "You've spoken with your brother?"

"During the brief moment he was lucid. I apologize for the imposition. As soon as he's fit to travel, I'm removing him to Fairwood."

"It was no imposition, Miles… just a shock to the system to find an unconscious body on one's front step."

"For which I cannot sufficiently apologize." He gazed at Reggie and Mary. "Ned should get on his knees and beg your forgiveness. I thank you for taking such good care of my errant brother, and please refer the physician's fees to me."

Reggie waved his hand in a dismissive fashion. "Mary, do you suppose we might have a moment of privacy?" Reggie kissed his wife's cheek and held her gaze in some sort of silent communication that husbands seemed to have with their wives.

"Of course. Come find me when you are done discussing things 'not fit for tender ears'," she complained with a smile and left, closing the door behind her. Reggie immediately dug in his coat and pulled out a ragged piece of paper which he handed to Miles.

"I took this off Ned's unconscious body."

Miles read the clumsily scrawled message written in grease pencil on what looked like a corner of newsprint.

£15,000 in a fortnight or we finish the job

"Has Ned seen this?"

Reggie shook his head. "He hasn't been fully aware of his surroundings until today. I thought you should know in case…" He sighed. "In case trouble follows you to Newmarket."

Miles closed his eyes, anger and distress vying with each other for a place of prominence.

"The physician said he has a broken nose, two cracked ribs and to watch his piss for blood. As far as he could determine, all Ned's other injuries, while painful, are not as serious as those. They beat him to a fare-thee-well, but someone took care not to cause him permanent disability. I have little doubt that if their terms are not met, these ruffians will attempt to see the job properly done. I don't suppose there is any hope of applying to Edgar for the funds?"

Miles caught and held Reggie in a direct gaze ripe with cynicism.

The man simply shrugged. "It was worth a mention."

"We both know these types. If I thought for one moment that this was a legitimate debt gained through honest play, I'd insist Ned work out some sort of repayment, but I'm certain it is not. Paying these bullies and cheats will just make them worse. The only thing these sorts understand is force. Well, if required, I'm not above using a little intimidation myself. As soon as they realize that I will not be blackmailed or cowed by their threats, the better off we'll all be. And if they think to extract money from Edgar...well, I wish them joy." Miles caught Reggie's gaze with his. "Did the physician say when he thought Ned could travel?"

"If you take it in easy stages, he can travel now, but you know you are—"

Miles put his hand on Reggie's shoulder. "...welcome for however long. You are too good, Stanton. I'll stay tonight, but tomorrow I'm removing my brother to Fairwood. Permanently. I've moved the Dowager Duchess Julia in, and she will be glad of the opportunity to smother Ned in maternal care."

"You've installed your mother at Fairwood?"

"Yes. I've given her full run of the place. The Duke treated her with cold indifference, and she lacked all but the bare necessities of life at Chelsony Hall. While she never complained, it was obvious to all who cared to see that she led a bleak existence. Removing her from under the oppressive hand of my half-brother was the first thing I did when I occupied Fairwood."

The expression on his friend's face made words unnecessary. "I cannot number any other persons of my acquaintance who possess such a sweet temperament as your mother...how..." Reggie sighed. "He's a thoroughgoing rotter, Miles, even if he is your brother."

"Half-brother and I agree."

Reggie's traveling coach was the height of modern luxury, but even its superb suspension with the latest in new design for springs couldn't smooth all the jolts from the road, and while Ned maintained a stoic expression, his occasional hitch of breath at any significant lurch said all that need be said about his physical condition. Miles sympathized, but he wasn't about to tell Ned that.

"Tell me how you came to this point, Lord Edmund."

His brother hunched a little more at his formal address, but drew in a careful breath through distorted lips and peered at Miles through the one eye that wasn't swollen shut. He spoke more slowly than normal, and carefully shaped his words as if it hurt to speak—which it probably did. "It's not what you think. I never went back to those gaming dens." His brow wrinkled. "I didn't, Miles. I know I haven't been a paragon of virtue, but I gave you my word, and I kept it. Miles? Please tell me you believe me."

"I believe you. So, finish your story."

"The day after I spoke with you, I secured your draft and searched for the lender, but I couldn't find the man who'd made me the original loan. I left messages for him everywhere that I had his money. Days went by without a word from him, and then a fortnight and still nothing, and I suppose I just thought ..." His brother let out a groan. "I've been such an incredible gull. Finally, I received a message to pay up with a time and place. Five nights ago, I appeared at the agreed-upon place," his mouth curled in disgust, "some stew near the docks, and met with three 'associates' of Mr. Smith."

Miles snorted. "Smith?"

Ned closed his eye. "Yes...I know. Not his real name, certainly. I just wanted to pay what I owed and leave, but they wouldn't let me. Said it wasn't £5,000 anymore but £15,000 due to daily interest! Interest, Miles! I explained that I'd tried to pay them back weeks ago, but ... well, stupid as I am, I finally realized they were playing me for a pigeon." He rested his head gingerly against the squabs of the coach's interior. "I became angry and said I knew their game and they'd not get more than what I owed. One of 'Mr. Smith's' associates said he thought I was worth more than £5,000 to my brother, and someone bashed me in the back of the head. The three of them set on me with cudgels and fists. I attempted to defend myself but after being blindsided and with the numbers against me... well, the results are plain. I don't remember much about what happened after that, other than I woke up in bed at Baron Stanton's, less the draft for £5,000."

Miles fished in his inner pocket and withdrew the ragged piece of newsprint and laid it on Ned's thigh. "This was pinned to your coat when Reggie found you."

Ned regarded the message as if Miles had placed a poisonous spider in his lap. "Damn it to perdition, Miles. I'm so sorry. I've been a complete embarrassment to you, and you've already done more than you should have. As soon as I'm able to travel on my own, I'll go into hiding somewhere until this blows over."

"No, you will not. You do not retreat from bullies. We will confront them with the only language this sort understands—force. I refuse to succumb to their extortion. You are going to make a life with Mother and me at Fairwood, and I swear to Almighty God, I will protect you."

"I don't deserve you."

"No, you don't, but you are stuck with me nevertheless, and trust me, Ned, I will extract a full day's work from you as soon as you are able." He held his younger brother in a stern gaze, but Ned appeared so woebegone that he couldn't sustain his anger. "Are you in a lot of pain?" he said softly. "The doctor gave me some laudanum if it gets too bad."

The corners of Ned's misshapen mouth twitched. "A vile concoction. I'd rather endure the discomfort." With a few grimaces, Ned arranged himself lengthwise on the seat, his arms wrapped around his ribs, and stared at the ceiling of the carriage. "First Mother and then me … who will you rescue next?" he murmured.

Chapter Eleven

Dreamer stretched into full, effortless flight beneath Eleanor. It was as if Dreamer's equine body escaped earth and took her rider to a transcendent place where there remained only speed. All else became a blur as wind assaulted her face and tears obscured Eleanor's vision. It didn't matter. The emerald green surface over which her mount flew stretched uninterrupted for miles. In her left hand, Eleanor fisted a heavy hank of blonde mane with only enough rein to keep the excess out of Dreamer's way while her other hand pumped the air as she stood in her stirrups and whooped and laughed and cried with uncontainable jubilation—for how could one participate in such perfection and not give voice to it?

Her exaltation couldn't continue indefinitely for a living creature of flesh and bone, heart and sinew, and fragile, fragile legs carried her—the tremendous forces of combined speed and weight borne by one slender pastern no bigger than a man's wrist. Gently, Eleanor sat, took the reins up in both hands and restored a measure of control, shortening Dreamer's stride from twenty-two-feet to twenty and then to eighteen and then to fifteen, and finally down to a nine-foot trot.

She whispered heartfelt thanks to Lord Miles Everleigh for his stunning generosity. She hadn't known him for an extensive period, but what she knew of him gave her to realize he well understood the value of her bride gift. She supposed it did her no credit, but she'd never entertained for one instant the thought of returning the three-year-old.

As she turned for home and rose and fell with the filly's springy gait, she leaned down and hugged her chestnut neck. "You glorious, glorious girl! We're going to do fabulous things, you and I."

Eleanor pulled Dreamer down to a walk quite a distance from where Fedder, Bitters, and Jemmy sat their mounts and watched. As she approached at Dreamer's free-swinging walk, the expressions on Bitters' and Jemmy's faces never altered in their mimicry of her cheek-to-cheek grin. Her trainer, Fedder, was another manner.

"Fedder, I want Joshua Crane as her jockey. He's light enough to make the weight and has excellent hands. Plus, he'll know how to handle her speed. Assign Bedham as her exercise boy." Eleanor leaned down and patted Dreamer's sweaty neck. "He's a kind, patient rider and she likes to play before settling in."

Her trainer gave a curt nod, his gaze focused on his stopwatch. He tapped the crystal with his fingernail. "I think something's wrong with my watch. This can't be right." He gave Eleanor a look of disbelief. "She's done six furlongs in a minute, ten."

Eleanor's head flopped back, and she laughed to the sky. Bitters grinned like a boy, his eyes never leaving the filly.

"Ain't she somethin', my lady?" Awe filled Jemmy's hushed voice. "Never seen nothing like her." He sighed the heartfelt sigh of a young man hopelessly in love.

"She's everything you say and more, Jemmy." Eleanor slid off Dreamer and swapped horses with Jemmy. "Let's get her cooled off. Hand-walk her for a couple of hours before you stall her. I'm sure she'd appreciate some green grass, and mud her legs before you leave for the evening."

Back in the stable block, Eleanor couldn't wait to share the time of Dreamer's workout with her father and hurried to change out of her breeches and into a day gown. Her maid was just adding a necklace to her ensemble when a rap sounded on her door. "Yes?"

Walters responded through the closed door. "Lady Eleanor, a Mister Ludlow, personal agent to His Royal Highness Prince George is here and is asking to speak with Lord Miles Ever—

Eleanor strode to the door, yanked it open and regarded Walters with wide eyes.

Walters didn't so much as blink. "...leigh. I have advised him that Lord Miles is not receiving and the man has demanded to speak with you. I told him I would inquire if you are accepting callers. He is in the blue room." Walters offered her a white calling card.

All the joyous feelings that her morning with Day Dreamer had produced popped one after the other like so many laundry bubbles. "Thank you, Walters. Tell Mister Ludlow I'll be down presently." She paused for a moment. "Offer him some of Father's port. Ensure his glass stays filled."

"Ma'am."

It may have been her imagination, but she thought she detected approval in Walters' voice before he bowed and made his unhurried way down the hall.

Crossing to her dressing table, she pulled out the chair and slowly sank onto its seat while her thumb ran over the raised letters on the man's business card. Her grim reflection stared back at her. She clenched her jaw and raised her chin. The white day dress with its printed sprigs of yellow flowers would never do. Neither would the simple braid that hung over her shoulder.

"Sally, help me out of this dimity. I want the purple damask with the jet trim and ring for May. She is very good with hair. I wish mine up."

"Ma'am? The purple damask?"

"Yes, it strikes exactly the right note."

"Yes, ma'am."

It took her an hour to reach a state where *she* felt ready to receive an agent of the Prince Regent and another hour before she felt the agent might be ready to receive *her*.

"Mr. Ludlow. I am Lady Miles Everleigh. How may I help you?"

Eleanor swept into what she'd always considered an overly-ornate and incredibly-ugly blue parlor, a holdover from a deplorable splurge on gilded French Rococo excess inflicted upon Rutledge Manor by one of her father's predecessors and addressed the gentleman staring at the vaulted ceiling painted sky blue with a baroque scene of naked cherubs and white clouds. She knew why he stared.

Several of the cherubs were engaged in amorous activities that were anything but celestial. He smelled strongly of fortified wine and cupped a large crystal goblet in one hand. An impassive footman in formal livery stood immediately inside the door beside a gilt and blue paint console and held a decanter less than half-full of golden brown liquor.

Her visitor stopped his staring, cleared his throat with a loud, "Ahem," and acknowledged her with a brief bow. Irritation edged his voice. "Ivan Ludlow, Senior Investigative Agent to His Royal Highness George Augustus Frederick of Hanover, Prince of Wales, Earl of Chester, Duke of Cornwall, Duke of Rothesay, Earl of Carrick, and Baron of Renfrew." He sniffed. "My lady, is it your intention to fog my mind with drink? I'll have you know, it won't work." He held her in a glassy-eyed gaze of indignation and swayed ever so slightly.

"I cannot imagine what you mean, sir." Her charming smile oozed naiveté. "I merely thought to provide you with a high treat while I rid myself of the stables and changed into something more suitable to receive an agent of His Royal Highness. You are partaking of The Earl of Rutledge's favorite port. He never shares it with anyone." She perched on the edge of a diminutive, powder-blue, satin double-sofa and indicated an unusually low-to-the-ground, eminently fragile-looking, slipper chair. "Please, be seated, sir. Take your ease." She smiled brightly. "Tell me what business the Prince Regent can have with me."

The agent eyed the unstable-looking furniture with obvious doubt and descended onto the narrow seat with an overabundance of caution. When he was fully seated, the chair creaked in an ominous fashion, and his knees lacked only a foot of being at his chin.

"I don't desire concourse with you, madam, I want to speak with your master, Lord Miles Everleigh, but I am informed he is not receiving. Equally, I am given to understand that your father is too ill. So…since neither of the heads of this household are available, I must make do with you."

He must "make do" with her? Eleanor wanted to hurl the Meissen shepherdess figurine on the sofa table at his head, but she "made do" with smiling vacuously and blinking like an ingénue. "For the second time, how may I help you?"

The agent regarded her with a narrowing of the eyes.

She smiled wider and if possible, more vacantly, with much batting of her eyelashes.

"The Prince Regent has come into possession of the premarital contract signed by yourself and your husband and has strong misgivings as to the legitimate nature of your union."

"Heaven save me!" She sprang to her feet necessitating that Mr. Ludlow rise also. The man's knees produced multiple sounds resembling a dead chicken being disjointed. "Are you suggesting we are not legally married?" Before he could answer, she sank back onto the sofa.

The agent clenched his jaw, and slowly returned his posterior to the fragile chair, which once again complained about his weight. "I, on behalf of the Prince, have several questions to put to Lord Miles Everleigh concerning the financial settlements accruing to him upon his marriage to you."

Once more she bolted upright in alarm. "My husband and I enjoy the greatest of domestic harmony. Do you imply that Lord Miles received recompense to marry me! What an infamous suggestion."

Forced to his feet again, Ludlow grimaced and cleared his throat with some exasperation. "Ma'am, I cannot have a rational discussion with you popping up and down like... like... some demented gopher."

"Sir! Your comments are beyond insulting." Eleanor clutched her hand to her breast and gave every evidence of being mortally offended as she once more sank to the love seat. She tried, unsuccessfully, to manufacture tears, though she did dab at her eyes with a hastily procured handkerchief and was quite proud of the quiver she injected into her normally direct tones.

With obvious ill-ease, Ludlow once again perched his buttocks on the tiny chair with all accompanying sound effects and scrubbed his face. "Apologies, ma'am. Can't think what..." He blinked as if to clear his vision. "When *might* I speak with Lord Miles Everleigh?"

Eleanor rose and drew herself up to her full six-foot height. She snickered internally as the agent regained his feet with an unmistakable grunt and much protest from his joints.

"That I cannot tell you, sir. Lord Miles has gone to the continent on a horse buying trip. The date of his return is uncertain. I have your card. I will send notice to you upon Lord Miles' return to Rutledge. Now, good day." Having issued the latter in her most imperious voice, she turned and swept out of the room.

As she gained the second-floor landing, she met her butler coming from the direction of her parents' apartments and paused. "Brilliant move putting him in the Blue Parlor, Walters. He was half disguised on Father's port and much distracted by the ceiling."

The man inclined his head. The corner of his mouth twitched slightly. "Yes, madam."

She lowered her voice. "Did you advise Father of Ludlow's presence?"

"Yes, madam."

"Ludlow won't be satisfied until he speaks with Lord Miles." With a long sigh, she smoothed the front of her elegant gown and played with the pieces of black jet that adorned the skirt. "I can think of no other option than to make a personal appeal to Lord Miles and throw myself on his mercy."

"Yes, madam."

"I suppose I should consult with Father before taking any action, though I do hate to burden him."

"Yes, madam."

Eleanor smiled wryly. "Enlightening conversation, Walters. I appreciate your always astute contributions."

"Yes, madam."

The Earl of Rutledge watched from his bed as his daughter left his bedchamber and closed the door quietly behind her.

"Laura, please step outside. I'll ring when you may return."

"Yes, sir." The pretty nurse rose from the chair where she sat stitching and dipped a curtsy.

When she, too, had exited, he reached an age-spotted hand sideways and clasped that of his wife. "You wanted private speech with me?"

She gazed at him, intelligence alive in her blue eyes.

"Rutledge, I'm worried that our daughter will make a misstep in this tricky business with the prince, and she has one hand tied behind her back in her efforts to keep her true standing with Lord Miles from us. Shouldn't we tell her we know? Offer her our support?"

He lay back and closed his eyes. "If we confess to our knowledge, we will also have to confess to how we came by such knowledge. Knowing Eleanor, she will be gravely wounded by our manipulation of what she very rightly considers her private affairs." He paused, laboring for breath. The simplest things had become such a struggle. It quite wore him out. "I still think silence is our best ally. She'll do the right thing. She made the correct choice for a husband, after all."

His beloved wife considered his comment in thoughtful silence then offered in a quavery voice, "I quite like Julia's eldest. Lord Miles was an excellent selection, darling, but really… you and Penwick offered her little else to choose from." She gave a theatrical shudder. "A drunkard with eleven children … I'd as soon have had the opium-eater or the Nancy boy."

He chuckled dryly. "I'd have preferred the older brother, Duncan, for her, but he removed himself from consideration when he bought his commission. A dead husband is of no use to me. I couldn't take the chance of some mishap on the battlefield. As you know, I have always liked that family; we would not have introduced Lady Julia to His Grace otherwise. Still… there is something very havey-cavey going on with the first son. The old Duke was tireless in his lauds for all but his first-born. Retreated into tight-lipped silence whenever Edgar's name was mentioned."

"Still, I do wish we could openly help her, and I can only wonder what happened between her and Lord Miles that she should refuse to offer him the hospitality of Rutledge for even one night."

He squeezed his wife's hand gently. "Don't worry, my love. It will all come right. They have too much in common and are too sensible not to see it in the end."

"Do you suppose I should write to Julia and ask her to … assist?"

"I have already done so. The Dowager Duchess of Chelsony replied that she will do whatever she can manage discreetly. It helps that Lord Miles has moved her into his new property and out from under Chelsony's neglect."

"Poor Julia. I wonder sometimes if we did the right thing in introducing such a young woman to such an older gentleman…but, she so loved her duke—and he her." His wife squeezed his hand. "Rutledge, I want for our daughter what you and I have, what Julia found." Tears stood in her eyes. "I want her to find love."

He raised her hand to his lips and kissed the paper-thin skin. "As do I, darling. As do I."

Chapter Twelve

The following morning, crumpled sheets of ink-stained paper littered the carpet in front of the fireplace in the library where Eleanor labored to compose a letter that would both be diplomatic—not her strongest attribute—and yet convey the urgency of the situation. She propped her forehead on the heels of her palms and gazed unseeing at the padded leather protecting the surface of the desk. Straightening, she rang for her footman. Her orders were direct.

"Tell John Coachman to put the grays to the light carriage. I'm going to Newmarket. I want to leave within the hour."

As the miles rapidly passed, she prepared her words, rehearsing them aloud in the carriage.

"Lord Miles, as your wife, I command your presence at Rutledge … *no* … Everleigh, you *must* accompany me to Rutledge immediately… *no* … Lord Miles, if you have any regard for me whatsoever, I wish you to… *no*." She sighed. She couldn't address him while prickling like a hedgehog.

For once in her life, she needed to unbend her pride and confess to needing his assistance if she was to stave off disaster. She'd already penned a letter to him in which she thanked him profusely for Day Dreamer, but she'd passed the mail coach to Newmarket at the last toll gate. Now she could express her immense gratitude in person.

Perhaps it would be best to start with the thanks? So how would that go? "I want to express my deepest joy over the gift of Day Dreamer. I'm willing to let bygones be bygones. Now, having said that, I require you to abandon Fairwood and return with me to Rutledge Manor for an indeterminate length of time and enter into your role as my husband—in name only of course; you'll not participate in the day-to-day activities at Rutledge. *For how long?* Probably for months. Perhaps as much as a year. I feel you must stay through the probation of my father's will. *And how shall I occupy myself as I while away the months?* Well…I've been told our library has an outstanding collection of …"

She slumped into the cushions of the coach and moaned. Oh yes, *that* would send him sprinting to her side. Somehow, she had to soften her tone, put away all her defenses and allow her sincere feelings to guide her words. She had another three hours to cobble together a speech that would sway him. Pastoral scenes of English countryside rolled past unnoticed as she stared glumly out the window.

Eleanor looked around the elegantly appointed drawing room with great curiosity. Cream plastered walls and French doors overlooking a covered portico gave the intimate space an openness it might otherwise lack. When she'd driven through the gatehouse to Fairwood Stud and had first glimpsed the manor house outlined on the horizon, she'd been unwillingly impressed with its graceful antiquity. After knocking at the front door for several minutes before the housekeeper answered, she'd requested speech with Lord Miles Everleigh and had been shown into this cozy chamber. That had been forty minutes ago. She was becoming impatient—and increasingly nervous.

The door opened and a lovely brunette of indeterminate age, certainly not in her first bloom of youth but not aged either, entered, followed closely by a footman bearing a tea service which he placed on the low table in front of her loveseat. Eleanor stood.

"Hello." The brunette smiled sweetly. "I'm the Dowager Duchess of Chelsony, but I wish you will call me Julia, and you must be Eleanor, Miles' wife."

This youthful woman with a slight French accent was Miles' *mother*? Eleanor dipped into a curtsy. "Your Grace."

"*S'il vous plait*, please, I shall be very distressed if you don't call me Julia, and perhaps in the future, *ma mère,* Mother? After all, you are now my daughter, and I've so longed for a daughter. Besides, I've never felt family should stand on ceremony. Please sit. May I offer you some tea?"

Such was the gentle kindness of the request that Eleanor couldn't refuse, though she felt one hundred kinds of a fraud for doing so and wondered what in the name of heaven Miles had told his mother about her. She collected her skirts and sat. "Tea would be lovely. Milk, one sugar."

Miles' mother poured her tea and handed Eleanor the cup and saucer. She then poured her own and settled back onto the facing loveseat and addressed Eleanor over genteel sips. "Miles tells me that your marriage is a business arrangement to preserve your inheritance and protect you from the greedy fingers of His Royal Highness." *Sip.* "He states neither of you harbors tender feelings for each other." *Sip.* She smiled innocently at Eleanor. "Bah. Men can be so blind—even intuitive men like my son." *Sip.* "Don't you agree?"

If someone had whacked Eleanor alongside the head with a coal shovel, she could not have been more dumbstruck. She held her teacup suspended in front of her mouth and blinked.

The lovely brunette pursed her lips and shrugged delicately. "It is plain to me that you have engaged Miles' affections, and you cannot be indifferent to him."

Eleanor shook herself and set her cup and saucer on the table in front of her. "How did you arrive at that conclusion…ah, Julia?"

A lovely trill of laughter filled the intimate room. "Oh, my sweet Eleanor. The three-year-old filly. To have given you *such* a horse, Miles must hold you in the highest regard... and, well…" Julia raised one elegant shoulder. "Miles is Miles." She shook her head ruefully. "*Oui,* I am his *maman*, but nevertheless, Miles is *irrésistible*. I would never tell him that, of course. It would give him the big head, but you'd be a very odd woman if you hadn't fallen a little under his spell."

She had fallen under his spell. Eleanor conceded it was her unwanted feelings that made his existence such a trial. Such a damning truth to confront and in front of his mother of all people.

In the last few months, emotions of unrelenting worry, ecstatic joy, profound humiliation, and building grief had played havoc with her normally rock-steady equilibrium, jerking it hither and yon until the slightest overset provoked unreasoned emotion. At least, that was the justification she gave herself for the slow filling of her eyes. One blink and the tears released to wet her cheeks.

"Oh, my darling girl, you have been through so much and with no one to help you carry the burden. *Donc très courageux*. So very brave. Here, you must let me… " Julia swept across the space dividing them and pulled a lace and linen handkerchief from her cuff. She daubed at Eleanor's tears and hugged her gently to her breast with soft murmurings of comfort.

Eleanor's discomposure was such that, without thought, she permitted Julia to cuddle her, an action her own mother hadn't dared since Eleanor was six.

"Now…my lovely Eleanor, please tell me how I can help you? I solemnly vow whatever you say to me shall never leave this room; it will remain between only you and me."

Snugged in the comforting embrace of the Dowager Duchess, Eleanor gave ragged voice to her distress. "Your Grace, I am not myself anymore. I hardly recognize the woman I have become. I have never spilled tears for any man until your son, and now it seems I cannot stop. I am *so* weary of it." She sniffed back her tears and swiped at her eyes and cheeks with the ball of her thumb.

The Dowager Duchess petted the crown of her head with gentle strokes. "*Mon petite*, men are very good at making us women cry. They can be wearisome and vexing. I must apologize on behalf of my son as he isn't here to make his apologies himself. He was summoned to London."

"London?" Eleanor stiffened in alarm and straightened. "When do you expect him back?"

"He should be home tomorrow or the next day." The Dowager Duchess's sympathetic gaze captured hers. "Now, why are you here? Is there anything *I* can do to help you?"

Eleanor poured out the entire story. The Dowager Duchess sat and listened with only an occasional nod and murmur of commiseration and sympathy. Such was Eleanor's comfort with the maternal air of nurture and warm concern projected by the Dowager Duchess, she revealed much more than she had planned.

"Well, my dear, you must first speak with Miles." His lovely mother cast an inquiring look at Eleanor. "I assume I cannot entice you to remain at Fairwood until my son returns?"

Eleanor shook her head. "I don't wish to be gone from my parents for even these few days."

Julia clasped Eleanor's hands in hers. "Completely understandable. I will send Miles straight to you the very moment he is back. Must you leave immediately? Or will you stay for tea and a light repast?"

Eleanor sat at the desk in her father's library, her cheek propped on her closed fist and stared at the unrelenting rain and sleet pounding the windows in wind-whipped onslaughts. It seemed everything was working in opposition to her, and that included the weather. For the last week, the warm sunny days of mid-May had vanished to be replaced with dreary cold and wet more appropriate to early March. The exercise boys had complained about having to take the horses out in such filthy weather, but at least no one would willingly travel, so while she didn't expect Miles, neither did she expect Mr. Ludlow.

A knock at the library door straightened her in her chair.

"My lady, Lord Miles Everleigh is here asking to speak with you."

"Oh, good heavens! By all means, show him in, and send Milly to attend this fire. I'm sure the poor man is chilled to the bone. Have Cook send up some of her hot spiced cider with a few dashes of rum and some bread toasted with cheese."

Next she knew, her husband stood before her and made an exceedingly elegant leg. How someone whose hair was plastered to his skull, whose finely tailored clothes hung ruined with wet and whose every step squelched, could still pleasure the eyes was beyond her.

"Madam, I trust I find you well?" He closed his eyes in obvious impatience. "Dash it all, Eleanor, I've no stomach for platitudes. I've been twelve hours on the road in the vilest of weather. What is wrong? Mother said you came to Fairwood in search of me. I know nothing but the direst of emergencies would drive you to do so. I rode here straight away."

"Miles, thank you for coming. Here…please, take this chair by the fire. You are soaked through and must be freezing." She stood and moved a wing chair as close to the fireplace as she dared and motioned for him to sit.

He chuckled wryly and indicated his disheveled and dripping ensemble. "Unless you insist, I'll spare the furniture, but thank you for the courtesy." He moved to stand in front of the fire and turned to face her. Small drips of water shed from his attire hissed as they hit the hearth.

She couldn't take her eyes from his. Now that he stood patiently before her, she was unprepared with words. So much had happened to advance her understanding; he'd done little to deserve her wrath, and he was so dreadfully kind and handsome. She felt a blush rise to her face, and she finally tore her gaze away from him and looked down. "Oh…how awful! Your boots look entirely ruined. You must let mc rcplacc thcm. I cxpect Hobby in London has your lasts? I'll send the order right away. Were the roads quagmires of mud? They must have been, or you would have driven. I ordered hot rum cider for you—and toast with cheese…"

"Eleanor, that all sounds welcome." He paused, weary forbearance inherent in his voice, "Now, will you please tell me what is amiss. What do you require of me?"

"Your mother didn't say?"

"She told me only that I should come to you with all haste."

Eleanor sat abruptly on the desk chair making a mental note that the Dowager Duchess had been true to her word not to speak of what passed between them. It would have been far easier for her had the Dowager Duchess spoken. She opened the top right desk drawer and rummaged through a stack of papers until she found the letter from Elsington & Elsington and held it out to Miles. "Read this."

He read it carefully and looked up when he'd finished. "I take it you have been visited by Prinny's agent?"

"Over two weeks ago, yes. He was most insistent on speaking with *Lord* Miles Everleigh. Said he had some questions pertinent to our marital contract."

"Indeed. What was your response?"

"That you were away on the continent on a buying trip. That I would advise him upon your return."

A rap at the door sounded, and the chambermaid entered to attend the fire followed by a footman bearing a tray with a covered plate and a steaming mug with odors of cinnamon and apple emanating from it.

"Ah, your rum cider and toast." Eleanor motioned for the footman to set the tray within easy reach of Miles and watched with some satisfaction as he wrapped a hand around the amply-sized mug, raised it to his lips and took several hearty swallows.

"And?" His gaze held hers steadily.

She closed her eyes for a moment. She couldn't think when he looked at her so. "I would be very grateful if you could see your way to remaining here, at Rutledge, and conduct however many interviews it may take with the agent of His Royal Highness, until such time as Mr. Ludlow considers us legitimately living as man and wife."

"I see." He removed the silver dome covering the toast, selected one of the thick slices and raised it to his mouth. The melted cheddar cheese elongated into yellow strands which broke and wrapped his hand. His tongue licked them into his mouth. His white teeth made a circular bite into the hearty fare, and he chewed with apparent appreciation, bite following bite until he had finished the entire piece.

She watched his movements with fascination, taken from herself by his almost sensual pleasure in the simple fare until his direct look of inquiry returned her to the subject at hand.

"Should Father... pass... in the near future, I would be most appreciative if you could see your way clear to remaining until the will has been probated." She again watched as Miles consumed the other piece of toast and drank what remained in his mug.

Miles carefully wiped his hands on a linen towel provided with the tray. "You are asking me to be absent from Fairwood for a period that could easily span a year's time—possibly more."

"Yes. I am well aware that the only beneficiary to dispelling any further inquiry will be me. The marital contract was drawn up in such a fashion as to assure you of your monies in perpetuity. Your funds come out of the Earl's private holdings and not the entail." She looked out the window. "I will, of course, facilitate whatever travel or communication you feel is necessary between Rutledge and Fairwood, and will instruct my staff to be at your disposal."

"Good of you."

Eleanor closed her eyes and wilted at the dryness of Miles' voice. "I'm sorry. I'm doing what I always do. I'm as prickly as a hedgehog and making an utter toss-up of this." She offered Miles a glance of apology before her gaze returned to the window and her tone softened considerably. "I'd meant to throw myself on your mercy and impress you with my sincerity and womanly vulnerability. Instead, I've offered to replace your boots and fed you toast." She wrapped her arms around herself and hung her head. He would refuse to help her, and she had no one but herself to blame. His low chuckle was the last thing she expected to hear.

"I'll stay until the agent is satisfied and your father's will is probated—however long that takes."

She turned and faced him. "You will?" An upwelling of intense gratitude made it difficult for her to speak. "Thank you. I… I… I cannot thank you enough. You are everything that is kind, and I cannot imagine why you should be. I have been absolutely hateful to you."

"Not absolutely."

She winced.

He gave her a crooked smile "As a point of curiosity, just where will I be sleeping?"

Eleanor's face blanked of all expression. She'd never considered... "Of necessity, I suppose in my bed. It would seem uncommon and give rise to damaging gossip for a new groom not to attend his bride every night."

"To lie inches from you for months on end? I have not been gelded, Eleanor. I cannot promise to remain a gentleman under such intimate circumstances."

His appraising look and the unusual glint in his eye gave her pause. "You would take an unwilling woman?"

"I never have."

Relief flooded her. "Well, I should hope not."

"You mistake my meaning. You will be willing."

Her mouth opened and closed without uttering a sound.

Chapter Thirteen

Miles manfully repressed the absurd grin that fought to emerge in response to her wide-eyed look of utter consternation. Oh, he meant to have her, and if she thought she'd be unwilling, then she very much mistook her man. He hadn't realized until that precise moment, but he wanted her—permanently. If he were going to reside at Rutledge for the indefinite future, he had the luxury of time at his disposal and the rudiments of a plan to win Eleanor began to take shape.

Between them, the silence deepened and lengthened; Eleanor still had not uttered a sound, just stood there and stared at him with wide eyes. As the well-bred gentleman that he was—most of the time—he rescued her.

"I would like to change out of these wet things and take a hot bath. I am free to use your apartments?"

She nodded.

"Still second floor, end of the hall?"

She nodded.

"Right. If you could have someone take the portmanteau I left in the entry hall up to your suite, I'd be appreciative. Do you keep country hours for dining?"

She nodded and worked her mouth around a preoccupied response. "The small dining room."

"Will we have the pleasure of your parents' company?"

"No…"

"Pity. I would enjoy seeing them again."

"I'll ask if they will join us."

He bowed. "I'll take my leave of you, Eleanor. Until dinner."

He was to see her much sooner.

"You have hair on your chest." Eleanor's matter-of-fact voice roused him.

He blinked his eyes open and with a swoosh of water, sat up in the amazing tub—amazing because it fit his length and submerged him to midway up his chest when he reclined. A moment's reflection reminded him that Eleanor was also tall. Perhaps she'd had it custom made for her. The hot water had been such bliss after the wet, frigid ride to Rutledge that he'd nodded off.

She stood half in and half out of the door to the ensuite bath chamber—an elegant room done in Carrara marble. Her gaze dropped to the floor, only to slowly regain his as if she were helpless to look anywhere else but at him. A slight pink colored her cheeks.

"I meant to wash my face and change for dinner. I'd forgotten you'd be here." She ran her index finger up and down her forehead and gave a snort of helpless bewilderment. "Your presence has put me at sixes and sevens. I'm completely disordered in my mind. Please forgive my intrusion." She shook her head and laughed, her chagrin apparent. Turning, she made to leave.

"Yes, most men have hair on their chests."

She paused in the doorway, her back to him.

"Have you ever seen a nude male, Eleanor?"

Still facing away from him, she shook her head.

"Turn around."

Her spine stiffened.

"Coward. Aren't you at all curious?"

She gasped audibly, released her breath in a huff and with painstaking slowness turned to face him, her hand resting on the door handle. Her gaze found his with unmistakable challenge.

Holding her in an unblinking stare, he rose slowly from the water, took as wide a stance as the tub would allow, and put his hands on his hips. From mid-calf to the top of his head, there was nothing to obscure her vision.

Her gaze dropped to his groin and then flew back up to his eyes. He fought not to grin. She cleared her throat and proceeded to assess him for an appreciable length of time with eyes that he suspected cataloged every detail. The rosy tint that had appeared on her cheeks migrated down her neck and into her décolleté. She cleared her throat again. "Ummm, turn around, please."

He did as she requested and only then, with his back to her, did he allow a half-smile to emerge. A long sigh met his ears and then her murmur.

"You are as beautiful out of your clothes as you are in them, though all the hair comes as something of a shock."

She thought him beautiful? He snorted softly and turned back around, but the door was closing. Eleanor had fled. He would give a goodly sum of money to have her return. He'd only just begun with Lady Eleanor.

He was in the process of toweling off when, with a rap, the door opened an inch or two. "My lord?"

"Yes?"

A middle-aged male dressed in garments that indicated he occupied the top rungs of the hierarchy of hired staff pushed the door fully open and bowed. "I'm Elmer Hopwood, my lord, first under-butler to Mr. Walters. He has instructed me to serve as your valet until such time as your man can come from Fairwood. I've taken the liberty of cleaning and pressing some of the Earl's dinner attire. You are both of a size. Shall I assist you in dressing, my lord?"

"Yes, thank you, Mr. Hopwood."

"Might I suggest we begin with a shave, my lord?"

"Excellent idea. You have some skill with a straight razor?" Miles said lightly. "I need to live long enough to speak with the agent of His Royal Highness."

The under-butler-turned-valet looked at the marble floor before raising a face where amusement flirted with solemnity. "Yes, my lord. I was gentleman's gentleman to The Lord Henry Devaunt of Hob Oaks in York for ten years prior to taking service here. He provided me a fulsome recommendation. I can assure you of my personal loyalty to the Russell family, of which you are now one." He inclined his head. "Does that explanation suffice, my lord?"

"Why did you leave Lord Devaunt's employ?"

"Through personal choice, my lord. Lord Devaunt had a yearning to see the untamed 'Wild West' of America. I far preferred to stay in a more civilized clime."

"Understood." Miles grinned. "Where would you like me, Mr. Hopwood?"

Once shaved by Hopwood, expertly Miles was glad to observe, the valet dressed him in pantaloons of white silk over white silk stockings tied at the knee with white satin ribbons. He added black pumps and a finely pleated white muslin shirt with long ruffled cuffs and an attached collar of moderate height. The pumps fit snugly but would do for short periods of time. Over the immaculate white shirt, Hopwood buttoned him into a gold, figured-silk waistcoat with flat buttons of mother of pearl.

"Do you have a preference as to the knot on your cravat, my lord?"

"I have always favored the Mathematical, but I'm not particular. Something simple and not too high, please. I would like to be able to freely turn my head."

"Of course, my lord." The valet proceeded to tie a moderately high, starched, pristine white cravat in an excellent example of the Mathematical. "And now, sir, if I may help you into your coat?" He held up a double-breasted, cut-away, tail coat of deep blue with gilt buttons, easing it over Miles' shoulders and doing up the gold buttons on the front. He then reached into the sleeves, pulled free the cuffs of Miles' shirt and arranged them in a froth of white ruffles that fell to Miles' knuckles.

"You are going to make me into quite the peacock, Mr. Hopwood."

His new valet eyed the result of his work with a gleam of satisfaction. "If I might be so free, my lord, you will be a pleasure to dress."

Miles entered the family dining room to find Eleanor standing by a massive oak sideboard looking pensive and sipping a small glass of red wine. She was beautifully attired in a three-quarter sleeved, empire gown of sheer ecru silk heavily embroidered with curlicues and floral figures in shimmery golden thread. The gold embroidery on the gown matched that of a sleeveless over-robe of a more substantial, deep lavender silk. The toes of crème-colored slippers peeked from the gold-encrusted hem. Her ash blonde hair was swept up into a simple chignon with soft tendrils left down to curl around the nape of her slender neck. Amethysts set in gold filigree dangled from her earlobes, but she wore no other jewelry. He found her immensely attractive.

"Lady Miles." He bowed.

Her large hazel eyes evaluated him over the rim of her goblet. "Lord Miles. I'm sure Father never wore those clothes half so well." Eleanor gave him a tentative smile then looked away. "Please help yourself to whatever appeals. There is wine, both red and white, and gin or ale if you prefer."

Miles walked to the sideboard, inches from Eleanor, and poured himself a half glass of ale. "I do hope we won't always be awkward with each other."

Eleanor turned on him with a snort, which she quickly muffled. "How awful of you to use my own words against me. I should very much like to be easy with you. I suppose I will have to stop surprising you in the bath."

He grinned and raised his glass to her. "Yes. Some things once seen cannot be unseen."

Mid-sip, she swallowed wrong and started coughing. He set his beer down and pulled a serviette from the sideboard, silently handing it to her in exchange for her wine glass. He casually sipped at his beer, and when she had composed herself to the point where a breath did not set her off into another paroxysm of coughing, she glared at him, half in accusation and half in amusement.

"Wretched man. I believe you timed your comment purposefully."

He chuckled and held up a palm. "Absolve me of any ill intent. I should hate for you to ruin that lovely gown for you look all the crack, and I would enjoy seeing you in it again."

She dipped into a small curtsy. "Thank you." Her eyes avoided his direct gaze, but a tiny smile tipped one corner of her mouth.

Miles felt a pang that she should take such obvious pleasure from a simple compliment and vowed, wherever possible, to sincerely compliment her again. If he did nothing else during his sojourn to Rutledge, he would restore her previous ease of interaction with him; although he hoped for much, much more.

"My lord…" Eleanor began.

"Miles."

She inclined her head. "Miles. I want to thank you…" Her head turned, and her eyebrows rose in surprise; she smiled brilliantly. "Father. Mamma. You are joining us."

Two sturdy footmen wheeled chairs occupied by the Earl of Rutledge and his countess into the dining room. Miles crossed immediately to Lady Rutledge, acknowledged the Earl of Rutledge with a nod, "Lord Rutledge," and offered Eleanor's mother his arm. "Good evening, Lady Rutledge. I'm pleased you and Lord Rutledge will be joining us. I was disappointed not to be able to stay previously but…business called. May I help you to a chair at the table?"

She offered him the sweetest of smiles. "Good evening, Lord Miles. Rutledge and I are delighted you are back in residence." She patted his forearm and confided, "We have decided to take dinner with you and Eleanor as often as our health allows." She indicated an armchair at the end of the cozy dining table set for four persons. "Just there, please." Miles helped her into the chair while a footman assisted the Earl into his place at the opposing end.

"Eleanor?" He offered her an arm and seated her before a footman pulled out the remaining chair for him.

As the dinner courses were served and removed, the Earl directed the conversation to Fairwood with an initial inquiry. "Eleanor tells us that you have been attending to a recently purchased property in Newmarket."

"Yes, I acquired the old Woodward farm from Lord Marlburl. Perhaps you know of it? Lord Marlburl is one of your contemporaries, I believe."

The Earl harrumphed. "Know the property and him well. The old fox got the better of me…" and marched off into a humorous complaint about how Marlburl had refused to sell Day Dreamer back to Rutledge. Miles looked across the table at a stricken Eleanor.

When the Earl ended his story, before Miles could draw a breath, she blurted, "I don't suppose you ever got my letter thanking you for your exceedingly thoughtful and much-appreciated bride gift."

He shook his head with a slight smile.

"I wrote to you immediately, but…" Her face transformed with demonstrable joy. "I adore her. I don't know how you could have given her up. Would you like to join me for the morning workouts? Watch her and the rest of the mob train?"

"It would please me greatly."

"We keep very early hours. We try to have the horses out by 6:00 a.m."

"I will require coffee. Large amounts of strong, black coffee."

Eleanor's eyes lit with humor. "I'll tell Cook."

The Earl regained Miles attention by asking, "Is it your intent to stay permanently at Rutledge? Or will you take up residence at the Woodward farm? I should call it Fairwood, I suppose. Eleanor says you have renamed it."

Miles glanced at Eleanor, but her intense engagement in tearing an innocent dinner roll into dozens of pieces of a size to feed a love bird gave him no indication as to how she wished him to answer. "My intention is to reside at Rutledge Manor for the foreseeable future."

"Excellent. I would like to share some of my thoughts on the operation of the estate and prospective changes I had wanted to implement going forward."

"I will welcome any insight you can provide, Lord Rutledge," Miles said. Lady Rutledge sat quietly and beamed—as she had done from the beginning of their meal.

Eleanor considered him from across the table, the beginnings of apprehension in her gaze.

"Eleanor has done a capital job of administering Rutledge, but now that she is married, it is natural and appropriate that, you, as her husband, should assume the administration of the estate. That said, you will need assistance conducting the affairs of a property this large. As you take on the burden of the day-to-day operations of Rutledge, don't hesitate to lean on Eleanor. She will be of the greatest help to you. Won't you, m'dear?"

"Ummm… yes, of course, Father." Eleanor shot Miles a wary glance and then dropped her gaze to her plate, stabbing fitfully at a Brussels sprout.

"I suggest you and I meet several times a week in my study to review existing practices and potential areas for improvement. We can begin tomorrow at 2:00."

"I will place myself at your service, Lord Rutledge," Miles said.

After the Earl's announcement, Lady Rutledge directed the conversation to a multitude of innocent topics. They chatted politely until the dessert course was finished and both the earl and his countess pled fatigue and retired to bed. Miles had risen out of politeness as Lady Rutledge left the dining room. Afterward, he rounded the table to help Eleanor from her chair, and as she stood, she addressed him from over her shoulder.

"My mother is high in alt because you are here. Does every woman who crosses your path fall in love with you on the instant?"

With a crooked smile, Miles returned Eleanor's sharp question with an equally direct response. "No. Present company a case in point." He pushed her chair back to the table as she turned to face him.

Eleanor visibly wilted. "I'm sorry. I deserved that set down. I didn't mean to sound so… snappish." She sighed. "It must be nice to woo total strangers to your side so effortlessly. It's not an ability I've ever had." Her expression softened. "I envy you. You've not been here twelve hours, and you've already won over my both my parents."

Both his eyebrows rose. "I've won over your father?"

"Oh, yes. He grumps and huffs, but he respects you. As you heard, you will have the management of Rutledge." She appeared stricken.

"Eleanor," he paused thoughtfully. "I win people over because I must. Until your unexpected offer, my continuing welfare depended upon my being universally agreeable. It was an attribute I took pains to cultivate, but it is not easy to hold onto one's self when you must always contort your speech and behavior to what is most pleasing to those around you. You say you envy me? Well, I envy you." At her surprised expression, he smiled wryly. "When was the last time you withheld your opinion because speaking would offend those in your company? When was the last time you had to give any thought whatsoever to your speech? You say you are blunt to a fault as if that were always a bad thing. I should rather say that you lack pretense, and you don't dissemble. You are honest and genuine. In my eyes, those are admirable qualities."

She frowned as though the concept was foreign to her. "But your circumstances have changed dramatically, and you are still…" Her arms made vague gestures in the air as she searched for words.

"I have fallen into the habit of being congenial. Civility does smooth one's way."

"Then I am doomed to a rocky path." She sighed. "Would you like to adjourn to the library? I can offer you ink and paper to write to the Prince Regent's agent and also give whatever directions you think necessary to your steward at Fairwood. I'm certain you will want your man here with the rest of your things."

His lips canted in a crooked smile. "I am practicing certain economies and have not engaged a valet at Fairwood. I would like to continue with Mr. Hopwood if it does not create inconvenience."

"Of course, if he suits."

"I will need my clothes, and I suppose I should tell *Maman* to run the house as she wills and to send me the accounts. My steward, Mr. Weldon, is wholly competent to carry on without me and if truth be known, would prefer not to see me at present." Miles answered Eleanor's look of inquiry with a wrinkled brow and a twist of his mouth. "He took the loss of Day Dreamer rather hard."

"The poor man. I sympathize completely, but you cannot have her back."

"I'm glad you like her, and thank you for keeping Jemmy."

She rolled her eyes. "Of course I kept him, as you well knew I would. I should have felt as if I'd devastated his young life for all time had I separated the two."

Miles threw his head back and laughed. "Heinous indeed... and Eleanor... I agreed to meet with your father as it was the respectful thing to do. It is not my intention to supplant you or interfere in your management of Rutledge."

She looked vastly relieved.

He offered his arm. "Shall we go compose letters?"

"It seems your schemes and machinations might come to fruition, Rutledge." The Countess lifted her eyes from the letter she read and gazed at her adored husband across the width of both their beds. "Julia writes that Eleanor's affections are decidedly engaged, and she is quite certain, as evidenced by the gift of the three-year-old filly, that Miles is far from indifferent." She turned to face him fully. "Now we must make *them* see it." Her aged face saddened and her eyes welled with unshed tears. "I absolutely forbid you to die before we see Eleanor and Miles settled happily. I forbid it. Do you hear me, Rutledge?"

"Yes, Lady Rutledge, I hear you." Her husband closed his eyes and released a long sigh. "I shall speak with the Almighty about accommodating you."

She settled back with a shaky breath and a small sniffle. "I can't think why He wouldn't. It's a small thing to ask."

Chapter Fourteen

"Here they come! Dreamer and Cinsyr! Oh! Look! Look! She has him by a nose!" Eleanor so forgot herself in her excitement that she grabbed Miles' upper arm and shook him as she jumped up and down. "Isn't she splendid, Miles! Isn't she simply splendid?" His rich laughter met her ears, and she felt him take her hand, but she didn't dare take her eyes from the two horses streaking toward them, urged on at every step by the slight men on their backs.

Sleek coats and rippling muscles thundered by not six feet from where they stood; clods of turf the size of her palm flew at them, sliced from the earth by the Thoroughbreds' churning hooves. Within moments the black tail and the chestnut tail disappeared in the heavy morning mist that obscured anything beyond a quarter mile. She could hear the faint voices of the exercise boys pulling up the filly and the young stallion with steady, "Whoa there, missy...whoa," and "Easy there, lad... go easy."

"Yes, she is glorious. They both are. Tell me about the black," Miles said.

As she watched for the two horses to reappear, she gave Miles chapter and verse on the two-year-old Rutledge stallion that had made such a name for himself in the short time he'd been racing.

"Impressive record."

"Yes. Cinsyr is one of the last of Absalom's foals. We lost the old man this past fall to colic. He will be hard to replace, but I'm hoping one of his sons, Dare To Dream, will be Rutledge's future."

"Well, if Day Dreamer is any indication of the quality of his offspring, I believe he will stand to a full book. It would be useful to see if you could find more of those Old Codger mares."

Eleanor nodded. "I've been trying. So far, I only know the whereabouts of two, the mare at Fairwood and one in Scotland, of all places. I've meant to ask you about a re-breeding." She chattered happily with Miles about other possible crosses on Dare until a chestnut and black materialized out of the fog followed closely by Charles Fedder mounted on his familiar brown gelding.

From their equine perches, the two exercise boys were laughing and jabbering back and forth.

"Don't get all top lofty, ya little toad. Cin woulda had ya in another eighth of a mile."

"You've daft and blind, Henry. The lass led him by a head and was gaining ground afore we pulled up."

Eleanor laughed along with them. "Well, I doubt we'll match them again anytime soon. Fedder wanted to see them together to give Dreamer a challenge, see how she'd react to being pushed." As she spoke, her gaze flew to her unsmiling trainer. "Well, Mr. Fedder?"

His gaze swung to the two exercise boys walking their charges in circles around their small group. "You lads get Cin and Dreamer cooled off and put away right. I'll be by to check on them later." He returned his attention to Eleanor and held up his stopwatch. "Time tells the tale, my lady." She detected an air of satisfaction about his sober person. "I believe we should run her in the Welborn Cup as a prep race for the Derby." His gaze settled on Miles. "If you concur, my lord. You've more experience with her than we do."

"Two months more experience." Miles laughed. "I still find it hard to believe you want her in the Derby where she'll have to run against colts and not the Oaks where she'll run against her sex." Miles shrugged. "As a rule, at three years old, stallions have greater physical development than fillies, but Dreamer has given me no reason to think she couldn't hold her own. Strength does not always equate to speed, and her times indicate she could win against colts. The distance at the Welborn Cup is good for her, and the field shouldn't be too challenging." He paused for a moment, thinking. "She could use the extra practice at the starter's tape. If you are set on that, I see no reason to object."

"I'll see to it, then. My lord. My lady." Fedder tipped his cap, and she and Miles watched him trot after the two youngsters, barking a continuing stream of instruction to their riders before she returned her attention to Miles and responded to his question.

"I am set on it. The Derby is more prestigious and for a filly to win against colts will capture the race world's attention. Dare will have the highest quality mares for his book. Besides, she's one of the rare females who could win the Epsom Derby. She deserves the opportunity to put her name in the history books." Exuberance welled inside her, and she wrapped her arms around herself to contain her joy. Her gaze found and held that of her handsome husband. The upwelling of happiness expanded to include the facilitator of her joy. "Miles, thank you—again. It has been my most longstanding and heartfelt desire to win the Derby with a homebred filly."

She looked away, somewhat embarrassed by what she planned to confess to him. "My father named me after a horse." At Miles' bark of amused disbelief, she looked back quickly and held up an admonishing finger while holding in check a smile of her own. "But! She was a very *special* horse, the only filly ever to win the Epsom Derby. Her name was Eleanor." She hemmed and hawed. "I have never told that to anyone other than you for the very reasons writ large across your face."

"I admit to initial shock that your mother agreed, but upon further thought... your father is horse mad and your mother adoring." His grey eyes sparkled with humor as he shrugged. "Your secret is safe with me, Lady Eleanor."

She linked her arm through his, thoroughly happy with the world at large, and sauntered toward the top of the rise, pulling Miles' solid body along with her. Not even the thought of another night lying stiffly next to him, attentive to his every twitch, could ruin her mood. "Come along, Lord Miles, we have some two-year-olds to observe. It will be the first time for them to run in company and then it's on to the broodmares and foals. After lunch, I believe Father expects you. I'll change and leave the two of you to maunder on while I go into the village to speak with a man about drainage tiles. He wishes to establish a business making them in Stelton. Apparently, we '*have good dirt.*' As his landlady, I must attend to estate affairs." She crossed her eyes and made a face. "Such is the elegant life of a lady of leisure."

His arm shook with silent laughter. "A lady of leisure? Indeed, I thought some young lad, the son of a gamekeeper perhaps, had wandered into our rooms this morning. Imagine my surprise when upon further inspection that youth turned out to be none other than my lady wife."

"I find breeches and boots practical when out in the fields, and I vastly prefer riding astride. It is a more secure and balanced seat."

"I was not voicing criticism, merely making an observation."

She slowed and eyed him sideways. "So, you've no objection to my masculine attire?"

"None whatsoever. You needn't wear a pretty frock for me to find you a desirable woman."

She came to a halt and stared at the back of his head as he kept walking. He thought her desirable? She stumbled after him. For the second time in twenty-four hours, he'd stripped her of speech. Happily, by the time they reached the observation point for the two-year-olds, she'd recovered her wits and could tell him about each of the horses that worked out below.

Eleanor and her accompanying groom rode back into the courtyard of Rutledge Manor by the light of the moon set high in the sky. It seemed there was much more to drainage tiles than she had first assumed, and her appointment had run until considerably past dinner. As she'd been in the village closest to her home, she'd sent a message to advise Miles and her mother and father not to wait dinner on her.

Swinging her right leg off the horn of the sidesaddle and kicking off the left stirrup, she faced sideways and slid lightly off her horse. With a twitch of her long skirts, she handed Mouse off to Toby with a smile and a nod of thanks. "See you in the morning, Toby. Sleep well."

"My lady." Toby tipped his cap and walked off, leading both their mounts.

She stood in the courtyard, skirt in hand, and gazed at the entrance doors to the manor both eager and hesitant to enter her own home. *He* was there. No light shone from either the first or second floor, but she couldn't ascribe too much to that as her apartments were in the rear. Drawing in a deep breath, Eleanor straightened her spine, put her shoulders back and climbed the steps to the oak doors. As if possessed of some higher magic, the door on the right opened for her, and she swept in.

"Thank you, Jeffers." She paused. "Still on *Lady of the Lake*?"

"Yes, my lady. I must confess I find the poetry hard going. I prefer *Ivanhoe*."

"So you said. Well, persevere." With a smile, she proceeded to climb the stairs to the second floor and nodded to the night hallboy seated there. "Good evening, Rowland, has Lord Miles retired?"

"Yes, ma'am. Shall I ring down for Miss Conway?"

"Yes, I would appreciate that. Thank you."

She slipped into the sitting room and closed the door quietly behind her. The door to the bedchamber that she now shared with Miles stood ajar. A faint gold glow outlined it in the door casing. He was still up. A light rap alerted her to Sally's entrance. Her personal maid bobbed an abbreviated curtsy and moved to her. "My lady?"

"Help me out of this riding habit and into my nightdress."

As she went through her nightly routine of washing her face and brushing her teeth, combing out her waist-length hair and re-braiding it, changing into bedclothes of shapeless, opaque, white muslin, with none of the allure of those Lady Florence had selected for her, Eleanor studied the bedchamber door. Had he left it open with a light burning as some sort of invitation? Or was a lamp left lit simply out of consideration for her?

The first part of this day, the part spent with Miles, had been immense fun. It was difficult to inject enthusiasm into drainage tiles, but her morning had been splendid. Part of her enjoyment was due to her optimism about Day Dreamer, but she'd be lying to herself if she didn't credit her husband with being a personable, charming companion...who said he found her desirable as a woman.

His casual utterance provoked emotions that had lain dormant in her breast for the latter half of the day— unwieldy, churning emotions that she refused to put a name to. Somehow she had to get through the coming months without becoming ensnared in *feelings*. She slumped in her chair with her hands in her lap, shoulders rounded, and glared at herself in the dressing table mirror. She could not summon any optimism for a hopeful outcome. Lord Miles Everleigh was an excessively handsome gentleman—she'd never erase from her mind the stunning glory of him in the bath—and he possessed an amiable and chivalrous manner. The Dowager Duchess had it rightly. No female that drew breath could resist him.

Her intellectual curiosity about what happened between men and women already warred with her desire to protect her heart. Could she have amorous congress with

Miles and remain unentangled? What if the result produced children? Lady Florence had instructed her in ways to prevent such an outcome but also advised her that such efforts were notoriously unreliable. If she gave herself to Miles, she feared she would cede to him the power to disorder her world, yet his proximity every night would prove difficult to resist. A quiet scoff left her lips. She was the most ridiculous of creatures, an infatuated woman. She briskly rose to her feet and stuck her tongue out at her reflection. *Infatuation or no, it is not necessary to turn oneself into a mawkish, peagoose.*

As she entered the bedchamber, her eyes went to the form of her husband asleep in a wing chair lit by the fading glow of the fireplace. A bed table lamp with the wick turned low provided the only additional light. Miles looked at ease in her father's old velvet dressing gown and slippers. Even in sartorial disarray, she could have stood and gorged upon his features for endless minutes. A weighty tome lay open on his lap. Interested to know the topic of his reading, she peered over his shoulder and scanned the pages. *Poor man.* A soft giggle shook her shoulders. She clapped a hand to her mouth immediately. Lady Miles Everleigh *never* giggled.

He stirred, coming awake, and straightened in the chair to regard her through warm, sleepy eyes. "Eleanor…good, you have returned. Now I can seek my bed without worry. So, tell me, tomorrow, will you be able to school me in all the varieties of drainage tile?"

He had worried for her? "Apparently, as I am a female, my understanding must be deficient, and thus, I will need to return to Mr. Abram's ovens for further edification. I insist that you accompany me next time. The scintillating topic of which types of earth make the best clay—

accompanied by examples of said earth—is not to be missed, though my favorite pair of tan riding gloves is quite ruined."

He responded to her quip with a light chuckle and closed the book on his lap with a snap, laying it on a petite side table next to the chair. He rose, and his gaze slid to her as he crossed to the bed, disrobed to his nightshirt and got under the covers, settling back into the fluffy white pillows with a groan of appreciation. "I, on the other hand, have spent the last four hours acquainting myself with the pages of *The English Landed Estate—Its Administration and Management*. Shall I educate you on the various advantages of chicken guano versus bullock manure and the dispersion rate of each per acre of turnips?"

Struggling to maintain a serious demeanor, Eleanor joined him in the great bed, lying on her back to stare at the ceiling, her arms straight at her sides. "Father is a great proponent of bullock manure. Perhaps the Hurst farm would benefit from your study. They grow turnips." She almost managed her suggestion without snickering.

He threw her a conspiratorial grin. "An evening spent reading about the beneficial properties of manure does not match with my boyhood dreams of owning a private estate." Miles reached and extinguished the bedside lamp and returned to lie on his back with his hands behind his head.

"You don't grow turnips at Fairwood?" she teased. The dim light from the dying fire cast soft illumination throughout the chamber. Eleanor thought it… romantic …and promptly shied away from the thought.

"I don't really know …I must make a note to ask Weldon." He rolled to his side, propped his head up on an elbow and studied her.

In their intimate situation, each time he inhaled or exhaled, his every subtle movement, the woody smell of the soap he used, the glint as the dim light caught his eyes …in short, each detail of his person, aggravated her feeling of vulnerability, and the easy sense of comradery their banter had established became something else, something more fraught with expectancy. She bore the growing silent tension as long as she could.

"Why do you look at me so? What is it you want?"

"Mmm… *that* is a dangerous question with a variety of answers. I'll offer you a simple one. I should like it very much if you would kiss me again." His smile gleamed white in the dim light.

"Will you forever repeat my words to me?" She had spoken those exact words to Miles on her wedding night. She also remembered ensuing the kiss. The memory spurred her onto precarious ground. "If you wish."

She rolled to her side and faced him. He did not move, merely waited—and watched. The distance between them lessened as she leaned toward him, closed her eyes and placed her lips fully on his. A rigid part of her softened in submission when he cupped her cheek and then wrapped an arm around her waist to bring her with him as he rolled over and laid her flat on her back. He took command of what she had initiated and deepened their kiss, breaking off only to use his lips to place butterfly-soft kisses on her cheekbones, her temples, under her jaw and down her neck before returning to her mouth. His arm left her waist, and his hand rose to the nape of her neck. Using both hands, he directed the position and attitude of her head with gentle pressure, moving her face to accommodate the infinite variety of kisses he bestowed on her. Pleasure followed pleasure until sensation drowned her, dragged her down into a world of melting bliss, a timeless world she could dwell in forever.

"Put your hands on me, Eleanor. Touch me," he ordered and recaptured her mouth.

She didn't fully understand what he wanted. Either her response was too slow, or he understood her confusion, for one at a time, each of his hands wrapped hers where they still fisted the bedding and placed them on his shoulders. Her palms opened on the smooth silkiness of his lawn nightshirt and then broadened to awareness of the warmth coming from the hard muscles working underneath. His kisses intensified as her hands, like two explorers on a quest of discovery, charted the unfamiliar territory of his shoulders, the hard column of his neck and sifted through the feathery softness of his hair. So lost was she to his seduction, that she stretched her length fully beneath him to revel in the press of his weight on her and held him with arms that wrapped his back. A languid warmth spread from her mouth to her breasts and lower to parts of her for which she knew no proper name. *More*. Her body demanded more of this bewitchment, for what he was doing to her was surely magic.

"Please," she begged in a whisper. "Please."

His dark form hovered above her. "Please what?" he murmured.

"I want more. Please …I'm…I'm willing."

A dark image looming in profile, he stilled completely and then pulled away to brace himself on his side and regard her. She wished the light was better so she could read the details of his face. A shudder ran through her when his forefinger traced the outline of her lips ever so gently.

He breathed a long sigh. "No… no, I'm not convinced you are. I would not like to be accused of forcing you."

With her body in aching rebellion at the cessation of his kisses, he rolled over, pulling the coverlet with him, and presented her with his back.

"Sleep well, Eleanor. I look forward to more of your kisses."

What! What did he mean he wasn't convinced? Had she not participated fully? This man continued to say and do things that confounded her, halted all the rational turnings of her mind and reduced her to a state of wordless confusion. Bewilderment colored her thoughts, but foremost among them was one clear question. What must she do to convince him?

Chapter Fifteen

Miles lay in bed in the early hours of the next morning and studied a sleeping Eleanor. At least sleep had found one of them. Following Eleanor's innocent kiss and subsequently more ardent ones, his cock had taken the bit between its teeth and bolted, refusing to be reined in. With no possibility of self-relief, he'd disciplined himself to lie quietly and thought of manure and guano until the recalcitrant part submitted to governance—a lengthy procedure as he was out of practice with such things. Thanks to his lusty patronesses, not since his early days at Oxford had he spent an entire night aroused and aching from unconsummated dalliance.

Nevertheless, he would willingly endure many more nights of the same in furtherance of his campaign to win Eleanor. Indeed, the only weakness in his plan had been the possibility Eleanor would no longer warm to his kisses. Last night had proved he could discard that worry. She would be a delight to teach. At the memory of her response, the anatomical part of him that had provoked hours of sleeplessness awoke with renewed interest. He had more than a simple physical interest in her, however.

Though obstinately independent, Eleanor needed him. Her money and elevated station insulated her from much ugliness, but the world they lived in was unkind to a woman with no male relation to protect her, witness his gentle mother. Fury still heated his blood at the belittlement she'd endured from Edgar, the economies of life she'd had to practice in a home that had formerly been hers. The Chelsony estate had a dower house of significant size to which she should have removed after the death of her husband. However, Edgar had complained of the expense to make it habitable after a vacancy of many years and consigned his step-mother to rooms in a seldom-used wing of Chelsony Hall. Out of sight and out of mind. That her widow's portion would have easily covered the costs of such renovation didn't loosen Edgar's purse. Had Miles wanted a permanent rift between him and his oldest brother, he would have pursued legal action to recover his mother's funds. He still might.

Presumably, Eleanor had met his mother at Fairwood. What had she made of the Dowager Duchess? What had his mother made of Eleanor? He'd have to ask, though, on his mother's part, he felt confident he knew. Her actions spoke of a sympathetic leaning toward his wife.

Just as he couldn't abide the thought of his mother under the management of the current Duke of Chelsony, neither could he stand the thought of Eleanor dealing alone after the death of her father and mother. Oh, she'd carry on in her independent and outwardly confident manner, but during the two weeks he had "courted" her in London, he'd seen another woman, one vulnerable and not self-assured, one easily wounded and lonely, one of lively wit and dry humor that only emerged when she felt in safe company.

He knew what she'd do. She'd entomb herself at Rutledge. What a wretched waste. More than most of her sex, a harmonious marriage would benefit Eleanor. He'd witnessed such a marriage between his mother and father, seen how the love between them had allowed his shy and retiring mother to flower into self-confident womanhood. He wanted such sympathetic companionship for himself. He wanted that for Eleanor.

Slipping quietly from their bed, he used the chamber pot and entering their shared dressing room, rang for Mr. Hopwood. Another day in borrowed clothes. While not a male milliner, he enjoyed knowing his turn-out was impeccable. He laughed at himself silently—his preoccupation with his dress a result of spending too much time in the company of ladies, no doubt. It was too much to hope for his instructions to have reached Fairwood in time to enable his mother to dispatch a return messenger to arrive with his bits and bobs by today. However, it was not too much to expect the arrival of a persistent nuisance in the guise of an agent of the Prince Regent. Hopwood arrived in conjunction with the early morning tray bearing Eleanor's hot chocolate and his coffee.

"Good morning, my lord. A housemaid will be up shortly with hot water. Mr. Walters took the liberty of preparing a selection of Lord Rutledge's attire suitable to receive such company as may call upon you today."

"Good morning to you, Mr. Hopwood." He digested what his valet had said. "Is there a particular guest anticipated by the omniscient Mr. Walters?"

Mr. Hopwood continued to lay out a display of morning coats in blacks, blues and greens, both single and double-breasted, some with high standing collars of black velvet and waistcoats that ranged from scarlet to an ordinary tan. "Mr. Walters didn't see fit to share that information with me, sir, but I might hazard a guess as to expect the Prince Regent's agent. He was seen in the common room of a local posting house last night."

"Indeed. He has made remarkable time. I shall marshal my forces to present a rousing defense." Miles shrugged out of his robe and nightclothes and threw a white shirt with frothy white cuffs on over his head. He next drew on a pair of black stockings and black breeches, forgoing the smalls Hopwood had set out—he drew the line at wearing someone else's linens—and pulled on his riding boots. He held his foot out and examined the immaculately clean and beautifully polished footwear. "Mr. Hopwood, my commendations. You have made an excellent job of bringing these tubes of sodden leather back from the dead. I believe I can see myself in the result. I confess to being astonished."

"Thank you, sir. The blacking formula has been handed down in my family from father to son and is a closely held secret. I *can* tell you that it contains a dash of champagne. Now, if you will be seated, I will shave you, and might I recommend a slight trim of your hair?"

"Good morning, my lord." Eleanor stood in the door to the bedroom, wrapped from toe to chin in her dressing gown and nodded at his valet. "Mr. Hopwood."

"Your ladyship," replied Mr. Hopwood.

One of the many things Miles found to like in Eleanor was her egalitarian treatment of her servants. She was not one to look through the staff who served her as if they were invisible. He supposed it was a result of growing up with only servants as confidants and friends instead of her own class. Unlike many aristocrats, she saw those who served her as people.

"Good morning to you, Lady Miles." While his valet had a very steady hand with the razor, Miles didn't wish to test the limits of his expertise by moving. He watched from the corner of his eye as she crossed to the small table by the door, picked up her chocolate and retreated once again to the bedroom. Hopwood continued the steady scraping of his chin and neck between applications of soap froth and hot towels.

Her voice came through the open door. "You may have the dressing room, my lord. Sally will attend me in the bedroom."

Fair enough. "It might be prudent to linger at the residence this morning... and wear a morning dress appropriate to receive callers."

"Oh?"

"Mr. Hopwood advises me that the agent for Prinny was observed in the salon at a local posting house."

His observation was met with silence from the bedroom.

He opened his mouth to ask her to attend the interview, but he was forestalled by Mr. Hopwood.

"My lord, if you will please refrain from moving your jaw?" his valet admonished. "It would expedite your shave and more than likely prolong your life."

Have been effectively silenced, he didn't speak to Eleanor again until breakfast was served at the unfashionably early of time of 9:00 a.m. At least the sun was up—a nice change from the previous morning. The country hours observed at Rutledge would take some getting used to.

"I told Walters we would serve ourselves," Eleanor said as he walked into the dining room. She glanced at him from her place at the table. "On the sideboard there are hot cakes with syrup and butter, sausages and fried potatoes."

After creating a pile of sausages and potatoes that threatened to spill over his plate at any movement, he joined her at the table. He loved sausages and fried potatoes. "I would like for you to be present during my interview with the Prince Regent's agent."

"I was going to insist on it. What will you say to him?"

"I will assure him that we are married in *every* way and conduct myself as to give him no reason to question my statement." While he steadily devoured the sausages, he checked with Eleanor and was amused by the pink flush that had arisen in her cheeks. She looked the image of a blushing bride, and that was why he wanted her present. Plus, he had some ideas about how to add to that becoming blush.

"So your intent is to perjure yourself to an agent of His Royal Highness."

"Perjure is a harsh term. Say, rather, a temporary bending of the truth." He forked another sausage into his mouth and offered her a benign smile as he chewed.

"A *temporary* lie?"

He patted his mouth with a serviette. "Yes. A false statement given with the surety it will imminently be made true." Large portions of fried potatoes marched into his mouth with the regularity of a dock laborer loading a sailing vessel. He was aware of her scrutiny the entire time. Once his plate was clean, he again bestowed a benevolent smile on Eleanor and took a large swallow of coffee. "Did you have some of these potatoes? They are exceptionally good. You must send my praise to the cook. I neglected to compliment you on how well turned out you are this morning. That rose color is particularly becoming to you, and your maid has done your hair in a most flattering style."

"Thank you. Go back to what you just said."

"About potatoes or the color of your dress?"

She stared at him and then snorted, pressing a hand to her mouth to halt a bark of laughter. Amusement lurked in her fine hazel eyes. "Wretched beast, you will make me ask."

"Ah, *that*." He shrugged. "You know my thoughts on the subject."

"But I told you last night I was willing, and you rolled over and presented me with your back."

"You lacked conviction."

Her mouth hung open for a moment before she closed it with a snap.

"If I eat another bite, I will surely gut founder, so I am away to the library to further acquaint myself with other improvements to cultivated earth such as gypsum and crop rotation. Will you join me, madam?"

She eyed him suspiciously. "Are you really going to bury yourself in some dry agricultural treatise?"

"Yes." Though, he could be distracted by other delights, Eleanor's elegant neck and the soft white skin on her slender shoulders for instance. Her lush lower lip, currently caught between her teeth might require further study. More of her sweet kisses wouldn't go amiss.

"Might I talk you into helping me research the owners of mares of the Old Codger bloodline instead? I mean to write to all of them and ask if they have mares they will sell. I have a copy of the General Stud Book current through last year. I'd like to accomplish it before Day Dreamer wins the Epsom Derby."

Ask him to research racehorses? You might as well ask a schoolboy if he wanted to put down his mathematics and go fishing. He was quick to assist her out of her chair. "I won't put up much of a fight, my lady. In fact, consider it done."

As she rose, he winged out an arm to escort her to the library. She wrapped her arm through his and observed, "It was remarkably easy to sway you, my lord. One would think you lack a true commitment to the science of land improvement."

"An accurate observation if ever I heard one," he muttered. "I'd as rather decline Latin nouns." From her gurgle of laughter, he'd found a co-conspirator.

"Then you will welcome the knowledge that we have a land manager who lives and breathes such things. Father had me read the exact same book you had last night only so that I would not be entirely ignorant."

"You have relieved my mind of a great weight."

They spent several hours in serious industry, borne out by the ink stains on his fingertips and the dust streak on Eleanor's cheek from venturing into some rarely-opened books containing maps of Ireland and Scotland. She shoved the latest one away with a groan.

"I cannot decipher these margin notes. My eyes are refusing to focus. Shall we take a break? I'll ring for some tea and biscuits. Cook made some lovely ginger ones yesterday."

"Excellent thought. It is coming on 2:00. Walters tells me that is the customary time the Earl set aside for business callers." He sent her a speaking look. "We should probably have to stop, regardless."

With a face as if she'd tasted something foul, Eleanor rose and stuck her head out of the library door to speak with a footman who would relay her message to the kitchen. Moving to where Miles sat at the desk, she picked up several large books with the obvious intention to reshelve them. He rose and followed her to the shelves.

"Here, let me help you," he offered, taking one out of her hand and sliding it into its place. With a smile, she handed him the others, one at a time. He misplaced the last volume on purpose.

"No." She stretched forward beside him, reaching across him for the errant book in such a fashion that her breast pressed into his side. "I believe it goes…"

He caught her about the waist and turned her toward him. "I know where it goes. We'll straighten it later." He leaned down and kissed her mouth, smiled against her lips and kissed her again before straightening. "I've meant to do that all morning."

She gazed at him wordlessly, then rose on her toes and kissed him back, her arms wrapping his neck, her fingers running through his hair in a delicious manner. Delighted with her boldness, he held her to him, one hand low on her back, pressing her against his falls where a particular male organ was rousing to life. Kiss followed lengthening kiss with Eleanor participating fully—so fully that he swept her up into his arms, carried her to the sofa and sat with her in his lap to further explore his willing wife. She made a warm, delectable bundle of rose silk and white skin, sensitive skin that he began to map with his fingers while continuing to occupy her mouth with increasing thoroughness. Her tongue danced with his eagerly while the innocent rocking of her arse incited misbehavior of the worst sort from his cock. His hand slipped into the front of her gown and cupped her bare breast. Her nipple hardened in reaction and she gave a low moan. If a man could die from raw need, she was going to be the death of him.

The rattle of china on a metal tray came from the open library door accompanied shortly thereafter by a clearing of a throat.

Eleanor drew back fractionally from a kiss she participated in with an untutored enthusiasm that was every bit as arousing as that of a skilled courtesan. "Miles … the servants."

"Ignore them. They will go away."

"But…" She gurgled with laughter. "I want my tea."

He drew back from an oral exploration of the delicious juncture of her neck and shoulder and with a sigh of regret, removed his hand from her bodice. "I'd prefer to nibble you instead."

"But you have yet to taste one of Cook's ginger biscuits."

He knew when he was defeated and by a ginger biscuit at that. But, he'd accomplished what he'd set out to do. The servants had caught them in a moment of amorous interchange and servants being servants, the gossip that Lord and Lady Miles Everleigh had been surprised in the library in an intimate moment would speed throughout the entire estate. If he could arrange several more of these moments of discovery in the odd location, it would shortly be common knowledge that Lord Miles was a randy sod and Lady Eleanor delighted in it.

He set her off him. Eleanor straightened the shoulders of her gown and glanced at his lap, noting the evidence of his enjoyment that had risen to prominence behind the falls of his too-revealing breeches. From behind her, she offered him a pillow for his lap. To call her grin triumphant would not be an overreach.

"See to your tea, Eleanor."

As it happened, the ginger biscuits were every bit as good as Eleanor professed.

Chapter Sixteen

As Miles had predicted, Mr. Ivan Ludlow arrived at the stroke of 2:00. As Miles and Eleanor were engaged in having tea in the library, Mr. Ludlow cooled his heels for a good hour before being shown into the Earl's study. Miles sat behind the Earl's great desk, at his ease, very much "lord of the manor" while the commoner, Mr. Ludlow, was offered an armchair positioned before the center of the desk, a place appropriate to a supplicant. Eleanor nested, cozily familial on a sofa near the window. She held an embroidery hoop and seemingly stitched, an expression of tranquil domesticity on her face which Miles found highly amusing given what he knew of the lady's character. The stage was set with the actors in their places. *Let the farce begin.*

"Let's not waste our time, Mr. Ludlow. I'll get straight to the point. Lady Miles advises that the Prince Regent questions the intent and validity of our union. Do I have the right of it?"

"Yes, my lord. There are elements of the circumstances surrounding your marriage that suggest intent to deprive the Crown of an entailed property that is legally theirs upon the passing of the present earl. We believe that yours is not a marriage entered into with the intention to beget children but to interfere with the legal reversion of property."

"Nonsense."

Ludlow narrowed his eyes. "I think not, my lord. The settlement of a significant sum of money upon you and the payment of a conditional annuity give rise to all sorts of conjecture. Furthermore, in interviewing the staff of the homes surrounding the Lady Miles Everleigh's property in London, I am told that on the very night of your wedding, when most brides and grooms are otherwise engaged, said lady was observed getting into her coach with baggage strapped to the roof and said coach was seen departing London at an excessive speed. Some minutes later, you exited the townhome and got into a hansom. Further inquiry revealed that you arrived at Baron Stanton's residence in Mayfair and departed his townhouse perhaps an hour later in great haste, arriving at Rutledge Manor shortly after the Lady Miles Everleigh's arrival." Ludlow checked his notes. "You remained less than an hour then rode out, not even staying for dinner. The ostlers at the posting inn on the road to Newmarket say that you came into the yard around 3:00 a.m. and asked for a change of horse, yours showing signs of hard use."

Ludlow settled back into his armchair with an air of satisfaction. "That does not paint a picture of wedded bliss. It smacks of a heated falling out between two business partners. I have reason to doubt this marriage was even consummated. What could possibly induce a high-born gentleman such as yourself to marry a plain spinster so senior to him if not for money?" He cast an uneasy glance at Eleanor. The expression of anger and offended outrage on her face would create trepidation in a much braver man than Ludlow. "Beg pardon, ma'am."

One booted ankle resting on his knee, Miles rocked back in the great chair and studied Ludlow, without sparing Eleanor a glance. "Let me address your last comment by referring you to the American, Benjamin Franklin. In a letter to a young friend, I believe he lists eight excellent reasons for welcoming, nay preferring, the affections of an older woman—none of which speak to money. You should familiarize yourself with them.

"As for the rest of your spewing, it is pure conjecture and balderdash. The financial settlement and annuity were not for me but for my mother, the Dowager Duchess of Chelsony. The funds happen to be in accounts under my name to protect them. You may have heard that my eldest half-brother acceded to the position of Duke of Chelsony. The man is a tyrannical skinflint. I would add unprincipled to that description as he is the trustee of Mother's widow's jointure and has used her monies for his benefit while she remained in mean circumstances. When I expressed my distress about my mother's situation to Lady Miles, my generous, kind-hearted wife offered to purchase a home for her and provide a yearly allowance for the running of the household. The property is Fairwood Stud in Newmarket, formerly the Woodward farm. It is easily found. You may verify this information with my mother if you desire. She is in residence." He wondered how fast a messenger could carry instructions to his mother about what to tell Ludlow. Certainly faster than Ludlow would care to travel.

"You can be certain I will, my lord. How do you explain both your and her ladyship's actions on the night of your wedding?"

Eleanor rose from the sofa, every inch of her quivering with offense. "Do you have a wife, Mr. Ludlow?"

"I haven't been so lucky, my lady."

"Then you will be unaware of the delicate sensibilities of well-bred females particularly when it relates to intimate matters of…of…amorous congress."

Ludlow squirmed in his chair and muttered something inaudible.

"When a virginal bride is confronted with the bare realities of what is expected of her, sometimes she needs…" Eleanor threw up her hands, gesturing vaguely. "A day… or two… to become adjusted to the idea. And, and, she wants her… her… mother."

She does? What a bouncer. With some difficulty, Miles arranged his features into an impassive expression. Eleanor's inventiveness fascinated him, but he had never met a woman less likely to run to her mother for anything—ever.

"Yes, I quit my townhome and returned to Rutledge as fast as my horses could take me, and yes, Lord Miles followed on my heels before proceeding to Newmarket. As my husband is a man of every consideration and kindness, he removed his person to allow me time to… adjust, and our marriage is now on a most congenial footing." Eleanor crossed the room and stood behind Miles with her hands on his shoulders. "Most congenial."

Miles picked up one of her hands, kissed her knuckles and replaced it on his shoulder, then held the agent with a featureless gaze. "Satisfied, Mr. Ludlow?"

The man studied them with an expression of lively suspicion. "For now. I have a few more interviews to perform before I'm ready to report my findings to His Royal Highness. I'll stop in again before I return to London." He stood and made a bow. "I'll see myself out. My lady, m'lord, good-day to you."

When Miles was certain Ludlow was no longer within hearing, he glanced over his shoulder at Eleanor, one eyebrow raised. "Your *mother*?"

She shrugged, her hands slipping off him. "At that moment, I couldn't think of anything else to explain my bolt to Rutledge other than to seek the comfort of my mother. Speaking of my dear parent, I told her I would sit with her in the garden this afternoon. I'm quite certain she will spend the time quizzing me about Mr. Ludlow."

Miles pulled out his watch. "I am closeted with your father for the next several hours. I expect the same treatment, but first, I must draft instructions to the Dowager Duchess on her response to Ludlow and dispatch them to Fairwood with all haste."

"Of course, she must have time to prepare. When you are ready, send a footman to Bitters. I think, Jemmy as our rider? He is conscientious and familiar with the way."

"Excellent idea." He stood and moved to the sofa. "Over the first hurdle safely. I think we made a convincing domestic pair." He picked up the embroidery hoop she'd been stabbing at when Ludlow arrived and scrutinized it. "Though I won't be asking you to darn my stockings."

"Are you up to continuing, Lord Rutledge? We can resume tomorrow. We have been head down in estate accounts for the last four hours and will have to dress for dinner shortly, regardless." Miles eased back in the chair that he'd pulled up to a circular table placed in a sunny bay window in the library and regarded Eleanor's father with a quiet smile. The Earl sat in his wheeled chair beside Miles with a lap robe covering his legs.

Lord Rutledge's mind remained keen. Sadly, the body that housed that impressive mind was failing. Miles suspected Eleanor's father lived on from sheer stubborn will. The Earl labored to catch his breath, and elaborating on a subject of particular significance required an effort on the old gentleman's part that was painful to watch. Miles knew a pang of regret that he had not met the Earl in the gentleman's younger days. He thought he should have liked him exceedingly well. His respect, tinged with a growing fondness for the crusty old man, gave him a measure of insight into the heartbreak for which Eleanor prepared herself.

He, too, had lost a beloved parent. He'd been at Oxford when his father had fallen ill and had nearly crippled his horse, so hard had he pressed the poor beast in a headlong race to reach his father's bedside. When the Duke succumbed to his illness and died, if not for the necessity to be strong for his mother, he should have spent weeks closeted with his grief.

The Earl of Rutledge impressed Miles with his vast and varied knowledge about the workings of Rutledge and its attached farms and villages and with his determination to ensure he imparted all of it to the younger man—as if Miles would have an active hand in the administration of the estate. Without saying a word, the Earl of Rutledge gave him to understand that he loved his land and his people and had cared for them with unstinting effort—a legacy he expected Miles to carry on. Caught up in the fabrication of his "loving" marriage to Eleanor, Miles couldn't tell Lord Rutledge that the older gentleman's hours of painstaking explanation were wasted, but it didn't signify. Some of the information the Earl imparted could be useful at Fairwood.

The man's winter-blue eyes caught Miles' and held his gaze for several moments before the Earl's lids dropped as if the effort to keep his eyes open was too great. "On this Ludlow business. All of the properties we discussed today, I hold privately. They are not subject to entail and are mine to give as I see fit. I have seen fit to leave them to you.

"I have amended my will and petitioned the House of Lords for a waiver that will allow me to adopt you as my legal heir. Elsington submitted the waiver to the House of Lords the day your marriage was announced in the Times. I still carry some influence in the House of Lords, and as I fully expected, the waiver was granted in a timely manner."

The old gentleman paused to catch his breath while Miles sat, stunned into silence.

"You will inherit the entirety of Rutledge, the entail plus all lands in freehold, thus keeping the estate intact. The title conveys with the entail. Furthermore…" the Earl opened his eyes and directed a fierce, uncompromising glare at Miles, "… you *will* set aside that ridiculous codicil to your marriage contract requiring you to separate yourself from Eleanor, and you *will* take up your residence here. Upon my death you will accede to the title of the 11th Earl of Rutledge and Eleanor shall be your countess."

"I beg your pardon?"

The Earl's voice lost its stridency, and his expression became weary. "This is the best way I know of to protect Eleanor. She has lived a life far removed from the avarice and the legal manipulations perpetrated upon vulnerable females by unscrupulous men. In many ways, she is naïve and artless, and altogether too trusting, though she does not consider herself so, and that makes her doubly vulnerable." His gaze sought Miles again. "Elsington has noted that in naming you my heir, I will bolster the authenticity of your marriage. This Act of Lords will put paid to any attempt by HRH to interfere in your marriage." Again his lids fell, and the room filled with his sonorous breathing. "You should get her with child at the earliest. It is always best to have a male heir *in situ*."

"Lord Rutledge, I... I..."

The old gentleman continued as if he hadn't spoken. "I can only pray my trust in you is not misplaced. I rely upon you to provide for my daughter in a manner that allows her to retain the freedoms she has enjoyed all her life. She has not had a conventional upbringing and should not be restricted to a conventional life. Her spirit would shrivel and die. Should Lady Rutledge survive me, I would deeply appreciate it if you would extend to her such tender considerations as may be necessary."

"Sir... I feel I must tell you—"

The Earl held up a trembling hand as if to forestall Miles' statement. "I will finish. Lady Rutledge wishes to tell Eleanor that we know about the circumstances surrounding your marriage. Penwick Elsington wrote to me over a year ago when Eleanor first presented him with her scheme. After that, it was simply a matter of our determining who might suit and then making her choice easy. It was at my direction that Elsington added your name to that list of appalling reprobates."

Miles straightened in his chair, his attention wholly captured. He held the Earl's gaze with narrowed eyes. A degree of irritation arose at the extent to which the Earl had interfered with both he and Eleanor, although he made certain to conceal any such sentiment from his dry statement. "In view of my circumstances at the time Elsington approached me, I am surprised you didn't consider me simply one more reprobate. You have been so remarkably thorough that I cannot conceive you were ignorant of the manner in which I lived."

The Earl returned Miles' stare with a piercing one of his own, his lips twisted in cynical amusement. The shrewd old gentleman was perfectly capable of interpreting the misleading lack of emotion behind Miles' flat statement.

"I knew of your circumstances. More to the point, I knew the reason for them." The Earl of Rutledge laughed dryly. "I felt you demonstrated an affinity for the weaker sex and would deal with Eleanor better than most. Unlike many men, it appears you are not threatened by a strong woman. I also felt you would treat Lady Rutledge with kindness." The Earl regarded him with knowing eyes. "And then there is your breeding. I thought highly of your father and have met few women more intelligent and charming than your mother—even if she is French. You put me very much in mind of her. Except for the odd outcrop— I cannot like the present Duke—the Everleigh bloodline has bred true. You were an acceptable choice."

Bloody hell. Just when had the Earl come to know his mother? Miles sat utterly silent and simply stared at the Earl of Rutledge.

The Earl's lips quirked. "Through the years, I have found Lady Rutledge's counsel to be wise, but in this instance, I disagree with her. Eleanor would be profoundly hurt by knowledge of my interference and with what she would rightly construe as my management of her. She must always believe you were *her* choice. I trust you will keep my confidence. I cannot see any benefit in her knowing the truth."

"You may rely upon it." He could not conceive how telling Eleanor what he just learned would in any way advance his cause. At some point in the near future, he would go from inconsequential, penniless, younger brother of the Duke of Chelsony to the immensely wealthy and thus vastly influential, Eleventh Earl of Rutledge. It took no imagination whatsoever to picture Eleanor's reaction when presented with this *fait accompli. Bloody, bloody hell!* Miles slammed down his disgruntlement, cleared his throat and searched for some response to the Earl's astounding revelations that did not include extensive profanity. He opened his mouth… and closed it. He didn't trust himself to speak.

The Earl waived him off with a feeble flip of his hand and leaned back. "Eleanor does not distinguish herself upon first acquaintance; rather she improves upon knowing until you wonder how you ever could have overlooked her. I hope the two of you will come to terms and make this a true marriage. You'll not find any better than her. She is honest, loyal and of sound disposition and judgment. She has heart and will go the distance. I think she'll be an excellent mother."

Dislike of the fact her father felt the need to defend Eleanor to him when Miles considered the woman succeeded on her own merits drove his sincere response. "I am aware of her worth, my lord. She occupies a place in my heart I'd not thought to ever offer a woman. The difficulty lies in convincing Eleanor of that—among certain other obstacles," he drawled.

Until he'd spoken the words, Miles hadn't crystallized in his brain the reason behind his campaign to win Eleanor to him, but having said them, he recognized their truth. He loved her. He had been falling in love with her from almost their first meeting.

The Earl grunted. "As I thought." His canny gaze settled on Miles as if he could read his thoughts. "I will be disappointed if you cannot mend whatever has gone amiss between you and my daughter."

Miles held her father's direct gaze without blinking. "So will I, sir. So will I."

"Then pray do so quickly, Lord Miles. My days on this earth are numbered."

Chapter Seventeen

E yeing the nightdress laid out for her on the bed, Eleanor turned to her maid with a stern look and a raised eyebrow.

"I know it's not my place… but… it's a lovely gown, ma'am. Much nicer than your old ones and as Lord Miles is sharing your…" Sally's voice trailed off. "I just thought you might…" She sighed and gathered up the transparent confection of a nightdress. "I spoke out of turn, ma'am. I had no right. I'll lay out one of the others."

"No. It is very pretty. Leave it, Sally. I'll wear it." Perhaps in this way, Miles might be enticed into continuing those activities he had begun in the library. His kisses and physical handling of her person had so engrossed her in sensation that, just as the night before, she'd lost herself. If not for the arrival of the tea tray… She hesitated to speculate on what might have occurred.

Eleanor shrugged out of her robe and Sally flipped the nightdress over her head. The gossamer material settled on her shoulders with a mere wisp of presence. She felt as if she wore air. A glance down confirmed the transparency of the garment. It was an astoundingly bold and provoking article of clothing, and her heart picked up pace at her daring. "Thank you. You may find your bed, Sally. I won't require you further this evening."

With a low, "Ma'am," and a curtsy, her attendant left, and Eleanor settled into bed, sitting propped on pillows against the headboard, her bedcovers pulled to waist high and with an eye to the open door. Thoughts of Miles' kisses and caresses had kept her in a restless and agitated mood all day. She dropped her gaze and fiddled idly with the coverlet. She wanted to have done with the mystery and find out once and for all what every other married woman knew. Some subtle disturbance made her look up.

Dressed in only a fine lawn nightshirt that fell to his knees, Miles' tall, broad-shouldered form filled the doorway. He paused to lean one shoulder against the frame and study her. She knew a purely feminine thrill that this virile specimen of masculinity was *hers*. She'd always been attracted to beautiful animals…and Lord Miles was certainly that. Would he ask for her kisses tonight? She hoped so. She would do her best to convince him she wanted more than kisses. As she watched, his posture became languid, and a half smile tipped his lips.

"You are a picture to warm a man, madam."

He sauntered toward her, and it took a certain amount of determination not to shrink under the covers, but she was dogged in her resolve to stay the course. He stopped at her side of the bed, and leaning down, with no display of haste or urgency, his forefinger gently traced a line on the skin exposed just above her breasts.

"Fetching nightgown, though I'd vastly prefer you in nothing at all."

She swallowed audibly. She wanted to rub her breasts to relieve the ache he'd created with his feather-light touches, but his grey eyes held her mesmerized.

"What are you about, Eleanor?"

Unable to maintain the intimate connection, she closed her eyes and forced words through her lips. "I'm trying to convince you I'm willing."

"Mmm."

His warm hand gently cupped her breast.

"Oh!" she gasped, and her eyes flew open and held his as he thumbed her nipple with a glancing back-and-forth motion.

"Do you like that?"

"No...I don't know? Yes...? Yes...but it feels strange."

The mattress sagged as he sat next to her, never stopping the gentle back and forth of his thumb that seemed to produce such foreign sensations in parts of her body quite south of her breasts, sensations that prompted a restless movement of her legs. His low chuckle tickled something inside of her.

"What do you know of intimate congress between men and women?" he softly asked. His hand left her breast. He took both of her hands in his and held them as his eyes searched her face with what she could only describe as tender patience.

"I've watched a stallion cover a mare." Heat rose up her neck, and she studied her lap where Miles' hands held hers.

Miles raised one of her hands, kissed the back of it and returned it to her lap. "When conducted properly, matters between men and women bear only a passing resemblance to the mating of animals."

"Only a passing resemblance?" She glanced up and was captured by his warm gaze.

"Yes."

Gathering all her courage, she whispered, "Will you demonstrate the difference?"

"With great pleasure." He stood and pulled back the bed covers, exposing her entircly. "While that is an eminently provocative garment which I will undoubtedly enjoy many times in the future, for tonight, let's have you out of it." At her squeak, he flashed a teasing glance her way. "One of the differences between animals and men and women is there is an abundance of touching and kissing best done when both parties are bare. I believe you like my kisses?"

She nodded silently.

He ran a palm up her calf, over her thigh, and up her abdomen, lifting her gown as he did. "Lift your arms, sweetheart." Her flimsy wisp of nothingness floated up and over her head to be discarded thoughtlessly on the floor along with his nightshirt.

As in the bath, Eleanor devoured the muscled body bared to her, distracted from her own modesty by the enthralling sight of sculptured muscles, sinew, bone, and *hair*—the whirls of glossy brown on his chest that led to a single line trailing down his abdomen to his...yes...*that*. Miles surely had to be an exceptionally beautiful male, for if all men looked as he did, women would never leave their beds. Even his male part had a fearsome sort of beauty, standing proud and upright.

He spoke as he motioned to her to move over in the bed. "I will do only those things that you like. I simply ask that you open yourself to what will certainly seem, in the beginning, uncomfortable and strange; give your mind and body a chance to appreciate and respond to my touch."

"May I touch you, also?" Her hands itched to explore him. He grinned in such a playful manner, her feelings of uncertainty and awkwardness shrank, replaced by a growing sense of emboldenment and anticipation.

"I encourage your participation."

He crawled toward her and lay down at her side supported on his left arm, their bodies touching all along her length, his leg between hers. Without thought—she wouldn't allow her mind to remind herself she wore no clothes—she moved into him and slipped her right arm around his shoulders, marveling in his hard-bunched muscle so different from her soft length. Her other arm wrapped his neck as she gazed into gray eyes that seemed lit from within with a feral intensity at odds with his calm manner.

His head descended. The warm press of his lips in a litany of kisses and the tender stroking of his hand up and down her body began her journey into thoughtless, mindless pleasure. Miles composed a melody of physical delight that demanded a four-part chorus of response from parts of her that Eleanor had given little thought. Her body sang. A fever flushed her, and she reveled in a physical euphoria she'd never considered possible.

Lances of intense pleasure streaked through her as his lips pulled her tightly ruched nipples into his hot mouth to suckle and lave first one and then the other until she whimpered and writhed as if in pain. Miles paused and lifted his head casting a silent question at her.

"I'm fine…oh, please…don't you dare stop," she gasped.

With a low chuckle, he resumed. His long-fingered hand found its way between her legs to her female parts, now plump and slippery with the dew of her body, and teased with light strokes inciting the conflagration of erotic sensation within her to burn ever hotter. A broad finger made the beginnings of a foray into her opening while the pad of his thumb found a place at the apex of her sex and circled with the lightest of touches. The converging sensations drove her to arch her back and push her hips into his hand, lodging his finger deeper within her. It wasn't enough. She pleaded, "Please…please, Miles…I need…I need…I don't know, but *do* something." Her head thrashed back and forth in desperation for surcease, for some ultimate culmination to the barrage of exquisite sensation driving her mindless.

He moved between her legs and pulled one of her knees up to his waist. He reached down and centered himself at her opening. The broad head of his organ stretched her open, and he paused with only the tip lodged within her.

"Eleanor…sweetheart, look at me." His voice sounded breathless and forced.

She reluctantly opened her eyes and tried to concentrate on something other than the physical imperative that rampaged unchecked through her.

"There is no way I can change the first time for you. It may hurt, but any pain will pass." His eyes conveyed such concern that she found herself consoling *him* for the discomfort he warned she might suffer.

"Please, Miles. I'll survive. Just do it!"

Her impatient and rash surge upward coincided with his drive forward, and she cried out at an unexpectedly sharp slice of pain. His groin collided with hers and stopped with him lodged fully within her as hurt radiated from her most tender parts. She felt rendered in half from within, stretched impossibly, and with whimpers of objection, she tried to shift her hips while her hands pushed futilely against his body, attempting to dislodge the implement of her physical distress. Her thrashing was futile. The heavy weight of his hips flattened her, immobile, into the mattress.

"Dash it, Eleanor!" Miles swore a soft oath as he held motionless within her, impervious to her actions. His breath punched in and out of his chest, and the well-muscled arms that supported his upper body trembled as if they had palsy. "In this one regard, trust me to lead. You have caused yourself far more hurt than necessary." He continued to remain unmoving and watched her intently. "Still yourself. The hurt will pass."

Her hands paused their futile clawing, and Eleanor held his gaze for many long moments, her breath coming in pants until gradually, the distressing pain muted. She became more or less accustomed to the entirely alien feeling of Miles inside her. Finally, she relaxed under him, and a long sigh escaped her.

"Is it bearable now?" Miles raised his eyebrows in question.

She responded with a slight nod. "In the future, I shall be more sympathetic to the maiden mares."

A grin flashed across his face. "It gets better, I promise." With a soft groan, he began to move in and out of her in long, slow, gentle strokes, accompanied by hushed words of encouragement and praise. Every entry and exit glided his thick organ along that portion of her he had earlier stimulated with his thumb.

Initially, she tensed, expecting more pain, but there was only soreness and a strange feeling of fullness gradually replaced by the same growing, exquisite tension he had built in her before. She hadn't been prepared for the intimacy of this act, but now she reveled in his weight, the press of his heavy body on hers. She wrapped herself in the smell and feel of him and leaped with abandon into the morass of the unfamiliar, swirling sensations that bombarded her. Seemingly endless minutes passed, and an urgency within her coiled tighter and tighter as ecstasy compounded ecstasy. Her eyes flew open in surprise and met his. "Oh!"

He watched her, his face a study in leashed ferocity, but his slow, gentle stroke never varied.

The amount of pleasure she could endure reached culmination and her body exploded in a pinnacle of the senses that clouded her vision with red spots. She screamed her ecstasy into the night and shook with each convulsive clench of her sex around the still thrusting male organ within her. Miles' hips stuttered, slammed into her and held. He gave a forceful grunt, and his arms collapsed. His considerable weight draped her and again pinned her to the featherbed. She could not have moved had she wanted to. Happily, she didn't want to.

As her body floated in a bliss-filled state of tranquility, her emotions erupted in a riot of joy. A grin of pure elation stretched her mouth, and she laughed out loud. "Why did no one ever tell me?"

Miles raised his head, observed her delighted countenance and fell back onto her once more. His muffled voice emerged from the pillows beside her ear. "I shall count my job well done."

Her delighted laughter followed his comment, and after a time of wondrous amazement, she sobered. "I doubt many virgins have had such an ultimately agreeable dénouement. Thank you for your care of me. I suppose I have Dorchance and Norwalk to thank..." Her voice trailed off at the end.

Miles rolled off her and lay on his back, eyes closed with one arm behind his head. The other drew her close to his side. "Pray tell, who are they? I have no memory of any woman but you."

As they had on most mornings for the past few years, Miles' eyes came open on this gray dawn to the view of a warm, naked female nestled on his chest. He lay there quiescent, a mixture of wonder and apprehension muddling his sensibilities. For him, their lovemaking last night had been transcendental, without match, unprecedented. The irony that both his awe and his apprehension derived from the same source did not elude him.

Beyond the pure physical pleasure of amorous congress with a woman who was *his*—and the pleasure had been significant, to be repeated at the earliest opportunity—when he'd retrieved his scattered wits, a feeling of profound caring and responsibility settled on him. He wished to cherish and protect the independent and forthright spirit that Providence had thrown in his path, to stand between her and all harm for the rest of his days—and there was the wonder of it.

Eleanor murmured in her sleep and nuzzled into him. Her arm wrapped his waist. With an indulgent sigh, he pulled her closer.

Whether he wished to acknowledge it or not—and he didn't—he had fallen madly in love with his wife—and therein was the source of his apprehension.

She did not love him, and he doubted she would welcome the entanglement of his emotions. Well…without burdening her with unwanted sentiments, he could still introduce her to the joys of the flesh and satisfy his promise to the Earl by protecting her from the vagaries of life. He smiled. Plus, there was nothing to prevent him from trying to win Eleanor to him.

The Eleanor Campaign was still on.

Chapter Eighteen

Eleanor awoke alone in the great bed immersed in a sense of well-being. The case clock in the room indicated the morning somewhat advanced. She smiled to herself. She was certain that Miles, in a thoughtful gesture typical of him, had cautioned the staff to allow her to sleep. She rolled to her side and hugged a pillow to her breasts. With a certain degree of caution, she stretched her legs. Other than a slight soreness 'down there' and some light spotting on the sheets, there was nothing to remind her of the activities of the previous night. She chuckled to herself. Finally, she knew what the fuss was about. She'd been initiated into the secret society of married women. She felt like opening the windows and crowing to the world, "Now I know! I'm one of you!" In many respects, with its physical pleasures and Miles' whispered words of praise, last night had gone a long way toward mitigating the slights and rejections she'd suffered years ago.

Why had no one told her of the profound degree of pleasure to be had with a man? Why had no one told her of the profound effect such an intimate act would have on a woman's heart? To strip her body naked, spread her legs and admit a man's breeding organ into her most female of places created an intimacy and a baring of self that had no parallel. She had recognized her vulnerability to Miles from their very first meeting. Even though she had done her best to maintain a certain emotional distance, last night turned all such attempts into wasted effort. She was perilously close to falling tail-over-tea-kettle in love with her husband, indeed, if that ship had not already sailed.

How was an aging former spinster supposed to keep a handsome, charming male like Miles at her side? She had no womanly wiles—besides, he would see right through her if she tried something as ridiculous as simpering and batting her eyes at him. He would know it for what it was— a sham. After several minutes of contemplation, she concluded she had no recourse other than to simply be herself; she'd seek his company, include him in the day-to-day workings of the estate and allow the majesty of Rutledge to woo him. However, there was no reason not to exert herself to be winning and to display herself at her feminine best.

When Eleanor went down to a very late breakfast, rather than the manly outfits she was accustomed to stride out in, Sally dressed her in one of the becoming riding habits Lady Florence had insisted she buy with matching half boots and a smart hat. The family dining room was deserted, so she found Walters.

"Walters, just the man I need. Do you know the whereabouts of Lord Miles?"

Walters acknowledged her with an abbreviated bow. "I believe Lord Miles mentioned his intent to find Mr. Bitters on a horse-related matter."

"Thank you, Walters." Eleanor smiled. "I'll look in the stables."

By following the sounds of men's laughter, she found him closeted with her stud manager, sharing a cheroot and a glass of brandy. Both men were engaged in hearty laughter of the hail-fellow-well-met variety. Her heart softened even more. How very like Miles to make immediate friends with her staff. If only it was that easy for her. Putting a smile on her face, she peeked her head around the door. "May a lady enter? Or is this just a gentlemen's affair?"

"Eleanor! You are always welcome. We are just blowing a cloud." Miles stood and offered her his seat on the sofa. He made to stub out a cigar he had obviously just begun, and Eleanor placed a gloved hand on his arm.

"Please don't let me stop you," she said. "I've always enjoyed the smell of a fine cigar." With a bright smile on her face, she continued. "As a matter of fact…I think I'd like to try one. I'll have some of that brandy also."

"Eleanor…" Miles began in a hesitant voice.

"I like the smell of cigars very well, so I think it's time I tried the taste." She smiled brilliantly.

John Bitters gazed across the room at Miles and raised his shoulders in a shrug. Flipping open a wooden box on his desk, he handed her a tube of rolled tobacco, lit a piece of kindling from the fire and held it to the end of her thin cigar. "Pull the smoke into your mouth in tugs, Lady Miles, but don't inhale it," instructed her stud manager.

Bitter, acrid, smoke-filled her mouth, and despite her efforts, some went into her lungs. It was only by the grace of God she didn't hack it out. She coughed daintily and with a smile pasted on her face, took another puff. That was no better. A lazy curl of pungent smoke rose to sting her eyes. She ventured a surreptitious swipe at the tears that pooled on her lower lid. Miles, his face one of concern, handed her a tumbler that held a scant finger of brandy. She swallowed a gulp and restrained a painful wince as the brandy scalded its way down her throat. *By all that was holy, what did men see in this?* With a voice somewhat more hoarse than normal, she inquired, "What were you speaking about when I interrupted?"

"I was just feeling Mr. Bitters out about Day Dreamer's chances of being the second filly in history to win the Epsom Derby," Miles said, his eyes never leaving her.

"I told his lordship that I favored her chances highly." Bitters grinned. "The speeds she's been clocking at home are…" Her stud manager looked heavenward and shook his head. "I suggested that we all make the trek to Newmarket to watch her run in the Welborn Cup—the Earl and the Countess, too, should they be up to it."

Miles arched an eyebrow and Bitters directed an inquisitive look her way.

"Merciful heavens, you want *me* to decide? Miles…" Eleanor puffed, coughed and turned it into a light laugh by the imposition of will. She caught Miles' eyes, "Well, my lord? What say you?" She took several more puffs on the cigar. Those went more smoothly though she thought the taste vile—not at all like the smell—and she felt very lightheaded.

His forehead wrinkled in a frown that vanished as quickly as it formed. "If you are leaving the decision to me, my lady, then I say we go. We can take the trip in easy stages if your father and mother wish to come as well. I'll alert my mother to expect house guests for weekend next."

Eleanor set down the partially smoked cigar and gulped the remainder of the brandy, stifling a shiver as it burned its way to her stomach. A hint of nausea threatened but she ignored it. "Good, it's settled. We can ask Father and Mother at dinner. I'm certain they will want to accompany us if their health is up to it." Holding Miles in an intent gaze, a smile tipping her lips, she stood and walked up to within inches of him. "I'm going to inspect a mill in the village of Warringford. It's a lovely ride out and back that will take much of the day. I would like it very well if you would accompany me." She ruined what she had planned as an enticing foray by coughing several times into her glove. Her stomach lurched unhappily, and she ignored it.

Miles smiled. "I'll be happy to join you, though if you are expecting me to weigh in with any intelligence on the running or maintenance of a grist mill, you will be sadly disappointed."

"No." She returned his smile. "I would just enjoy your company, and you will see some of the most charming aspects of the estate."

"I am at your disposal, my lady."

"Are you certain you are up to an all-day ride, Eleanor?" Miles murmured as he wrapped his hands around his wife's waist, put her up on her flea-bitten gray, and found the left stirrup for her foot.

"Why ever would I not?"

He shrugged slightly and with a slight smile sent her a telling upwards glance while he arranged her skirts to fall neatly.

"Oh…" She colored a pretty pink. "Um, no…I feel quite fine. I took no lasting injury," she stated softly. "But it was kind of you to ask."

He took the reins of his horse from the groom and turned to mount his bay. He withheld his response until they had cleared the stable yard and were out of hearing of any staff. When Eleanor headed them down the carriage drive and into a narrow lane edged by hedgerows, he judged them sufficiently private. "When you appeared in that habit—you look quite the thing, by the way—rather than your customary breeches and boots, I wondered if you had suffered some ill effects from our activities of last evening and chose not to ride astride."

"No, no ill effects." She shook her head shyly. "I liked it. Well…most of it, but the part I didn't like won't happen again. Will it?" she asked hesitantly.

"No," he assured her.

Eleanor straightened and directed a forthright gaze at him. "Well then…I liked what we did, and I hope...I hope we will do that again." As he grinned and began to reply, a faint look of alarm crossed her face, and she put her gloved fingers to her mouth and swallowed several times. "Pardon me a moment, please," she blurted and urged her horse with leg and whip through a gap in the hedgerow, whereupon she slid off her animal and vanished from his sight. Her disappearance was closely followed by the sound of violent retching.

He sent his own horse through the gap after her and dismounted, tying up the reins on both their animals and knelt beside Eleanor, wrapping an arm around her waist to help support her as she continued to be comprehensively ill. When it seemed she had emptied her stomach, he helped her to stand and steadied her while digging in his jacket for his handkerchief.

"Here, Eleanor."

She took his white linen square with a garbled, "Thank you," and wiped the tears streaming from her eyes and then blew her nose. "I'm so sorry. I can't imagine what brought that on. I am mortified beyond words."

"Please don't be," he laughed. He knew it was not well done of him to laugh, but he couldn't help it. She flashed him a disgruntled look, and he sobered though still smiled broadly. "It was the cigar. It is common knowledge the first experience with any sort of tobacco frequently ends with a casting up of one's accounts."

His handkerchief clutched in one hand, she pulled back and stared. "Really? Then why do you men do it? There is nothing about the experience that I can recommend."

He shrugged still grinning. "It is a rite of passage to adulthood, I suppose. Come here." He pulled her into his arms, and she came willingly. She fit perfectly against him. "I'm sorry you were sick. Would it help to know I did exactly the same thing after my first experience?"

"I suppose. How old were you?"

"Twelve."

She snorted in self-derision. "Twelve, not thirty." With a sigh, she straightened out of his arms. "You are sworn to secrecy. If you tell Bitters, I will devise some awful retribution."

He chuckled and caught their horses. They hadn't wandered far. He handed Eleanor the reins to her gray along with a hip flask he fished from a broad pocket of his coat. "Here, rinse your mouth."

Eleanor eyed the flask with suspicion. "What's in it?"

He smiled. "Does it really matter?"

"I suppose not," she huffed as she unscrewed the cap and took a swig, swished it around her mouth and then spat it out. "Ugh, brandy." Grimacing, she recapped the flask and handed it back. "Thank you."

Once more, he put her up on her horse, arranged her skirts and mounted his own. When they were both through the hedge and back on their way, Eleanor sighed heavily and muttered something under her breath.

"Yes?"

With a roll of her eyes at the heavens and another heavy sigh, she responded, "I was chastising myself for being three kinds of a fool. I heard you and Bitters sharing such jolly laughter that I yearned to be a part of it." She glanced at him and then straight ahead. "You are of such an easy and considerate nature that people like you the moment they meet you. What comes so naturally to you is awkward for me, and I made a cake of myself in an effort to appear congenial." She made a sound of disgust.

Miles considered her statement as they rode side-by-side along the shaded lane, then caught her attention. "You don't have to try with me, Eleanor."

She shot him a quick glance. "No?"

He recalled the warm, responsive woman he'd made love to last night and whom he planned on making love to again at the earliest opportunity. He gave her a slow, lazy smile that he made certain reflected his warm admiration. "No. I find the present version of Lady Miles Everleigh very much to my taste."

Her shy sidelong gaze was much longer this time. "The discrepancy in our ages doesn't bother you?"

"I can honestly say I've given it no thought whatsoever."

The corners of her mouth tipped up as she set her horse into a trot.

It would have been ungentlemanly of him to remind her of his past amours, so he did not add that she was the youngest bed partner he'd had in years.

Chapter Nineteen

The hilly forest land Eleanor guided him through startled Miles with its striking vistas. She stopped at one overlook where a break in the fir and hardwood trees displayed the vignette of a waterfall plunging fifty feet into a placid lake with cattle grazing the banks under willow trees. Eleanor explained that the waterfall was the end of the river that powered the water wheel at the mill in Wallingford. Another pause in their ride occurred by an apple orchard with the trees in the last of their blossom while Eleanor spoke with the wife of the tenant farmer as her young children played a noisy game of hide-and-seek among the trees. As they rode off, Eleanor confided, "The best hard cider in all of England comes from this orchard. We sell as much as we make. It turns a tidy profit."

"Is it the farmer or the apples that produce such a good result?"

Eleanor smiled. "Neither. It is the brewer who happens to be the woman I paused to speak with. I keep trying to glean her secrets so we can apply them at other farms, but she holds her methods and ingredients close."

"What do you find to be the sources of most revenue for Rutledge?"

Eleanor responded with a fascinating outpouring of information about the wide span of income-producing products that brought vast wealth to Rutledge and its farms and villages. She knew the people of Rutledge well and regaled Miles with many humorous anecdotes interwoven with facts and figures about crop-yield and such. Miles had no difficulty appearing interested as she captured and held his attention completely, and he knew a moment of wistfulness, wishing he could halt time and preserve this perfect afternoon spent in uncomplicated interaction with an intelligent and vivacious woman of easy laughter and animated expression.

Such passed several hours of companionable travel until they came upon the village of Wallingford and the new mill race that Eleanor wanted to view for herself. She pointed to a partial diversion of the river into a stone-lined chute that fed the four-story waterwheel attached to the multi-story mill.

"We had some very bad flooding here last spring, and the water overran the millrace, eroding the mortar and displacing the stones. The miller called in a stone mason to repair the damage, and I wanted to view the results. We grind wheat and corn here in quantity. When the miller opens the flume fully, the flume is the box where the water from the millrace enters the mill, we can grind upwards of 2,500 pounds of corn flour per day and double that of wheat. Would you like to meet the miller and see the mill in operation? Mr. Townsend is also a millwright, which makes him of greater value to Rutledge than a simple miller, as he can repair the inner workings of the mill as well as see to the grinding of the grain."

"Yes, I would be very interested to see the workings."

"We can tie the horses in that copse of trees."

The grove of trees was situated such that it enclosed them in the idyllic privacy of dense green boughs, lush spring grass and a scattering of bluebells while the river burbled as a backdrop of sound, and after a glance around to appreciate the beauty of the setting, Miles dismounted to assist Eleanor from her horse. As she had done the last few times that day when he'd wrapped his hands around her waist to assist her on or off her horse, her body softened as if she welcomed his touch, and assured of no onlookers, he took advantage of her pliancy, holding her to him when her feet touched the ground, to place a kiss on her full, upturned lips.

After a moment of startlement, she relaxed into him, wrapped her arms around his neck and kissed him back. The kiss started as a simple, spontaneous demonstration of his burgeoning feelings for Eleanor, but with her enthusiastic participation, it flourished into something far less innocent. When his hand strayed to massage her breast and pass his thumb over the hard nub of her nipple, she made a sound of encouragement and pressed herself more fully into him. She might as well have set alight oiled straw, so quickly did he catch fire. He could only indulge his desire for a finite time. With an effort, he wrenched himself away from her and dropped his hands to still her hips and hold her from him. Her arms still draped his shoulders, and her kiss-swollen lips shone with wetness. Her hazel eyes opened and held his in question.

"If we don't stop now, Eleanor, I will have you in the bluebells."

"Really? In the bluebells? Outside?" A slow smile grew on her face, and her expression held a certain smug satisfaction. She shrugged lightly, and her hands dropped to her sides. "I can think of places more onerous."

"Behave yourself," he admonished in a teasing voice. "Your inexperience demands a week of amorous activity that occurs in a comfortable bed, accompanied by all the niceties such as hot baths and clean sheets. There will be time enough to venture into the wilds." He traced a knuckle across her cheek and stepped back to put more than a hand's span between them.

"As you wish, my lord." She looked away, appearing very much like a barn cat who'd discovered a spill of cream. "The horses are wandering off."

And so they were. With a snort, Miles went about catching them. It was just the diversion certain parts of him needed to restore equilibrium.

After securing the horses, he and Eleanor spent in excess of an hour with the miller as the man showed Miles the massive, four-story shaft that turned four stone wheels and all the cogs and gears that connected them to the water wheel to produce power. Mr. Townsend was justifiably proud of his mill and Miles left with a greater appreciation for the labor required to provide the flour for his daily bread—and a growing understanding of the assets Eleanor fought so hard to retain.

When he and Eleanor rode into the courtyard of Rutledge, the sun cast lengthy shadows. It had been a long, but interesting, day. A bass chord of desire for his wife had strummed in the background of his awareness the entire time, and he wondered if they might forego a formal dinner for a tray in their apartments. He assisted Eleanor off her horse and handed their horses off to the grooms. Turning,

Miles offered his arm, and with a smile, she entwined hers with his as they both sauntered across the cobblestones to the great oak doors of Rutledge Manor.

"I've only seen a portion of the Rutledge holdings, but I am gaining an ever-growing insight into the vast diversity of knowledge required to efficiently manage this estate."

"I cannot pretend to have an in-depth knowledge about many of the trades. I have several land stewards that manage most of the day-to-day issues, but tenants always benefit from the eye of the landowner. That precept is one my father imprinted on me from my earliest days. The people who are entrusted to work the land need to know that the master or mistress of Rutledge is aware and engaged in their efforts. At some point in the future, we will do a comprehensive tour of the estate and introduce you as the new master." She cocked her head and glanced at him. "Is Chelsony a large property? Did your father involve you in its workings?"

"Chelsony is a fair size at 35,000 acres but small in comparison to Rutledge. As to my involvement? I wasn't really…or at least not in any depth." Miles frowned. "As the third son, I was expected to go into the Church, not a vocation to which I felt called; law, again not a field that suited me; or enter the military. Father strongly opposed buying a commission for me commenting that one son at risk of death was enough and when Mother added her heartfelt pleas, I conceded the field." He shrugged. "I had developed a passion for the breeding and racing of the Thoroughbred horse, and my understanding with Father was that, upon my graduation from university, he would grant me an independence sufficient to pursue my desires. Unfortunately, he died without amending his will, and when Edgar acceded to the title, he shut down what he considered frivolous expenditures. He sold off all the racing stock Father and I had so painstakingly put together, indeed sold all our horses but those that pulled the carriages and a few personal mounts. My Badger was on the block in the knacker's yard when Ned rescued him and brought him to me in London. Baron Stanton was kind enough to stand for Badger's upkeep as I lacked the ready. Edgar left my younger brother and me to find our own way on a pittance, enough to hold body and soul together…but little else—certainly not keep a horse in London."

"Your half-brother appears deficient in brotherly love," Eleanor observed dryly. Miles snorted and dropped Eleanor's arm, so she could use both hands to manage her skirts as they climbed the steps to the front doors. Gaining the wide porch, she paused and once again wrapped her arm around his when he offered it, casting a shy smile at Miles as she did so.

"Edgar's greatest sin was treating Mother poorly for which I will never forgive him. Had Duncan been home, he might have been able to shame Edgar into doing properly by her, but he is fighting somewhere in France. I hope, still alive. My letters to him have gone unanswered for almost a year."

"Duncan is your father's second son by his first wife?"

"Yes." He made to open the door for Eleanor, but it swung inward of its own accord.

"Good evening, Lady Miles. Lord Miles." The doorman nodded as they walked through.

"Good evening, Jeffers. How is *Lady of the Lake* going?"

"You have not kept up, your ladyship." He grinned. "I'm now into a popular novel that's all the rage, *Frankenstein* by Mary Wollstonecraft Shelley." He shuddered. "A gruesome tale I'd not have thought penned by a woman."

"Truly?"

Miles cleared his throat. "It deals with the reanimation of the dead."

Eleanor turned to him. "So you've read it?"

He pulled her away gently and continued to walk toward the stairs to the second floor. "Yes, I have not always been as usefully occupied as I've been the last few months. In the past, I've had to fill large stretches of idle time, so I read extensively."

Eleanor cast a sidelong glance his way and considered Miles' last words and all that he had *not* said. How it must have chafed this young, active man of sharp intellect to be reduced to the beck and call of single, aging females. Was she any better? Yes. Yes, she was. She had offered him an honorable escape from that life. She was like any other bride that came to her groom with a large dowry, and look how he had responded—not by squandering his monies on high town living and stylish equipage. He'd purchased a working estate and set up his mother.

He'd thrown himself into smoothing her way as well; and then there was the gift of Day Dreamer and Miles' inexplicable ability to kiss her into forgetting all reason. He worked some sort of strange alchemy on her body that liquefied her bones and melted her flesh in surrender to stunning pleasure. Was it any wonder she was powerless not to love him? She acknowledged her ability to resist him had never been worth a tinker's damn. Emotion welled in her breast, and she vowed he would not regret his many kindnesses to her, and she cringed inside when she recalled the vile slur she had hurled at him in anger. She would do whatever was required to make Miles happy—even if it meant a life lived apart. But until that calamitous day, she'd do all in her power to make him love her, beginning with a much overdue apology.

Chapter Twenty

They had reached the door to their second-floor apartments and Miles ushered her in. She paused in the sitting room, removed her smart hat and tan string gloves and placed them on a low table. She turned to him as he closed the door. "Miles?"

He raised an eyebrow and offered her an inquisitive smile.

She closed her eyes and took a breath, praying she could, for once in her life, manage to say what was in her heart. "The day you followed me here from London…I most profoundly apologize for the undeserved and hateful words I spoke in anger in this very room. I said detestable things deliberately meant to hurt, and I have bitterly regretted those words ever since." She looked at the floor, ashamed to meet his gaze. "I don't think you are without pride. I think you lived as needs must, in difficult circumstances, and you have always comported yourself with dignity and integrity while I…" she faltered, "I have not. Indeed, it would be impossible for me to hold you in any higher regard or be more disgusted with my own past behavior. I can only hope that you will find it in your heart to forgive me," she finished quietly.

He had moved to stand in front of her, and she raised her head to find grey eyes filled with tender consideration. "Forgiven and forgotten. And for my part in so bitterly disappointing you, I beg your forgiveness."

"I think you have already apologized most admirably, but..." a smile trembled on her lips, "Forgiven and forgotten," she whispered.

His hand cupped the nape of her neck, and he bent slightly to kiss her, angling his head to better fit his mouth to hers. With a moan of pleasure, she opened to him, and his tongue invaded to tangle with hers. Once again, with an effortlessness that mystified her, Miles reduced her to a senseless abandonment, her body aware only of him.

After a prolonged interval wherein he seduced her with breathless kiss after breathless kiss, pulling her into his body with a strong arm around her waist while his other hand traced light fingertips down her flanks and back, he paused and murmured against her lips, "Let's have dinner in our rooms. I'll be your lady's maid, and you can be my valet."

She flattened her palms against his chest and pushed gently. He released her, watching for her response. She gave him a mysterious smile and rang the bell to summon a hallboy. The young man assigned to their wing of the second floor answered almost immediately. "Advise the kitchen that Lord Miles and I will be taking dinner in our apartments. You may leave the tray trolleys outside the door, and tell Mr. Hopwood and Miss Conway they are free for the rest of the evening. Please send up hot water for a bath. After that, we are not to be disturbed until morning."

The hallboy acknowledged her orders and bowed. "I'll see to it immediately, your ladyship."

Eleanor closed the door, set the lock and turned to face Miles. "Is that what you had in mind, my lord?" She shivered at his wicked grin as he shrugged out of his black tailcoat, placed it over the back of a chair and stood before her in a white shirt and fawn waistcoat.

"Come stand here, lady wife." His forefinger pointed to the carpet directly in front of him. He pulled the tails of his cravat out of his waistcoat and proceeded with dispatch to disassemble the Mathematical his valet had painstakingly tied that morning. With a jerk of one hand, the long piece of folded, starched linen joined the tailcoat across the back of the chair.

She closed the nine feet between them with a growing sense of wariness provoked by the piratical expression on his face. The closer she got to him, the more her feet dragged. He didn't wait for her to reach him before striding to her and hoisting her over his shoulder, head down, her posterior in the air, as she shrieked in laughter.

"Miles! Whatever are you doing? Put me down!" She landed with a bounce in the middle of their bed and giggled, until her husband's body landed on hers, punching all the air from her lungs. With his face inches from hers, she flailed at him and in breathless pants complained, "I can't breathe. Off me, you oaf. You are a very troublesome maid. Sally has never behaved so."

With a low chuckle, he rolled to the side and braced himself on one elbow. "I suspect I will behave in many ways that would scandalize the good Miss Conway."

She gasped as he nuzzled into the sensitive juncture of her neck and shoulder and placed sucking kisses and tiny nips, soothed by licks of his tongue all along her neck and the underside of her jaw. All the while, his busy fingers played havoc with the high-collared front of her habit, undoing the hooks of her tight-fitting jacket and then the buttons on her white lawn blouse to expose her fine linen shift. She'd forgone all stays as the tight-fitting jacket didn't allow for anything other than her naturally slender shape. Consequently, he had no difficulty slipping his fingers into the bodice of her loose shift to cup her bare breast in his warm palm and roll her tightly gathered nipple, inciting tumult between her legs. His kisses reached her lips, and she greedily grabbed the back of his head to hold him to her. She groaned loudly into his mouth when the hand that had been at her breast moved to gather up her full skirts and bare her thighs. Beneath her shift, she was nude.

"Hush," he whispered. "The servants are filling the bath, and they will hear you."

As his fingers stroked her outer and inner thighs in a provocative fashion certain to result in her ultimate madness, she tried to listen for sounds of the servants leaving the bathroom through the service door. She gasped audibly and whimpered with pleasure when his mouth settled on the nipple his fingers had teased into inordinate sensitivity.

"You cannot be quiet, can you, Eleanor?" he murmured around kisses as the sounds of light chatter and water being poured into the great tub filtered through the walls.

"Devil...fiend...oh!" His tongue did something particularly nice at her breast at the same time his fingers stroked with great delicacy between her legs, and she cried out at the pulse of sensation.

He lifted his head off her breast. "Shhh...you'll set the servants talking."

The laughter in his voice finished her. "Off! Off me, until we can be private." She laughed. "You cannot be relied upon to behave in a seemly fashion, and I am defenseless against your trespasses on my person." She accompanied her words by scooting out from under him and batting at the hand between her legs.

With a quiet chuckle, he complied and rolled to a sitting position at the side of the bed. "Come and make yourself useful. Pull my boots off."

Eleanor snorted and proceeded to tug on his top boots, grimacing at their refusal to part company with Miles' leg by even so much as an inch. Frowning, she eyed a languid Miles. "Is there a secret to this?"

He grinned, immediately arousing her suspicions. "Straddle my leg with your back to me."

She did as he instructed. With a narrowing of her eyes, she glanced over her shoulder. He gazed at her with a cheerful demeanor, and her suspicions increased.

"Now…one hand at my heel and another at the toe, clasp my boot between your legs. Good. Now, bend over and pull and I will assist you."

As she followed his instructions, he placed his other foot on her buttocks and pushed. Abruptly, the boot gave up its death grip on his leg. With an exclamation of alarm, she sprawled forward onto her elbows and knees on the carpet, holding the foot of his boot between her legs. Silently she rose, boot in hand, and turned, bestowing her most ferocious glare on him. "I cannot believe Mr. Hopwood tolerates such personal abuse every night. How do you remove your boots when you have no assistance, for it is patently impossible for the wearer to pull off such tightly fitted boots as these without aid."

"I use a boot jack," he replied amiably, lounging on his elbows on the bed.

She rolled her tongue in her mouth. "I see. And is such an item present in these rooms?"

"Oh yes. There is a perfectly good boot jack in the dressing room, but I dislike using it as it mars the polish on the heels. Mr. Hopwood works very diligently to achieve that shine."

Eleanor held up the offending article and examined the glossy black leather of the boot's heel. "Resign yourself to marring your other boot."

Miles sighed and shook his head, though his eyes held laughter as he rose and wandered into the dressing room. A minute or two later he returned in stocking feet, took his boot from her and placed a quick kiss on her lips. "Thank you, lady wife." He tossed his boot toward the open door to the dressing room and faced her holding his arms out straight to either side. "You have some more work to do before I'm fit to bathe." He waggled his eyebrows in a comical manner, and she stifled a laugh.

"Wretched beast." She stepped up to him and unbuttoned his waistcoat, then the four buttons at the very neck of his shirt. She pulled the tails of his shirt out of his breeches, slid the waistcoat off his shoulders and pulled his shirt over his head. She tossed both toward the dressing room and paused at the sight of his well-muscled upper body so very different from her own. Unable to resist the temptation, she ran gentle fingers through the whorls of springy hair on his chest.

"Ahem. Stockings then breeches."

Her mouth thinned, and she glanced at her grinning husband. She sank to the floor; at the bend of his knee, she undid the buttons on his breeches and removed one stocking and then the other from well-formed calves covered with additional fine brown hair. She looked up at him from the floor and swallowed. One more piece of apparel and he would be bare.

He extended a hand and helped her to stand. "My breeches, if you would be so kind."

She inhaled deeply and unbuttoned the fall of his breeches and then the small buttons in the center of the waistband encircling his trim waist. His inexpressibles sagged and fell from his hips, and she finally allowed herself to examine the male part of him that had grown rapidly to stand upright in yet more tight curls of brown hair. Fascinated, she reached out a finger to touch and let out a squeak when it jumped on his belly.

Miles' rich laughter sounded in the room. "He will not bite. Hold me in your hand."

Eleanor shot a doubtful glance at him but did as he asked and wrapped her entire hand around what felt like a hot wooden rod covered in velvet, but no wooden rod in her memory had pulsed in her hand with a life of its own. She tightened her grip, but her fingers would not quite encompass the whole of him.

Miles exhaled in a grunt.

"What do men call this part?"

"There are many names. Prick, rod, Adam's staff, Arbor Vitae are but a few. I use 'cock'."

She looked at him bemused. "Like a male fowl? A rooster?"

He nodded with a chuckle, and his "cock" jerked in her hand. She released her grip and stroked up his length to the tip where it mushroomed out and formed a dusty rose cap. "So this is the part of you that I took inside me," she mused. She caught her lower lip between her teeth. "I know I was able to accommodate you, but it still seems quite unlikely. Are you considered abnormally large?" She once again attempted to wrap him in her hand.

Miles choked on a laugh and looked heavenward. "I would like to observe that this is a most unseemly topic for conversation. However…" He cleared his throat. "It may be that the Almighty has blessed me with an abundance, but I have no definitive answer as I have not gone about making a study of men's erect parts. There is a vast difference in size between an aroused male organ and one flaccid." He lifted a shoulder and eyed her with amusement, and she returned to her intent study of his cock.

"I should hope so. I would think it terribly awkward to go through the day with a part of this immensity in one's trousers." He didn't respond, simply laughed silently, his cock leaping in the grip of her hand. A clear drop of liquid appeared, poised at the very center of the broad tip. She ran the pad of her index finger around the head and through the glistening drop. She was startled when Miles hissed and wrapped a firm hand around her wrist. "I'm terribly sorry. Did I hurt you?"

"No. Quite the opposite. Enough of that for now." He worked his breeches down his calves and stepped out of them. The part of him that so held her fascination slapped against his abdomen.

Miles turned to her. "I'm neglecting my duties as lady's maid." He had her out of her clothes and down to her shift in half the time she'd spent on him. "Do you want to take down your hair?"

"Please."

With an ease of practice, she didn't wish to think about, he removed all her hairpins and unraveled her braid, finger-combing her hair and massaging her scalp in a pleasure-inducing caress that raised goose bumps on her arms.

"And now your shift, my lady." He had it off over her head, and before she registered what had happened, she stood before him just a naked as he.

Her arms crept toward her breasts and the juncture of her legs.

"Ah, ah…we'll have none of that." Miles placed her arms at her sides. "You have a lovely body, and I enjoy looking at it. I know you may feel hideously uncomfortable, but you need never hide from me."

She straightened and held him in a direct gaze. "I feel wretchedly awkward and thoroughly embarrassed, but if the sight of me naked as a babe pleases you, I will strut around thusly at every available opportunity."

He chuckled and placed a kiss in the middle of her forehead. "It will be sufficient if you forego clothing in our bedchamber before only your maid and your husband."

She blushed. "Of course. That's what I meant."

He took her hand. "The bath awaits."

She hadn't realized that Miles meant to get in with her. Sometime later, with half the contents of the tub on the floor due to some boisterous application of soap that devolved into finding what parts of Lady Miles Everleigh were ticklish, she stepped out of the tub and wrapped herself in a warm towel.

Miles grinned at her from the tub as he held up a foot and soaped it.

She offered him a soft smile in return. "Are all men such little boys at heart?"

"I can't speak for all men, but as a rule, I've found most things that cause embarrassment are best approached with an appreciation for the ridiculous and an ability to laugh at oneself. I'll chance a guess you didn't think of your nudity once."

She thought about that as she toweled her hair dry. "Thank you," she said quietly.

He glanced at her as he washed himself. "For what?"

She closed her eyes and let out a long breath before she opened them again and allowed her gaze to linger on him. "For your kindness. For your humor. For your patience with me." She lifted a shoulder, unable—and unwilling—to put into words all the different reasons she'd found to fall in love with him. She sighed and wondered what his reaction would be should she tell him *that*.

His gray eyes met hers soberly. "You are welcome." He continued to hold her in a steady, considering gaze. For a brief moment, Eleanor read something more profound in his expression, a warmth of feeling that answered her own, but he looked away and began to sluice water over his chest, and she decided what she had seen was a product of wishful thinking.

Chapter Twenty-One

Wearing only her delicate silk robe, Eleanor sat cross-legged in the middle of the bed surrounded by three empty wine bottles and multiple silver serving trays bearing the remnants of their dinner. She spooned the last bit of trifle into her mouth. "This appears the site of a bacchanal," she said around her mouthful of custard and waved her spoon in a haphazard fashion at the wreckage adorning the bed. "I feel exceedingly dissolute and…not precisely sober." She stuck her tongue out and leisurely licked the flat of the spoon.

Miles, also in only a thin robe, reclined against the headboard, one leg crossed over the other, and sipped his Madeira, slowly rolling the stem of the crystal wine glass between his thumb and forefinger. His eyes appeared half-lidded, and over the rim of his goblet, they tracked her. She'd offer odds he hadn't missed a single move she'd made in the last hour. His potent study of her raised gooseflesh on her arms and sent her thoughts careening in a thousand naughty directions.

With casual grace—Eleanor wondered if he ever did anything that wasn't graceful—Miles put his glass on the bedside table, got to his feet, and slid the trays abruptly off the bed and onto the floor. She jolted at the ensuing crash. Sitting on the side of the bed, he removed the empty bowl and spoon from her hands and with a careless clatter, they joined the rest of the plates, trays, and cutlery on the floor.

"A true bacchanal requires one additional ingredient."

Eleanor twisted her mouth into a crooked smile and squinted in an attempt to bring Miles' face into focus. "And that would be, sir?"

"Debauchery."

Her mouth formed an 'O'.

"Unless you are not feeling up to it?" he murmured.

Her teeth clicked as she shut her mouth. "I am in perfect health, good sir." She sat up primly and blinked, assuming a studious air. "I would very much like to be debauched." A rude burp erupted from her throat and quite ruined the serious effect for which she strove. She snorted and clapped her hand over her mouth to stifle a giggle.

"Would you now…" Miles slipped off his robe, dropped to all fours, and naked, slunk across the massive bed toward her. The salaciously intent expression on his face combined with the menacing threat of his fully erect member boded no good for her tender person.

"Miles…" She giggled and crabbed backward as a hint of apprehension traced ghostly fingers up her back.

He was on her in an instant. She laughed and shrieked in mock fear until her breath left her in a forceful "oof" when his weight flattened her to the mattress. He stilled, his face four inches above hers, his hips nested between her thighs and began to nuzzle her neck where her robe bared her skin. She arched her upper body into his kisses and tried to open the neck of her robe to allow him better access, but she could not move very well.

"You are very heavy, Miles," she panted, and never ceasing his attentions to her, he lifted up to support himself on his elbows.

"Better?" he murmured into her neck.

"Mmmhmm." His kisses, combined with her wine-induced euphoria, created such an aura of languid pleasure that she found it difficult to coordinate her muscles or even speak without slurring her words. She flopped her arms out to her sides and spread her legs. "Debauch me, Lord Miles Everleigh. I have no idea what that entails, but whatever it is, I know I'll love it. I love everything you do."

"Eleanor…"

"Mmm?"

"I think you *have* been dipping rather deeply."

She sniffed and thought about it as he kissed his way down to her breasts. "Most likely. I recall consuming the entire third bottle unassisted. Oh! Do that again! The tongue thing…please." She lifted her head and beamed at him before releasing her head to flop back on the bed. "Yes…precisely that."

His body shook with not so silent laughter as his hands undid the tie to her robe and pulled it from between their pressed bodies. She more or less lost track of his direction while she reveled in the glide of his smooth, bare flesh against hers—the press of his warm mouth on her belly, her hips, the vee of her groin, the insides of her thighs and on her…"Miles!"

Woozy from drink or not, she popped up like a jack-in-the-box and stared between her widespread legs. "Is this sort of thing really done? Is it a required part of debauching?" She cleared her throat. "Do you actually find pleasure in...*that*?"

The pad of Miles' thumb took over for his tongue and slipped in easy circles around the apex of her sex. The feeling produced was quite distracting and required she concentrate doubly hard on Miles' words. She'd given up trying to bring his features into focus. Her eyes wouldn't stop crossing.

"*That* is cunnilingus, and I enjoy it very much." He grinned. "You make the most adorable sounds as you rise in pleasure. I find it quite stimulating. Should you ever wish to return the favor, you need only indicate as such. That act is called 'fellatio'."

Her eyes widened in disbelief. "Put my mouth on your cock? Do you like women to do that?"

He smiled broadly and winked at her. "I should like it very well if my wife were to do it."

"I see." She collapsed backward on the bed, arms splayed and made a study of the ceiling. "There is much more skill to this debauching than I realized." The warm, wet caress of his lips and tongue began again, and now that she wasn't so startled, she had to confess...it felt, ah...*good*. "Miles?"

"Mmm?"

"Are there books I can study about debauching? I am determined I shall be very, very accomplished at it."

He laid the weight of his head on her thigh, and his laughter spilled into the room. "Yes, Eleanor, they exist. Some even have illustrations. Next I'm in London, I will look into obtaining the most instructive of debauching literature for you, and we will practice until you are very, very, accomplished at it."

By the time Miles finished with her many eye-opening hours later, she felt thoroughly and entirely debauched and even more hopelessly in love with her husband.

The next morning, Miles left Eleanor sleeping in with a note instructing her to consume the medicinal drink in the glass on her bedside table before rising. Unless he missed his mark, his endearing bride was going to awake with quite a bad head. He had risen at his normal time of 9:00 a.m. feeling thoroughly satiated and incapable of performing any task that required the slightest degree of physical effort or mental acuity. She'd kept him up until 4:00 that morning. *Up* in all meanings of the word. The night had been…memorable. He smiled into his cup of coffee as he sipped. After three bottles of wine, of which she had consumed the majority, his innocent wife had been devoid of inhibition, avidly curious—and wholly enchanting.

He now sat in the family dining room enjoying a breakfast of cold bread and butter, lovely chops swimming in meat juice and an egg omelet, all washed down with some excellent cider. He had been joined by the Earl and his Countess.

"Fedder and Bitters wish Day Dreamer to have a race before the Epsom Derby." Miles directed his comments to both Lord and Lady Rutledge, who sat opposite him, his gaze going first to one and then the other. "He has suggested a race in Newmarket this Saturday and has paid the late penalty for her entry. Eleanor wishes to attend. If the weather promises to be fair and you felt up to it, we would enjoy your company. We would stay at Fairwood. While it is not as grand as Rutledge, I can promise you will be comfortable. I would be able to introduce you to Mother and my younger brother, Edmund." As soon as he spoke the words, Miles remembered the Earl's comments implying an acquaintance with his *maman*, but he made no mention of it. This was not the appropriate time.

"My, what a lovely invitation." Lady Rutledge straightened, and she and her husband exchanged a lengthy gaze. "What do you say, Rutledge?"

Miles could have sworn some unheard conversation took place between them. The Earl's eyes rested on him and then Lady Rutledge, but no clue was to be had from their faces.

"You know I like pleasing you above all things, Lady Rutledge, but in this matter…" The Earl paused to catch his breath. "This beleaguered carcass might give up the ghost should I rattle off to Newmarket." Again he paused, breathing heavily, and with an arm that shook noticeably, he laid his hand on his wife's where she rested it on the table. "But, please don't let my infirmities prevent you if you wish to go."

"Well," her voice quavered, "I should take no enjoyment whatsoever if you were not there." Lady Rutledge turned her hand over and laced her fingers through her husband's. She directed a smile at Miles. "There you have it. You will have to bring us back a detailed account. Oh, it nearly slipped my mind. Your young groom returned late last evening and said a trunk is coming today with your clothes. When they arrive, I'll have Walters turn them over to Mr. Hopwood to be freshened. The groom also brought a letter for you. It's on the desk in the study."

At the rustle of silk, Miles looked toward the door and rose. A waxen-faced Eleanor entered the dining room, stepping cautiously, holding herself in such a manner as not to jar her head. He recognized the stratagem, having used it himself on the rare occasion he overindulged.

She smiled faintly. "Good morning, Mamma, Father," she said in a thready voice. Her gaze traveled to Miles and a genuine smile tilted her lips and warmed her eyes for a scant three seconds. "My lord. Pray be seated."

"Good morning, dearest," her mother chirped.

Eleanor winced and pressed her fingertips to her temple. "There is no need to shout, Mamma. I am in the same room." She scanned the food laid out on the sideboard with a muted moan while her hands pressed her stomach. "I don't believe I can eat." With guarded steps, she closed the few feet to stand beside Miles and allowed the footman to assist her into her chair.

Miles poured her a cup of tea, fixed it to her liking and placed it on the table in front of her.

"Thank you." Eleanor sat rigidly motionless and stared at her cup.

Miles leaned across the table and murmured, "Lady Miles awoke this morning with a vile head, a megrim. She doesn't feel at all the thing."

"A megrim? I cannot recall Eleanor ever having a megrim. She has always had quite a sturdy constitution. Whatever could have brought on a megrim?" Lady Rutledge's wobbly voice sounded innocent, but she shot an impish glance at her husband.

Eleanor rose abruptly. "This was a mistake. I'm returning to my bedchamber to lie down with a cool cloth on my forehead. Don't hold dinner for me. I bid all of you a good day."

Three pairs of eyes watched her leave.

Lady Rutledge made a sound of sympathetic concern and motioned to one of the footmen standing at attention around the dining room. "I am going to make sure Eleanor has what she needs." The male servant immediately moved to help the Countess into her wheeled chair and pushed her out of the room.

"Poor girl," murmured Miles, shaking his head and raising his coffee cup. "It was that third bottle of Spanish red. I warned her against it."

"Sounds carry better than you think they might in these vast estate houses. So much stone, you see," Lord Rutledge observed in a soft undertone. A dry humor wove itself through his words, and his eyes never left Miles.

Miles responded with a raised eyebrow as he sipped his coffee. "Merely mending what was amiss between your daughter and me."

"Will Eleanor think it worth the price paid?"

"I can say with all confidence she thought so at the time," Miles stated blandly as he took another sip of his coffee and then met the steady gaze of Lord Rutledge with an equally steady one of his own.

Later that evening, after spending the majority of the day with Bitters and Fedder arranging for Day Dreamer and entourage to leave for Newmarket, Miles entered their apartments with a tray of toast triangles, butter and jam, and strong, black tea. Eleanor sat in a wing chair wrapped in a dressing gown, a book open in her lap, though her head rested against the chair and her eyes were closed. She opened them and smiled faintly when he entered, but otherwise did not move. He set the tray on the small table beside the chair and removed the open book from her lap.

"I have brought you tea and toast. Feeling at all more the thing?"

"I feel as if I had been planted head down, uprooted by my heels and then dragged at a gallop through the hedgerows." She straightened slowly and offered Miles a wan smile. "Mostly it is my head. My stomach has finally settled. I have also faithfully ignored the amusement displayed by the staff when they think I don't see." She eyed the toast and with a minimum of motion, buttered several pieces before loading them with strawberry jam and consuming them and a cup of strong tea straight away. She then closed her eyes and sank back into the chair. "Thank you, my lord. I feel better."

"You are welcome. I've had a letter from the Dowager Duchess. She reports that Ludlow appeared shortly after she received my letter advising her he might call. She supported our story and says Ludlow departed rather cross."

"Hmm. That was good of her. I liked your mother."

"Yes, she's a lovely woman. I'm rather fond of her myself." He took her hand and gently pulled. "Come along, my dear."

Eleanor barely opened her eyes. "What?"

"I'm going to sit on the sofa and read, and you will put your head in my lap so that I can rub your temples."

He settled in with a popular novel, and groaning, Eleanor stretched out with her head resting on his left thigh. The book opened to the place he had marked and holding it in his right hand, he propped it on the arm of the sofa and began to read. His left hand stroked through her hair and massaged her temples in a gentle, repetitive pattern that drew a low moan of appreciation from Eleanor. He'd been rubbing her head for about an hour when her sleepy mumble broke the silence in the room.

"Miles, aside from my inebriation—Spanish red shall never pass my lips again—last night was perfectly splendid. You proved an exceptional lady's maid and have quite ruined Sally for me." She snuggled closer into his lap with a deep sigh.

Sometime much later and in the barest of whispers, he heard, "I'm so very glad I married you."

He smiled to himself and kept stroking as Eleanor fell asleep.

Chapter Twenty-Two

The ten days Eleanor spent at Fairwood with Miles, his mother, Julia and his brother, Lord Edmund, were days of unprecedented joy. She still worried about her parents, but her life could not become only a death watch. Neither her mother nor her father would countenance such and demanded that she "get on with her life". So she did.

Dreamer won her race handily as Eleanor screamed encouragement in a most unladylike manner, abetted by Jemmy, Bitters and Lord Edmund. Even Fedder was caught out in a genuine smile. After the race, sporting reporters from the London papers engulfed Bitters and Fedder. They shouted questions about Day Dreamer's blood lines and workout times and the races she was entered in. In the race barn at Newmarket, and later at Fairwood, Jemmy floated high on his new-found fame as the groom to the filly that had captured the fascination of the racing public. Eleanor was certain Day Dreamer would join Cinsyr as a rising star in the racing world and shortly, all of London would know of Rutledge's latest three-year-old prodigy.

Even Mr. Weldon unbent and welcomed the Rutledge contingent to Fairwood with well-justified pride. Everywhere her eye looked, the property and animals showed the results of conscientious care. Mr. Weldon may have been out of joint due to the loss of Day Dreamer, but he hadn't shorted his master in his care of Miles' property.

Julia lavished maternal affection on Eleanor, and Miles brother, Lord Edmund—who immediately insisted she call him Ned—charmed her by treating her from the start like the sister he'd never had. Eleanor considered Miles the most handsome man she'd ever set eyes upon, but had she not been so enamored of her husband, she would have awarded that title to Lord Edmund. Ned combined his devastating good looks with an engaging personality and an agile tongue—he could charm his way out of anything—and made her wonder at the wisdom of having left such a scamp on his own in London. While his intentions were usually good, trouble of some sort or another seemed to find Ned, even in a town such as Newmarket, hardly the center of vice. Ned redeemed himself in her eyes, though, for he worked magic with the young, fractious horses, and as that described every animal Eleanor had ever raced, he impressed her greatly.

"Has my brother seen you rigged out like that?" Ned flashed her a lascivious grin as they left the stable block one early dawn morning and headed toward the exercise green, mounted on two of Miles' young race prospects.

"Brat," Eleanor responded. "Of course, he's seen me. I can't very well gallop racehorses in a sidesaddle and skirts, can I?"

"You're the first female I've known brave enough to back a half-trained, two-year-old stallion, much less ride him at a full-out gallop."

As Ned replied, the youngster he rode demonstrated exactly why *any* person concerned with staying hale and hearty would avoid riding such an animal, for the young stallion reared skyward and as soon as its front feet hit the turf, bolted forward to flee some unseen provocation. When checked abruptly to a halt by Ned, the youngster proceeded to thrust its head between its front legs and engage in a display of leapfrogging and vaulting such as to pitch any normally-skilled rider into the clouds. Ned stuck like a burr and had the animal pulled to a quivering standstill with very little fuss and bother whereupon he immediately urged the animal forward into a trot with an audible kiss and a light pat on the neck as if naught had happened.

Eleanor's own mount had tried to emulate his companion, but forewarned, she'd immediately shortened one rein dramatically and pulled his head around until he eyed her right boot, and thus forced the young horse to constrain his histrionics to snorting and crabbing sideways in a tight circle. Thus having discouraged any airs above the ground, Eleanor loosened her rein on the young stud and drew alongside Ned. The pair of young horses proceeded to trot down the carriage path displaying, for the moment, acceptable manners.

"As to being brave… I've lived on a horse's back since the age of three, Ned," Eleanor scolded humorously. "Very few of the horses my father mounted me on were suitable for children for I was light enough to ride the yearlings, and as a young girl, I regularly limped back to the stable yard on foot, bedecked with mud and grass—my mount having returned home without me and long since been put back in its stall. The ensuing disgrace motivated me to try harder to stay atop the beasts." She looked at Ned as they bobbed down the lane and smiled. "I wouldn't say brave as much as accustomed to willful behavior. Where did you come by your exceptional seat?"

"Miles and our father, the old Duke, had acquired some young race prospects not yet trained to saddle. Miles was off at Oxford, and our head groom didn't have the time to spend with them—nor the interest, frankly. I was at loose ends, betwixt and between—not a man and yet not a boy— with far too much time on my hands. One thing led to another, and I discovered I enjoyed working with the young horses. Miles took note." Ned shrugged.

"There is great satisfaction in bringing a young animal into its full potential, and from what I've observed, the horses like you."

"Yes. I have a way with horses and women," Ned declared with unrepentant laughter. "Both adore me."

Eleanor snorted and rolled her eyes and they rode in companionable silence for a short while.

"He worries for you, you know." She cast a quick glance at Ned.

"Miles? Why, what has he said to you?" he asked sharply.

"He has said nothing to me other than you are an immense help. It is more the care I see on his face when you aren't aware he is watching you."

"Elle, tell him not to worry about me. He might listen to you. Nothing I say seems to matter." The clack of shod hooves filled the silence that followed Ned's clipped words. "Come on… race you to the gatehouse."

She won. Ned's mount, deciding he had behaved long enough, leaped and farted and generally behaved so poorly that Ned had to pull up or risk being unseated and she thundered by with a cackle of glee.

At the end of their visit, she and Ned were well on the way to being fast friends.

And Miles, her intoxicating husband … he filled her nights with physical pleasures that never failed to astonish her—though she stayed true to her vow never again to drink Spanish red. He filled her days with walks through the Fairwood pastures and barns examining promising young bloodstock all the while deep in discussion about their shared excitement at Day Dreamer's excellent prospects for winning the Epsom Derby.

On her knees at prayer on the evenings he didn't distract her with more earthy pursuits, she implored the Almighty to show her the way to win Miles' heart.

On the morning of the day they would return to Rutledge, Eleanor sat at breakfast alone with the Dowager Duchess of Chelsony, as the gentlemen had rushed off earlier in response to a summons from Mr. Weldon—a summons that had Miles and Ned frowning and looking troubled.

"I think, perhaps, I did not lie to Mr. Ludlow when I told him you and my son were a love match." The Dowager Duchess smiled at Eleanor and lavished butter on a warm scone. "You seem happier in your marriage than when I spoke with you last."

"Is it so very obvious?" Eleanor played her spoon through her congealing oatmeal.

"*Oui.* You have the appearance of a woman well-loved."

Eleanor raised her eyes to hold the gaze of Miles' mother, unable to conceal her feelings of baffled enchantment. "I wonder that my skin can contain such joy without bursting like an overstuffed Christmas goose."

"So Miles treats you well in the bedchamber? Pleasures you?" the Dowager Duchess inquired brightly. "Conjugal relations that gratify both parties create faithful spouses and a harmonious marriage, and it is universally acknowledged by the most educated physicians that a woman brought to her own supreme ecstasy is more likely to conceive. From the rumors that circulated, my son seems to have earned a reputation as a proficient cocksman." Julia raised an elegant shoulder. "But you never know how much to believe of such gossip." While ostensibly arranging the knife she'd used to butter the scone on her bread plate, she cast an upward glance at Eleanor through her lashes. "Is it true?"

In the midst of swallowing a sip of tea, Eleanor gulped it down hastily and pressed her napkin to her mouth. Her wide-eyed gaze found Julia's laughing eyes brimming with mischief, and slowly, feeling extraordinarily audacious, she made a slight movement of her head up and down. Behind her napkin, her tiny smile grew into a self-conscious grin. She dropped her hand into her lap, and she and the Dowager Duchess began to giggle like adolescent girls instead of the mature women they were.

"*Bien.* I will prepare a nursery for my future grandchildren."

I should like to give Miles a child. Eleanor became pensive. "But, Your Grace, I have him for only a short time. Just until the entailment is probated. Our agreement was a year at most, and then he returns to you and Fairwood." She slumped in her chair and picked at the stitching of her napkin's hem. "I love him. He grows more dear to me by the day." She smiled faintly. "It is as you said. Miles is irresistible. I find I want a marriage real in every way, not the cold arrangement spelled out in the contract we signed, but how do I make him desire me enough to remain at Rutledge? If I tell him I am in love with him, Miles will stay by my side out of a sense of duty and the abundant kindness inherent to his nature—for I have never met another soul on this earth as compassionate and giving as my husband. He would stay, and I would never know truly what was in his heart. You must promise not to tell him of my feelings." She gazed at Julia in raw appeal until she saw the older woman's reluctant agreement. "I want to win his love, but I lack the faintest clue as to how to go about it. I had thought to entice him with the magnificence of Rutledge…" She shook her head slowly and returned to unraveling her napkin. "…but Miles is not at all mercenary. Besides, no matter how grand the buildings or how expansive the lands, mere bricks and tilled fields cannot compensate for the love of family that enfolds him here at Fairwood." Eleanor cast another despairing glance toward the Dowager Duchess. "How do I win him?"

Bemused empathy shone from Julia's eyes as she broke off a piece of buttered scone and slathered it liberally with gooseberry jam. "My dearest girl, you already have," she murmured and then popped the morsel into her mouth halting further speech.

Eleanor wished she was privy to the insight the Dowager Duchess possessed that made her so certain, but in a contradictory departure from her normal confidence, she lacked the boldness to ask. Instead, Eleanor cast Julia a doubtful glance and ate a spoon of cold oatmeal.

Miles rose from where he and Ned had squatted to examine the black charring on some timbers that supported a section of the roof in the hay barn. Several of the grooms and farm laborers, begrimed and soot-covered, stood in a wide semi-circle around scorched floorboards and an overturned lantern that Miles was certain had been used to start the fire. The smell of burnt wood and hay hung heavy in the air. He faced Mr. Weldon. "I believe only the surface of the timbers have been burnt. We won't have to replace them. We are very lucky that one of the lads caught this fire early enough that we could put it out quickly."

"Yes, my lord, we certainly are, and then there is this." Weldon handed him a piece of paper with a grim expression. "It was tacked to the harness room door."

> Did you think we wouldn't find you? £20,000 now. You have a lovely mother. Pity if harm befell her or this property over such a petty sum. Be at Epsom for the Derby.

Reading over Miles' shoulder, Ned turned the air blue with his curses.

Miles appreciated the sentiment, but unfortunately, he could not succumb to anger. He had to remain rational and take the steps necessary to protect his family, his property and the four-footed inhabitants of Fairwood. "Mr. Weldon, how many men would we need to keep watch around the clock on the property? The manor house, the barns, and pastures?" Miles waited patiently as the man stood and considered.

"I should think eight armed men would be sufficient, Lord Miles. Two for the main house and grounds and six to patrol the pastures. They would work in shifts of twelve hours on, twelve off."

Miles frowned. "We have little staff we can spare, so I suppose you will need to find some able-bodied men from Newmarket."

Again, Weldon thought for several long moments before he answered. "Well…I can shift three of the stable lads I would trust to keep their wits about them and not shoot one of the horses by mistake. He shrugged. "Shouldn't be too difficult to find five more. These days there are always men who have mustered out and are looking for work."

Miles rubbed his forehead and tried to think where he'd find the money to hire five more staff for an indefinite period of time. He took a deep breath. He'd work the Fairwood accounts again and find the money somewhere. "I loathe that I cannot remain, but I am obligated to see my wife back to Rutledge. From there we will be going almost immediately to London and then on to Epsom Downs for Dreamer's run in the Derby. So…I am putting a great deal of trust in you, Mr. Weldon. Hire the men you need. Pay them something fair. Above all, see that my family and my property come to no harm."

Mr. Weldon nodded. "I'll keep them safe, my lord. You can count on it."

"I am." He gave his farm manager a tight smile and turned to his brother. "Ned, I am going to trust you to keep a level head about you. Ned?" His brother had looked away when he'd addressed him and stood with his hands on his hips staring out the open door. Miles reached out and gripped his brother's shoulder. "Ned...I am counting on you to help protect Mother."

His brother wilted out from under his hand and turned to regard him with a bleak expression. "Whatever you need, Miles."

He clapped his brother on the shoulder and smiled. "Right then...I'll see you in Epsom in a fortnight. It was our plan regardless of the new threat. Under the circumstances, I don't think it wise that you come alone. Bring a couple of Fairwood men with you." Miles paused. "And Ned...stay with them?"

"Yes." His brother closed his eyes and gave a pained chuff. "Bugger all," he whispered in an undertone. "This is my fault. I've caused you nothing but expense and worry. I'm so damnably sorry."

Miles raised his eyebrows and responded mildly, "Yes, I expect you are. We will muddle through this, Edmund. Chin up, and take care of the Dowager Duchess." Not for the first time, Miles wondered if he had done his younger brother any favors by standing between Ned and the worst of the repercussions of Ned's imprudent behavior. He could not have acted any differently, however, and still slept peacefully at night. He offered his brother a crooked grin. "In my study, in my desk, second drawer on the right, you will find a very fine pair of

Wogdon & Barton coaching pistols. Keep them loaded and close to hand."

"Wogdon & Barton?" Ned gave a long whistle. "Those must have cost you dearly."

"Oh, I didn't purchase them. I could never have afforded such precision pieces. They were a parting gift from a grateful lady, though I'd appreciate it if you didn't mention that detail to Lady Miles should the subject ever come up."

Ned rolled his eyes. "Of course. I'm not a complete nodcock."

"Speaking of my wife, I must find my lovely bride and get started for Rutledge or we shall run out of daylight and that road is the very devil at night." Memories assaulted him, and his mouth twisted in a wry smile. "I have reason to know. Mr. Weldon, please send word I want the team put to."

"Yes, my lord."

"We left Fairwood as if the devil was on our heels and you've been lost in thought ever since. From your grim features, those thoughts are not uplifting." Eleanor voiced her concern over the noise of the swaying traveling chariot as four superbly matched grays drew the ultra-light vehicle homeward to Rutledge at a smart trot interspersed with periods of cantering. They slowed to a walk occasionally to allow the team to blow and catch their air but picked up the rapid pace again as soon as deemed practical. At this rate, they were bound to far outstrip Sally and Mr. Hopwood who, along with the luggage, rode behind them at a more sedate pace in the drag, but Miles' instructions to the postillion riders had dictated their ground-covering pace, and she would not countermand him.

Miles turned his head from his sightless stare out the glass and regarded Eleanor with faint surprise as if he'd just realized another person sat beside him.

"What is troubling you? May I know?"

His stern features eased, and his mouth tipped in a faint smile, but he said nothing, rather, he appeared to be considering her request. She'd just about given up hope that he would share with her whatever plagued him when he relaxed back into the squabs with an audible sigh.

"Ned got himself into something of a bother in London some time ago, and I'm afraid it has followed him to Fairwood." Beginning with Ned's arrival in London prior to their wedding, Miles proceeded to explain the circumstances that led up to his and Ned's hasty departure from the breakfast table that morning.

"Good heavens, Miles! Someone set fire to the hay barn and threatened your mother? We must turn around immediately and return to Fairwood. Her Grace and Ned must be convinced to stay with us at Rutledge."

"It is immensely kind of you, but to what end? The villains who are trying to extort money from Ned will simply follow him there. These people have proven to be entirely without conscience and willing to sink to the vilest of behaviors." He shook his head. "No. I will not allow those at Rutledge to be imperiled because of my brother's folly."

Eleanor frowned at him, more upset than angry. "If it is a matter of money, I am happy to pay these people."

"No!" Miles snarled, and taken aback, she straightened in her seat. He closed his eyes briefly, and when he opened them again, he said softly, though his tone was no less stern, "I'm sorry. I did not mean to raise my voice to you. I know you mean well." He returned his gaze to the passing scenery and spoke to the glass. "You cannot pay people like this sort. Once you do, there will be no end to it. They will suck you dry. Ned satisfied his legitimate debt. Nothing more is owed. They simply see what they think is easy money." He shook his head. "They will find we are anything but."

The chariot rocked along for several minutes, and he retreated into sober silence, once again staring out the glass.

No…she wouldn't have it. He was not going to freeze her out.

Ten days ago, she wouldn't have contemplated taking the bold action she took now. Gathering up her skirts, she rose, turned and straddled Miles' lap. She released her gown, settled her hands on Miles' shoulders and from mere inches away and eye-to-eye, smiled at him.

"Lady Miles…what is this, my dear?" For the first time that day, his face lightened, and he returned her smile, a trace of his normal devilry apparent in the twist of his lips. The vehicle lurched, and he wrapped his hands around her waist to hold her steady.

"If I cannot relieve you of the cause of your blue devils, perhaps I can make you forget them for a while."

He arched a playful eyebrow at her. "And just how do you propose to do that?"

She felt her cheeks color. "I thought I would kiss you."

"And you thought a kiss would be sufficient to distract me?" His tone conveyed a misleading innocence. Eleanor was not deceived.

"Well...I..." she stammered. "I thought I would kiss you *several* times—with my tongue, a kiss in the, ah... I believe you called it the Florentine style...and at length."

His chuckle was deep and suggestive. "My sweet wife, there is much more fun to be had than simply kissing... even in the Florentine style."

As the rocking of their vehicle moved her back and forth, she wrinkled her brow and examined him for a long moment trying to discern what he implied. The growing hardness where her bare parts met his trousered lap cued her understanding. "Oh!" She frowned and cocked her head. "Really? In a moving carriage?"

He nodded, growing amusement apparent on his face.

She looked at the confined, intimate space of the two-person vehicle. "Truly? It doesn't seem there's enough room."

Biting his lip in what she felt certain was an effort to prevent another laugh, he nodded and reached to close the window curtains. The hand that had released her waist disappeared, flipping through the froth of her skirts to grasp her bare thigh above her garter and then move elsewhere. He held her gaze with mischievous intent until she felt his hard cock resting against the bare skin of her inner thigh. His talented fingers traced caresses up between her legs to her tenderest of flesh where he proceeded to incite her until she teetered on the brink of ultimate pleasure. He withdrew his hand.

"No! Miles! Don't stop."

"Rise up on your knees, Eleanor."

"Why did you stop? I was very happy with what you were doing."

"Yes, dearest, I'm sure you were. I, however, would like to participate more fully. Now, raise up on your knees."

"I fail to see how being on my knees will achieve anything." With a huff, she rose until she knelt over him.

"Come down slowly."

"Oh…" As she sank, he guided his rigid length into her until she rested fully seated on his thighs. The motion of the coach rocked her back and forth in his lap. "What a novel position. I feel all of you quite keenly."

Miles groaned softly, and his head fell back against the squabs.

After a few moments of rocking, her eyes widened. "Oh…Miles…?"

"Yes, Eleanor?" he said in a strained voice.

"Oh…Miles…this is very nice."

"I'm glad you think so," he ground out. "Now, be a very good girl and don't enhance the movement of the carriage, or I will be useless to you."

"Yes, Miles."

Of course, as he then set his hands to work teasing her flesh where his body joined with hers, ultimately she had to move as she couldn't stand not to. At that point, however, she was certain she had achieved her objective. The Ned problem had been put aside for an hour or so as Miles thoroughly acquainted her with the intimate delights to be had in a traveling chariot. Eleanor made a mental note never to sell this particular vehicle.

Chapter Twenty-Three

"I have been to Epsom many times, but I've never watched the Derby from a private box." Lady Florence beamed at Eleanor. "Such an improved view—one can see every detail, and you are not jostled by the crowd." She studied Eleanor and slowly shook her head. "You are all but climbing out of your skin. Go on, my dear, go to the barns or saddling circle or whatever it's called. Find your handsome husband and your trainer and satisfy yourself that all is well. I will be fine on my own."

Eleanor winced in apology. "I'm sorry to be so preoccupied. Females aren't welcomed in the saddling area, but I would dearly love to see for myself Dreamer is properly turned out. Miles and Mr. Fedder are more than capable but..." She frowned.

Lady Florence snorted. "But you must satisfy yourself, or your nerves will consume you." She made a shooing motion with her gloved hand. "Go. Go on."

"I'll be back before the start with Lord Miles." Eleanor gave her friend a hasty kiss on the cheek and strode from the owner's box with one hand on her hat and the other holding up her skirts.

"She looks in wonderful shape, Fedder. I am very hopeful for a win today." Miles hung over a stall door with the Rutledge trainer and watched Jemmy put the finishing polish on Day Dreamer with a soft rag. The lovely filly's copper coat gleamed with good health. Her step seemed to have an extra loft, and she exuded quiet power.

"Yes, my lord. You know as well as I if she runs as she ought, none in this field is her match." Fedder stepped back and picked up the bridle that hung next to the horse's stall. "That will do, Mr. Struthers. Bring the saddle and pad to the saddling enclosure. I'll take the filly. The call to summon the horses to the saddling area was sounded several minutes ago. We must be off." He turned to Miles. "My lord, as you did in Newmarket, would you like to give the jockey his instructions?" Fedder's lips twitched in what for Fedder was a broad smile. "That way I can always blame you if the filly doesn't run to form."

Miles laughed. "I would be honored, Mr. Fedder. The same man up as in Newmarket?"

"Yes, my lord. Mr. Crane did a good job for us in the filly's last two races. He knows how she likes to run. He deserves a crack at a Derby win."

"Miles!" Ned's voice rang down the aisle with a note of frantic impatience. "I must speak with you."

He raised his arm to acknowledge Ned. "Good enough, Mr. Fedder. I will see you in a few minutes." Miles clapped the trainer on the shoulder then turned and walked down the barn aisle to where Ned stood. Miles' heart sank at his first clear glimpse of him. Ned's left eyebrow was split and bloody. He was missing his hat, his cravat hung undone, and his clothes looked as if he'd rolled in the mud. He'd no more reached his younger brother than Ned grabbed him by the arm, jerked him into an empty stall and addressed him in a fierce undertone.

"Smith's gang have Mr. Morgan and Mr. Allen, the men I brought with me from Fairwood. Those thugs…they ambushed and overpowered us just outside the racecourse. Beat both Mr. Allen and Mr. Morgan unconscious… and…" Ned's face crumpled. "There were too many of them. I couldn't do a damnable thing. Allen and Morgan are being held pending the outcome of the Derby. They've threatened to kill them—and sooner or later get to Mother—if you don't cooperate." Ned looked down, blinking steadily. He raised his sleeve to his face as if to wipe away the evidence of tears.

"If I don't cooperate how?"

Ned flinched at the ice in his tone. "They want our jockey to throw the race," he said miserably. "They have bet on what they think is a sure thing but for our filly. Our man is to take the rail at the back and hold Dreamer there as we always do at the start." Ned looked at his feet. "But two horses will box her in—trap her against the rail. She'll not be allowed to make her run until it's too late. This Mr. Smith, the leader of these villains, stands to win a fortune." Ned raised his head and finally met Miles eye-to-eye. "If we comply with their demands, they will release Morgan and Allen… and leave us alone." Ned looked away, the muscles in his clenched jaw visibly working.

"Do you know where Morgan and Allen are being held?"

"Yes. In a shed not far off."

"How many men do they have?"

"Seven. At least, that was the number who waylaid us."

Miles scrubbed his face and then braced his forehead between his fingers and his thumb as he tried to formulate a workable solution for being two places at once. *What a damnable position to be in. Bloody, bloody hell.* He could not remember the last time he'd had to work so hard to discipline himself into a civilized response as he did at that moment. Miles raised his head and regarded Ned steadily, and as was his custom when volatile emotion of any sort threatened to overturn his self-control, he lowered his voice and spoke with little inflection. "Everything in me demands I confront the scoundrels face-to-face and have this out here and now. I swear nothing would give me greater pleasure than to leave them in bloody pieces on the ground … but I cannot. I cannot leave Lady Eleanor and Lady Floyd-Smythe vulnerable to such predators, and as her husband, my first duty is always to Eleanor."

Ned nodded and drew his mouth into a tight line. "Agreed. Nor can you concede to their extortion. I have quite made up my mind, brother. With you or without you, I am going back to get our Fairwood men. I have taken the liberty of assembling all the Rutledge staff. They are armed with pistols and clubs and merely wait for me to join them, but I thought it best to lay the details in front of you first."

Miles braced a hand on his brother's shoulder. "Ned…"

"No. I am determined. Nothing you say will make me cry off. We will have five men and the element of surprise. It should be enough. It is doubtful this gang would leave all seven to guard two unconscious men. I *will* do this, Miles. I am one and twenty. Though I have not always acted it, I am a grown man. My older brother cannot continue to fight my battles for me. Allow me some pride."

A grim smile twitched the corners of Miles' mouth. "Alright, little brother. Yours is as good a plan as any I suppose. I must go to the saddling paddock. Find me the instant you get back. I should be in the Rutledge box." Miles searched his brother's face. "And for God's sake, Ned, have a care for yourself. Were something to happen to you, I should be devastated, and I can't begin to think what I would say to *Maman*."

Ned offered him a shadow of his devil-may-care grin. "You must cut my lead line sometime, Miles. I know I have let you down in the past. I won't this time. You can trust me to do this."

Ned was correct. Miles had to let him grow up sometime. His heart in his throat, he nodded once, gripped Ned forcefully on the shoulder and then turned and strode out of the barn before he could change his mind. He walked into the sunlight with his thoughts and emotions in savage turmoil, though none of it showed on the agreeable face he presented to the outside world.

The saddling paddock was a confined space of organized chaos as jockeys found their mounts and trainers issued their last instructions all the while dodging nervous horses being saddled. Miles found Fedder and Crane in an isolated corner with a calm, composed Day Dreamer, her head up as her eyes surveyed her assembled competition with the serenity of a champion viewing those of lesser talent. Fedder appeared relieved to see Miles.

"Mr. Crane, glad you are in the irons today. Let's trust in a successful outcome." Miles nodded to the diminutive man wearing the blue and gold silks of the Rutledge stud.

"Yes, my lord. The filly felt good in the warm-ups. Very playful. She'll give those colts a run."

"Good man. A slight change in tactics. You are going to be the rabbit today. Do all in your power to get a clean start, go to the front immediately and stay there. Make them catch you." He reached to stroke Dreamer's chestnut neck before he gently grasped both reins under her chin, ran a hand up her forehead to pull at her forelock and murmured, "Show these boys nothing but your heels, my beauty. Win it all. Do it for your mistress." He returned his gaze to his jockey and stated crisply, "Keep her at the front and out of trouble."

Fedder frowned and sent an intent and considering look at Miles but remained silent as he put the jockey up on Day Dreamer. The call to assemble at the starter's tape was sounded, and both men stepped away from the filly.

"Good luck, Mr. Crane. I'll see you in the winner's circle." Miles nodded and turned to hustle his way to the owner's box, his thoughts divided between the race and the mission his brother spearheaded.

He hoped to heaven Ned would be successful. Otherwise, he might have sentenced two men to death. He didn't think this gang would make good on their threats as murder was a hanging offense, while extortion—assuming it could be proven—was simply imprisonment or deportation.

His other option was completely unpalatable. A horse with the speed and endurance of the chestnut filly was a once-in-a-lifetime gift. He would not deprive Eleanor of what might be her only opportunity to realize her greatest dream because of threats to men in his employ due to the regrettable actions of his brother.

He made his way into Rutledge's private box and was immediately greeted by Lady Florence Lloyd-Smyth.

"Lord Miles, I had thought Eleanor would return with you. She left to find you some time ago."

He frowned. "I didn't see her. Perhaps she got caught up in the crush? The crowd is rather heavy. I'm sure she will be here for the start of the race."

Lady Florence smiled. "Yes. She definitely won't miss that. Oh, look. The horses are under starter's orders. She'd better hurry, or she *will* miss the start." She held an opera glass to her eye. "Rutledge silks are blue and gold are they not?"

"Yes." Miles squinted at the tape where each racer was to place a nose. The jostling and back and forth milling of the horses made identifying an individual animal something of a challenge.

"I don't see them, but then perhaps I don't know what to look for." She handed Miles her jewel encrusted eyeglass. "I'm not very good at looking out of one eye. Would you like to try?"

Miles took the glass from her and intently scanned the field of starters. He came to an inescapable conclusion at the same time as the starter's tape fell and the field of racers for the Epsom Derby were off.

"Oh, Eleanor is going to kick herself for missing the start—"

"My profound apologies, Lady Lloyd-Smyth," Miles interjected. "I must get to the barns." He turned and ran, a sick feeling growing as he pushed and shoved his way through the throngs of cheering racegoers.

Turning into the aisle of the barn, he almost plowed into a glowering Mr. Fedder tearing out of the barn like hellhounds nipped at his heels. Fedder seemed blind to everything around him. Miles stopped the man's progress by grabbing his arm.

"What happened? Why didn't Day Dreamer start?"

The trainer's gaze swung to Miles as if he'd risen from the ground in front of him. The man gave an inarticulate growl of fury. "The Lady Miles Everleigh happened," he spat. "As to why the filly didn't start? You'll have to ask *her*. Mayhap she will give *you* a lucid answer." Fedder uttered his last words in a guttural snarl, and when he jerked his arm out of Miles' grasp, Miles released him unhindered.

Even more alarmed than before, he came to a stop in front of Day Dreamer's open stall door, and his consternation boiled over. "Eleanor, why didn't Dreamer start?"

Eleanor's heart beat as if to come out of her chest and her mouth went suddenly dry. She screwed up all her courage, determined to show no uncertainty and reminded herself one more time that she'd done the right thing. She finished adjusting the stable rug to fit without a wrinkle on the chestnut filly and then turned to face Miles.

"I made the decision to pull her from the race. I saw something off in her gait. She's too valuable to risk a permanent injury."

Miles frowned at her and moved to run his hands down the young horse's legs, an intent expression on his face. After a thorough examination, he rose and stood in front of Eleanor, shaking his head.

"I'd ask to see her trot out, but there's nothing wrong with her. We both know that. Why did you pull her from the race? And Eleanor, please grace me with the truth this time." His gray eyes held her steadily, stern accusation apparent.

As with Fedder, Miles disbelieved her spurious excuse, and she hated not being honest with him. Bracing herself for the furies of hell to descend upon her, she told him the truth.

"Your men are in fear for their lives. Lord Edmund and Her Grace have been threatened with physical peril, and I know how much you love them. It's only money. There will be other days and other Derbies."

"It is *not* only money, and there is only one Derby for Dreamer. Next year she will be too old." His intelligent eyes examined her for a long moment, then narrowed with an all too knowing consideration. "Lady Florence said you came to find me, and you did find me, didn't you?" He took a deep breath and let it out in a long exhale. "How much of my conversation with Ned did you overhear?"

Eleanor gave an internal gasp of relief. Miles was not going to fob her off with some Banbury tale. "I think I heard most of what Ned said to you... and I heard your instructions to Mr. Crane. You placed my hopes and dreams ahead of the physical jeopardy to your men, your brother, your mother—Fairwood and all those lovely horses. I couldn't allow you to put at risk so much you hold dear—not for some silly daydream of mine."

"Some silly..." He choked off the end of his thought. Everything about Miles' manner from his suddenly rigid stance to his clenched jaw and averted gaze indicated immense frustration or barely restrained anger. She didn't know which, but she feared she was in for a violent dressing down. Instead, he closed his eyes, visibly relaxed and when he opened them again, he took her hands into his and addressed her in a quiet voice.

"Eleanor, you must know by now. Isn't it apparent in all I do? As unfashionable as it is, I am a man in love with his wife. I count no cost too great to ensure your dreams come true." His eyes searched her face. "Please tell me my sentiments are not unwelcome for I am hopelessly and irrevocably in love with you."

She stood for a moment, stunned, as one shattered dream was supplanted by the sudden realization of another—one even more desperately longed for.

She'd been silent too long, for his hopeful expression faded and his face became a mask devoid of all expression. She made haste to recover lost ground and shook her head rapidly, removing her hand from his to lay her bare palm in a caress against his cheek.

"No. Oh…no, never unwelcome." Incredulous joy choked her throat and made speaking difficult. Her words emerged garbled, and she cleared her throat to speak more clearly. "Quite the opposite. Your sentiments are dearly welcomed."

She tasted the salt of uncontrollable tears on her lips when she stuttered in a husky rasp, "As anyone who has e-even a pa-passing acquaintance with me will tell you, I've never given a f-f-fig for being fashionable, and I have been yours from the moment you t-t-tipped your ha-hat to me at Tatter-sa-salls." She hiccupped emotional sobs as more tears flooded her cheeks. "Oh, M-Miles … I've been s-so very afraid you c-could ne-never love me." Try as she might, Eleanor could not temper her highly wrought emotions.

Her beloved gazed down at her, his eyes full of kindness. "Such an unnecessary fear, dearest, for I find you eminently lovable." His knuckles and then his thumb caught the fat tears that welled from her eyes. "I never spoke because I thought to spare you the burden of my unwanted sentiments."

Beaming a wobbly smile at him, she struggled ferociously to restrain her graceless, noisy hitches of breath and slow the dribble of tears down her face, but it was a fruitless venture. Whether it was the crushing disappointment of pulling her certain winner from the Derby or the unmitigated joy of hearing words of love spoken to her that she'd never thought to hear—or perhaps some combination of the two—emotion thoroughly overset Eleanor, and her body trembled with the violence of it. At the moment when she so desperately longed to be at her most appealing, she stood in front of the man she loved so very dearly and shuddered and hiccupped and laughed and leaked like some demented watering pot. With a wordless shrug of her shoulders, she gazed at her beloved and rolled her eyes, sharing her chagrin at her inability to compose herself.

Miles regarded her tenderly, reached into his coat and offered her his handkerchief.

With a watery laugh, she took his offering, swiped vigorously at the tears she couldn't seem to check and then blew her nose. "I have never mastered the knack of crying daintily. I must owe you at least a dozen of these by now." She grinned at him through blurred vision. "I love you so very, very much," she said, through a mix of half-checked sobs and laughter. "I must, for you are the only male of my acquaintance who regularly reduces me to ungoverned tears. Not even my father has such authority over my heart."

The next she knew, strong arms crushed her to Miles' hard chest, his firm hand cupped her chin and tilted her face upward, and his mouth descended on hers in a demonstration of his love that swept her from her present surroundings into the oblivion of physical desire that he'd schooled her in so well. Her bare hands clutched at the lapels of his tailored coat and clung for life as Miles rained kisses on her mouth, her face, and began to work his way down the long column of her bare neck accompanied by her whispered encouragement. His hat became dislodged and fell into the straw but neither of them moved to recover it.

A loud *harrumph* brought both of them back to a sense of time and place. They each gasped for breath as if they had been the runners on the race course. One glance over Miles' shoulder revealed Jemmy standing at the open stall door holding standing bandages and a lidded pottery crock while staring at the ground as if he wished it would swallow him up.

Miles put her away from him gently, straightened the lapels of his frock coat where she'd pulled them awry, returned an errant lock of her hair to behind her ear, resituated her hat and did up several buttons at the bodice of her day dress that had mysteriously come unfastened.

With a diffident smile, she straightened and smoothed his cravat.

"Lord Miles, my lady, pardon me, but Mr. Fedder directed me to poultice and wrap my girl's legs. He'll skin me raw if it ain't done immediate and proper like."

"Of course. If you'd give us a private moment?"

"Yes, sir. Sorry, my lord."

Miles bent and retrieved his hat and brushed the straw from it before snugging it on his head. He gazed at her with such open warmth that Eleanor wondered at her blindness for not having seen for herself how he felt.

He held his arms out. "Come here, dearest love."

She went to him immediately, and he enveloped her in a hug. Eleanor lay her head on his shoulder and snuggled into him. Only one issue stood in the way of her abandonment to total joy. "What about Lord Edmund, Miles? I am very afraid for him. I do hope your brother will return unscathed with your Mr. Allen and Mr. Morgan."

"I share your concern, dearest, but we will know something within the next hour or so. Ned is a competent marksman and not bad with his fists. Unless outnumbered again, he is fully capable of defending himself." Miles' chest rose and fell as he took a deep breath. "One can only hope the villains are too busy counting the money they won today to guard their captives."

"I want to help. What can I do?"

"Eleanor," he growled. He pushed her away just enough to look her in the eyes. "By God, you have done enough. The thought of you in harm's way is intolerable." His manner softened, and he pulled her to him again. "I would dearly love a respite from my thoughts for the next hour or so. I believe you had a small dinner planned in the Rutledge box with Lady Florence, Baron Stanton, and Lady Mary. Should we go find them? They might be just the diversion I need."

"Poor Florence. I quite abandoned her." Eleanor tightened her arms around her husband and nodded. "Yes, let's find our guests. Besides, we shouldn't embarrass Jemmy any further."

Miles' chest vibrated with rueful laughter. "So far, we have scandalized the downstairs footmen in the library, the upstairs maids, your father and mother and now young Jemmy. Suggestions for who should be next?"

"Father and Mother? Whenever did we scandalize them?"

Miles simply chuckled. She never did get him to tell her.

"The Eleanor that left this box in search of her husband is not the same Eleanor who returned. Whatever happened to you when you left, I wish it would happen to me, for despite the disappointment of an injury to your filly and having to scratch her from the race, I have never seen a person in such a state of elevated bliss as you." Lady Florence gave a soft snort. "Considering the adoring looks you and Lord Miles have been exchanging for the past hour, I very much suspect I know." Lady Florence delicately sipped her champagne punch while examining the cold buffet in front of her. "Wherever did you find pineapple at this time of year?"

Only listening with half an ear, Eleanor tore her eyes away from where her husband stood conversing with Baron Stanton and his wife and turned her attention to her dearest friend. Lady Florence immediately ceased her inspection of the pineapple slices.

"Indeed, I am not the same Eleanor. So filled am I with joy and lightness of spirit, I feel like one of those colossal observation balloons you see at ascensions. If I start to float away, please grab me, else I drift into the clouds." Eleanor put fingers to her lips and shook her head. "I can hardly credit it, Florence. Miles declared his love for me."

"Finally! Were we not in such a public venue, I would cheer and dance a jig. I am so very glad for you, dearest. No one deserves happiness more than you." Florence's tone of voice changed, and she chided Eleanor with a slight frown. "Since the two of you arrived in London, there were moments when you gazed upon Lord Miles with such hopeless yearning it has been all I could do not to seize your shoulders, shake you and demand you recognize what was before your very nose. The man adores you."

Eleanor became thoughtful. "I have been blind, haven't I? When last at Fairwood, the Dowager Duchess asserted with confidence that Miles loved me, and I wanted it to be true so fiercely I was afraid to believe her. I have steadfastly refused to examine our dealings together lest they prove the Dowager Duchess' assertion false." Bemusement colored her expression. "Upon further reflection, Miles has ever treated me with the most tender consideration and has regularly put his own purposes at disadvantage to forward my interests." A besotted smile grew as her thoughts once more dwelt on her husband. *Husband. Was there ever such a wonderful word as that?* Never taking her gaze from the source of her enthrallment, she murmured, "Florence…I do not deserve him."

Florence made a rude noise and rolled her eyes. "Such saccharine drivel is hard to endure. I had always held you to be such a practical woman." Florence stabbed a piece of pineapple as if it offended her and flopped it onto her plate. "I pray the good Lord spare me from the affliction of love if it turns a sensible woman such as you into a beetle-headed goose." Florence turned an admonishing glare on

Eleanor. "He is the lucky one. In your person, he is getting a jewel beyond price and don't you forget it."

She sniffed and pulled herself erect, directing an unwavering glare at Eleanor, but then her ire collapsed. "Please, dearest... pay no attention to my graceless comments. Love has never left its calling card at my door, and I am beset by the green-eyed monster of envy. Just once in my life, I should like to be so adored as you, though when I consider those gentlemen whose adoration I should welcome... well, it is quite disheartening for there are none." She cleared her throat awkwardly and continued in brisk tones. "Now, tell me. *Where* does one get pineapple in June?"

Eleanor opened her mouth to reply to Lady Florence but gave a glad cry when, with a determined step, Ned walked into the owner's box accompanied by two men dressed in serviceable but plain clothing.

She flew to him and pulled him aside, examining him frantically from head to toe.

"I am quite in one piece, Elle. Cease and desist with your fondling of my person or I shall be in more physical danger from my brother than ever I was from those thugs."

She growled at him but did stop running her hands over his extremities and patting his body. "You have caused me a great deal of worry, you wretched boy. I am quite put out with you." She crossed her arms over her breasts and scowled at him.

Ned gave her a smile so charming that she found it all but impossible to maintain her glare. "I'm sorry to have worried you, Elle, but as you can see, it all came right."

Ned turned his head and directed a look so intent, so charged with emotion, that Eleanor also turned to discover the recipient of such a potent gaze. From across the owner's box, Miles had paused in his conversation with Baron Stanton and the two brothers exchanged speaking looks. Eleanor watched their silent communication with fascination, her attention shifting back and forth from Ned to Miles, back to Ned, then to Miles and so on. Miles raised his eyebrows, asking a silent question. Ned smiled faintly and jerked his head to indicate the two men who'd entered with him. A smile tugged at one side of Mile's mouth and with an almost imperceptible bow, he saluted Ned with his flute of champagne before turning back to Baron Stanton. It had all happened in no more than the shake of a lamb's tail, but Eleanor knew what she had seen. Lord Edmund had officially come of age.

"Lady Miles, may I present to you Mr. Allen and Mr. Montgomery of the Fairwood Stud." Ned opened his arm to indicate the two gentlemen standing ill-at-ease behind him. Mr. Allen, Mr. Montgomery, your master's wife, and our hostess, Lady Miles Everleigh." Both men bowed and acknowledged the introduction then stood with their hats in their hands and tried to look as if they were not gawking at the elegant interior of the Rutledge box and the sumptuous food and drink to be had.

Eleanor smiled. "Gentlemen, I am delighted to have you here. Have you seen the cold buffet? We have a number of delicacies on offer. Come." Eleanor placed her hand on Mr. Allen's forearm. "You and Mr. Montgomery must try the iced pineapple. It is a particular favorite of mine and quite difficult to acquire."

The Tuesday following Ned's safe return found Eleanor placing a gloved hand on the crown of her hat to prevent the wind from taking it as she and Lady Florence waited on a little-known street in a lesser-traveled part of London's city center. They stood in front of an unprepossessing little shop whose grimy bay window bore an arc of gold letters spelling *Chesterton's Rare Books, Coloured Plates & Odd Curiosities* as the summer wind buffeted them and whipped their skirts.

"Florence, please don't take offense when I tell you that I'm not entirely certain Lord Miles meant for you to accompany me today. He said he had something of a particular and private nature to share with me."

Eleanor's groom stood perhaps fifteen feet away, and Lady Florence's groom and carriage waited a little further down the street.

Lady Florence slanted a playful gaze at Eleanor accompanied by an arch smile. "I won't intrude on your privacy. You won't even know I am there, but as soon as you told me you were to meet at Chesterton's, you could not have prevented me from coming."

"I can't imagine why. It's just a musty old bookstore and not even in a very tonnish part of town." Eleanor frowned. "I dislike standing on the street. Should we wait inside?"

Lady Florence gave Eleanor another one of "those" glances before Eleanor beckoned to her groom who escorted the ladies into the shop and took up a post by the front door.

At the tinkle of the bell above the entry, the proprietor, a small, rotund gentleman with a florid complexion and an appalling lack of pride in his personal dress—as evidenced by a waist coat bespattered with what had to have been the gentleman's latest meal—entered through a curtain from the back of the shop.

"Ladies, how may I be of service?"

"I'm not exactly certain, sir," Eleanor said with her normal reserve. "My friend and I are meeting my husband, Lord Miles Everleigh, here shortly." She looked at the shop clock on the wall behind several long glass display cases. "It is a quarter-past two. He is to meet us at half-past. We are a bit early."

"Lord Miles Everleigh, you say? Ah yes, I remember speaking with your husband just a day ago. A gentleman of discriminating taste," the proprietor remarked. "He indicated an interest in several of my more, ah… out of the ordinary and exotic…publications and had them put back for your perusal. I'll just go get them prepared for your viewing." He bobbed a bow and disappeared through the same curtain from which he had appeared.

Lady Florence began to peer into the glass cases that lined one wall. When she chuckled, Eleanor joined her and examined the contents of the display to see the source of her friend's amusement.

"Good heavens… is that what it appears to be? Florence…" She blinked in amazement and pointed "…that one has ballocks." Eleanor studied the assortment more closely. "Quite an astonishing variance in sizes. Is that true to life?"

Lady Florence laughed quietly. "I have heard them called dildos or godermiches. I should think a more proper name would be a widow's 'pleasure companion'. Yes, Eleanor, they are what they appear to be, a reproduction of a man's phallic part. Obviously, some are more realistic than others. What is of more interest to me, though, is why did Lord Miles wish to meet you at Chesterton's?

Precisely?" She smiled and batted her eyes at Eleanor. "This shop is well known for providing risqué literature and indecorous objects for people of an adventurous propensity.

Eleanor felt the rise of heat into her cheeks and squirmed. "Erm…I believe I said something one evening about wanting instructional literature? Lord Miles indicated he would obtain some for me." Her voice rose at the end of the sentence. She cleared her throat and waited for Florence to respond.

Her friend's face was alight with mischief. "Really? Ah, to have been a mouse in the corner."

Eleanor covered her face with her hand. "I detest being ignorant, always being… surprised…always needing explanations."

"Yes, I can see where that would not sit well with you. There is nothing wrong with being ignorant because you are innocent, dearest. It is a quality attractive to most men. I shouldn't be in such a rush to cure it."

Eleanor held her friend's eyes steadily. "You will think me a complete goose, but I want to be perfect for him."

"I don't think it silly at all. You'd be surprised at how well I understand." Florence stared sightlessly at the far wall, a wistful smile tipping her lips. "But, some of the greatest fun to be had on earth is in remedying one's inexperience with the right partner…" she shook herself and returned her attention to Eleanor "…and as you are married to an extraordinarily handsome and virile man who happens to adore you, were I you, I should look to curing my ignorance with *him* rather than some dry book." Florence's serious gaze held Eleanor's for some moments before she looked away.

As Eleanor considered the heartfelt advice of her friend, the tinkle of the bell above the entry door caused her to turn. Her beloved had entered the bookshop. Upon seeing Eleanor, Miles' face lit with a smile… and then after only a glimmer of pause—which Eleanor suspected no one other than she would detect—he smiled pleasantly at her companion.

"Lady Florence," he acknowledged with an elegant bow.

"I know I am *de trop*, Lord Miles. You needn't be so polite," she said with a laugh. "I quite forced myself upon Eleanor despite her protestations, but I could not miss an opportunity to see Chesterton's again.

The owner appeared through the curtain. "Ah! Lord Miles, you have arrived. I thought I heard the bell. Good. Good. All is in readiness in our private viewing room. Whenever you are ready, my lord."

Miles tipped his hat at the proprietor. "Indeed, yes. Lady Miles, Lady Florence, after you."

Lady Florence stepped forward and followed the proprietor through the red damask curtains, but Eleanor hung back. Slipping her arm through Miles', she leaned forward so that she could whisper. "Miles, have you brought me here to examine books about debauching?"

"I have."

Eleanor pursed her mouth. "Would you be disappointed if, after all, I decided I did not want to see such literature?"

Miles straightened and gazed at her, a question on his face. "Not disappointed, no, but curious as to what brought about your change of heart? Is it the presence of Lady Florence?"

She gazed into his grey eyes and with a faint smile on her mouth, murmured as she steered them toward the door, "Not her presence as much as something she said. I still wish to be skilled at debauching, but I have decided I would rather you teach me—time spent in the saddle as it were—and I do so enjoy your lessons. I'm certain you will be more entertaining than the dry pages of a book, even if it does have illustrations. Would you mind, terribly, being my tutor?"

His eyes crinkled in a smile and he drawled, "I will be delighted to be your instructor, Lady Miles." He gazed at her thoughtfully, then asked her in a level, matter-of-fact voice—the kind one would use if inquiring whether a guest took one or two lumps of sugar in their tea, "Would you like to begin your lessons immediately?"

A thrill of delight bubbled up her spine. She tilted her head and gazed at him considering. "I believe I would."

The bell above the door jingled as he opened it and escorted her out. They stopped briefly to send Lady Florence's groom to her to inform her of their departure, and then Lady Florence was quite forgotten until the hour was exceptionally advanced.

Chapter Twenty-Four

"Father, may I please have a word with you and Mother in private?"

"Certainly, my dear. We always have time for you." The Earl nodded at his nurse. "Will you leave us, please."

"Yes, my lord."

Eleanor waited until the door closed behind the young woman before coming to sit on the bed beside her father. Her mother put down the book she'd been reading and looked on with bright curiosity.

"I have been home from Epsom Downs for going on six weeks and in that time, I have done a vast amount of soul-searching. I think I finally have my thoughts in order and I want to put something before you."

The Earl raised his eyebrows. "Does this have anything to do with your floating about three feet off the ground with an ever-present smile?"

Eleanor hummed with joy and stroked her fingers across the sheer linen fabric of her skirt, suddenly shy. "I never realized what joy could be found in the love of a husband; how it could alter one's priorities; how it could overshadow everything that once felt important."

"I am glad you have found such joy in your marriage. It is what your mother and I have always wished for you."

Eleanor reached for his hand and held it in her lap. "Father, I have always been devoted to Rutledge to the exclusion of all else. This manor, the estates, its horses, have been the center, the driving purpose of my life." She paused and looked away, suddenly reticent to bare her heart to her father, as if speaking aloud of her stunning happiness would tempt fate into snatching it away. She shook off such silly apprehension. "While I still love them dearly, since my marriage, I have found a new center with a husband who is my partner and my friend. I have discovered the thought of returning to my day to day life independent of him holds little appeal." Her mouth twisted in a sad smile. "And above all things, I would detest it should society consider Lord Miles the lackey of his rich, eccentric wife. He has endured enough of those contemptuous insults to his honor already, and I cannot help but worry that a steady meal of such slanderous remarks would poison his feelings toward me." She straightened and regarded her father. "He and I have not spoken of what I am about to ask of you. Miles would never encroach in such a common fashion. Please be assured, I have arrived at my request without influence and quite independent of him." She held her father's gaze steadily until he snorted and patted her hand.

"Continue, Eleanor. You have always known your own mind to the point of obstinacy. I am confident that has not changed. What is it you wish of me?"

"I don't know what is possible with the laws of inheritance, but could it be arranged, somehow, to have

Rutledge pass to Lord Miles? He would make an excellent steward, and I know he would not discourage but rather, welcome and solicit my continued involvement."

Her father and mother exchanged a quick glance, before her father replied, "Do I understand you to say that you wish him to inherit Rutledge?"

"Yes."

"Go to my desk. The top drawer. Bring the papers to me."

Eleanor did as he asked and returned, handing him a sheaf of papers.

He flipped through them until he scanned one and grunted in satisfaction before handing it to Eleanor.

As she read, Eleanor's eyes widened.

Concerning a Petition for Adoption & Exception to the Laws of Inheritance

as submitted by the 10ʰ Earl of Rutledge
on the fourteenth day of March
in the one thousand eight hundred and
fourteenth year of our Lord

Be it known to all men:

It is herewith declared by majority vote of the House of Lords that an exception shall be made to wit:

Lord Miles Wrotham Everleigh shall be designated
the true and rightful heir of Victor Abernathy Russell,
being himself the 10th of his line to hold the title of
The Right Honorable, The Earl of Rutledge
as if he, Lord Miles Wrotham Everleigh,
were the legitimate offspring of such legal union between
Victor Abernathy Russell and Amelia Constance Russell,

though he, Lord Miles Wrotham
Everleigh bears
no consanguinity, nor affinity to
Victor Abernathy Russell or Amelia
Constance Russell.

As such sole heir,
Lord Miles Wrotham Everleigh
is due all titles and properties, real or otherwise
attendant,
as would legally and naturally convey at the
death of
Victor Abernathy Russell, and upon the
passing of
Victor Abernathy Russell,
Lord Miles Wrotham Everleigh shall
accede to the title of
The Right Honorable, The Earl of
Rutledge,
being the 11th of this line.

So say we, this the twenty-eighth day of May in the one thousand, eight hundred and fourteenth year of our Lord.

She hugged the paper to her, her eyes finding her father and mother, for whatever actions her father had taken, if it concerned her, her mother would have been intimately involved. "This is everything I could want." Her incredulous gaze returned to the page, and she read aloud the words that firmly fixed her future with Miles at Rutledge. "I can scarce believe it. It is really going to happen."

A weight she was not even aware she bore suddenly lifted from her shoulders, and she was almost giddy with joy. Her gaze studied the glorious words on the document before her, and she frowned. Her brow wrinkled, and she cocked her head, puzzled, for when she considered the date of her marriage—a marriage of which her parents had no knowledge—the date on the petition by her father seemed...premature. "But, this submission predates..."

Her father eyed her sharply, and her mother sat more erect against her pillows.

No. Eleanor decided on the instant; she did *not* want to examine this discrepancy too closely. She would adhere to the words of the proverb, "No man ought to look a gift horse in the mouth," and silenced her question. "Never mind. Whenever you did this, for whatever reason you decided to take such an action, I thank you. You have made me immensely happy. A woman could not ask for better parents."

Her mother, who'd remained silent during their entire discussion, regarded her with a hesitant smile. "My dearest child, we acted only to secure your future and your happiness."

Notes of apology threaded her voice, and Eleanor wondered what it was her mother thought to apologize for. But, while she wondered, her happiness on this day, at this moment, was impenetrable. Leaning forward, Eleanor kissed her father's cheek. "Does Lord Miles know of this?"

Her mother cleared her throat, but her father glanced at his wife with an almost imperceptible shake of his head and responded, "He has not seen this document, no."

Eleanor again dismissed the thought that there was more left unsaid than said in this interchange, but she would leave them to their secrets. She did not want to know. A heady feeling of anticipation built in her breast. "May I be the first to tell him?"

The old gentleman leaned back into his pillows and closed his eyes. A slight smile lingered on his mouth. "Be off with you, girl. Go find your lord and master and give him your news. Though I caution you, he may not greet such a burden—and Rutledge is a burden—with the enthusiasm with which you embrace it."

Heart brimming with excitement and joy, Eleanor flew out the door, only pausing to close it gently. She trotted down the stairs with unseemly haste and chirped a greeting at Walters who bore a tray of luncheon up the stairs to her father and mother. He paused, and his head followed her as she flew down the remaining steps. She reached the card room where she knew Miles to be engaged with Baron Stanton. Both men stood when she entered the room, and she made haste to Miles, placing a hand in the crook of his elbow. She smiled across the card table at Baron Stanton. "Please forgive me for interrupting your play, but I must speak with my husband on a matter of some import."

"Of course, Lady Miles. Perhaps this interruption will change my luck. As usual, your husband's skill at cards far exceeds mine."

"You are too kind, Baron Stanton."

Meeting all Miles' inquiries with mischievous silence, Eleanor led her mystified husband to their apartments. Vibrating with excitement, she thrust the legal document into his hands. "Read this," and then studied his face diligently for his reaction.

He flicked a glance at her, a frown creasing his brow before his gaze fell to the paper. His eyebrows rose and a look she could not interpret crossed his face. When finished, he rolled the document tightly and tapped it against his muscled thigh, all the while studying her with an inscrutable expression. He said nothing, nor gave any indication words would ever be forthcoming.

It was hardly the reaction she'd expected, and after waiting what she considered an inordinate amount of time, at least thirty seconds, she demanded, "Well? What do you think?"

A hint of caution tinted his slow words. "That depends entirely upon how you feel about it."

She beamed. "I could not be happier."

His eyes warmed, and he pulled her into his arms. "Then you don't mind that I will become the Eleventh Earl of Rutledge…that the governance of this vast estate will not come to you? You don't fear I will become autocratic, dictatorial, and render your life one of suppression and misery?"

She shook her head. "I would never have inherited. My previous hope was to keep Rutledge intact during my lifetime, and that was chancy, at best. Now, my soul can truly be at ease for I will never have to leave my beloved home, and I cannot think of a man more fitting to be the master of Rutledge than the master of my heart."

"And the other?"

Her face softened with love. "I have every confidence you will remain the man you have repeatedly demonstrated you are." She grinned. "I will revel in my unwomanly independence and behave with scandalous freedom secure in the knowledge I have your loving support."

The paper fell to the floor, and with an inarticulate sound, he cupped her head in his hands and kissed her. Taking a deep breath, he drew back a hand's width. "Dearest, I have something I wish to give you. This seems as propitious a time as any."

She wrinkled her forehead in question as he dropped his hands.

"Stand here and don't move." He crossed the room to an escritoire. From one of the drawers, he removed something from a small, black box. He turned and approached her, the object concealed in his closed hand.

She watched with puzzlement as he dropped to one knee before her.

"Lady Eleanor Constance, will you be my future countess? Will you marry me?"

Bemused and baffled, Eleanor murmured with a soft laugh. "I have already married you."

"Too many tender milestones that should mark a woman's life are sorely lacking from yours, but a proposal of marriage will not be one of them. Should our children ever ask, I want you to be able to freely respond that their besotted father proposed to their mother on bended knee and begged for the honor of her hand. Please, my dearest heart, I beg you. Will you marry me?"

Her smile wobbled. "Then, yes...of course, yes." She quite spoiled the solemnity of the occasion by sniffling and dabbing at her eyes with the back of her wrist.

Miles rose to his feet and placed a gold ring with a large central ruby surrounded by sapphires and diamonds on her finger. "My father gave this ring to my mother on the occasion of their marriage."

"Oh, Miles... it is stunning, but I cannot accept your mother's wedding ring. It must hold such cherished memories for her."

"Mother is the one who gave it to me and expressed the desire that I give it to the woman I loved, specifically, that I give it to you. She knew my heart long before I did."

"You have a very wise mother."

"Agreed."

"Almost as wise as my father."

"Hmm." Miles considered her with an unfathomable expression, a faint smile pulling up one corner of his mouth. His enigmatic examination was protracted as if some debate occurred within him and her curiosity stirred.

"A penny for your thoughts?"

He shook his head with a rueful snort then his mouth distracted her with a tender kiss that, in her opinion, was far too brief.

When he pulled back, she made a sound of complaint. "I want a more lengthy kiss..." She sighed. "...but I suppose we must get back to our guests. Lady Florence and Lady Stanton will tease that I've abandoned them again."

With a quiet chuckle, Miles continued to undo the small buttons at the top of her bodice. "I want far more from you than simple kisses...and our guests can wait."

His nurse excused herself from the Earl's room with a comment about getting another bottle of his tonic. The door closed with a quiet click as she exited.

From a freshly plumped pillow, the Countess of Rutledge gazed with jubilation at her earl who lay beside her in his bed. "We've done it, Rutledge. I believe we have secured Eleanor's happiness."

Her beloved opened one eye and peered at her before he grunted and settled more deeply into his covers.

"Do you suppose Lord Miles will ever tell her about our part—our plots and schemes?"

"He said he would not. I judge him a man of his word."

"Good, though I would not put it past Eleanor to winkle it out for herself. She is quite clever that way, a trait inherited from her sire, no doubt." She lay her head back into her pillow and closed her eyes with a happy sigh. Silence fell in the room. Briefly. "Rutledge?"

A delayed grunt sounded from the other bed.

She wiggled upright and peered in the direction of her husband. "I have it in mind to see our first grandchild into the world. It would cast a pall over my happiness were you not at my side for this auspicious event. Will you please try not to die just yet?"

"As much as I like to make you happy, Lady Rutledge, while my spirit is willing, this mortal flesh grows weary and longs for its maker."

"You shouldn't have to wait terribly long," she pleaded softly.

A lengthy silence followed her statement broken by a long-suffering sigh.

"Would you like to share the source of your prognostication with your ignorant spouse?"

"I initiated an enlightening conversation with Conway...you know, Eleanor's personal maid, wherein I asked her some specific, intimate questions regarding Eleanor." Lady Rutledge settled into her pillows with a happy hum. "I doubt even Eleanor realizes, but if all goes well, our first grandchild should arrive sometime next April. I must pen a note to Julia and advise her of our good news. Just seven more months, Rutledge. Oh, and do act surprised when Eleanor tells us."

A prolonged, weary sigh followed her imperative. "As I have ever done, my Countess, I will strive to please you in all things."

"Thank you, Rutledge."

"You are welcome, my love."

The End

Epilogue

The entire house party from Rutledge, Baron Stanton and his wife, Lady Florence Lloyd-Smythe, Lord Edmund and she and Miles, had traveled to Fairwood so that Miles could show the baron his estate. Several days after their arrival, very early on a soft, sun-kissed, late-summer morning—far too early to expect their guests to arise, Eleanor stood next to her husband, their arms crossed on the top rail of the pasture fence and watched the young horses gamboling in the green field beside their mothers. Some of the mares were already heavy with their next foal. She considered the mares with a particular sense of fondness, feeling some kinship with them as she, too, shared their condition. Initially, she'd put her queasy stomach and dragging fatigue down to over-exertion and too much rich food, but lately, she'd begun to suspect another reason altogether. Her last monthly had never arrived—nor the one before that—though she'd not taken note of their absence until recently. She'd been...preoccupied.

"I believe the new foals should start arriving in late March or early April," Miles murmured. "Fairwood stud's first foal crop." He looked at her with a smile. "Such a wealth of unspoiled potential to nurture and develop. I feel overwhelmed with responsibility."

She took a deep breath and gazed at the mares. "Perhaps our son or daughter will be as lucky as you were with Badger and a filly or colt will be foaled on their day of birth." She waited for him to realize the implication of what she'd just said. He remained silent. Straightening, she glanced at Miles and then with a tremulous smile turned to face him.

His face seemed fixed in an incredulous expression of awed delight. "You're… you're… oh by god… I'm… that is, we, will be…ah… parents." Panic erased his delight. "Good lord, I'm too young to be a father. I can't even manage Ned."

Laughter gurgled from her. "Finally, I have found something that displaces your unshakeable composure, my lord." Her voice softened. "Yes. You are to be a father. In April, I think." Using her fingers to count backwards, she sighed. "Yes, I think April." She placed a hand on his forearm. "In my opinion—a biased one I admit—I think you will make the finest of fathers for you are the best of husbands."

He gazed at her as if he had never beheld anything as precious. "My Eleanor. My wife." He caught her under her knees and swept her up into his arms, twirling her and kissing her until they were both dizzy and laughing. Miles allowed her to slide from his arms and held her until it was apparent she could stand on her own. "Have you told *Maman*? She will be over the moon." When she shook her head, he reached for her hand. "We must tell her immediately!" He set off down the carriage way toward the manor house, his strides brisk and long, towing Eleanor in his wake.

Laughing, she protested, "I cannot walk so fast, sir."

He turned and swept her up again. "Of course not, what am I thinking? I will carry you."

More laughter spilled from her. "Miles, put me down. I am breeding…not crippled. It is the dress that hobbles me."

He stopped and looked skyward. "I knew it. I knew it. A father not even five minutes and already I have lost all reason."

She slipped from his arms and they proceeded to the manor at a more sedate pace. They found the Dowager Duchess, fully dressed, in the kitchen discussing menus with Cook.

"*Maman*, will you come for a stroll outside with us? Eleanor has something she wishes to tell you."

Miles' mother eyed him suspiciously. "*Vraiment*? Will I be glad of this something, for it is too early in the morning to unsettle my day with worrisome news."

Miles glanced at Eleanor with a slight smile. "Yes. I believe this 'something' will be welcome."

"*Très bien alors.* Alright, I will stroll."

Once out of the front door and down the steps to the forecourt, the Dowager Duchess took Miles' left arm while Eleanor took his right.

Before they had taken another step, while Eleanor was formulating her thoughts on how exactly to break the big news to the Dowager Duchess, Julia announced, "You wish to tell me you are *enceinte*, *n'est pas*? You are in a 'delicate condition' as the English say."

Miles cleared his throat, and Eleanor shot him a quick grimace of question and then peered around him to regard her mother-in-law with bewilderment.

"And, you are pleased, *mon cher*?" asked Julia.

"Oh, ah, yes. Quite pleased. Ummm…how did you know?"

Julia gave a very gallic shrug. "I am French. We know these things." The Dowager Duchess exhaled with a happy warble, disentangled herself from her son's arm and enveloped Eleanor in a smothering hug. "I am delighted with your news. When will my grandchild enter this world?"

"I think… sometime this spring?" She pushed back gently from her mother-in-law's arms
and made a face. "April… if I count correctly."

"*Bien*, I will come to Rutledge at the beginning of March. It will be good to see your *maman* and the Earl again. You should request your friend, Lady Florence Lloyd Smythe ."

"Wait…again?"

"I heard my name mentioned." Lady Florence paid the porch steps unusual attention as she made her way down to join the trio. "Why are you up at the crack of dawn and what is it you should request of me?" She smiled through a yawn. "I'm all agog…or as agog as one can be at this ungodly time of day. Lord Miles, you are familiar with the hours the civilized world keeps. Cannot you break Eleanor of this loathsome habit of rising at dawn?"

Eleanor snorted. "Well…hardly dawn, Florence. It is coming on half-past eight. The sun has been up for a good two hours. I'm afraid I shall be rising even earlier than ever, though. Children are wont to rouse their parents at all hours with no regard for time of day."

Her friend blinked as she gazed at Eleanor and finally murmured, "Children? You?"

"In April." Eleanor beamed at her friend. "I think."

Florence blinked more, did an about-face and announced as she ascended the steps she had just come down, "I cannot deal with such earth shattering news before I drink some coffee and the hour is more advanced. I will be in the family dining room attempting to awaken my muzzy brain."

The three of them watched as Lady Florence disappeared back through the front door, and then burst into laughter.

"She is not suited to country life, I think," commented the Dowager Duchess.

"No. Not in the slightest," Eleanor said. "It is a testament to our friendship that she visits me at all."

Miles cleared his throat. "Well, I don't know about the two of you, but I, for one, could do with some coffee—or a stiff brandy. Shall we join Lady Florence?" He held out his arms for Eleanor and Julia.

The three of them entered the family dining room to see Lady Florence standing before one of the floor-to-ceiling windows that overlooked the forecourt and carriage drive. She held a cup of coffee to her mouth. Pausing mid-sip, she peered more closely through the window. "Are you expecting visitors, Lord Miles? There are two disreputable and rather dangerous looking military types riding down the center of the carriage way just a bold as brass." She stepped closer to the window and abandoned her coffee to a side table.

All four stood looking out windows at the figures riding up the approach to the manor house, their weary horses moving at a dragging walk.

"Should you remove all the dirt and dress him in clean clothes, the one on the right would be tolerably good looking. I do believe the gentleman on the left is hurt as he looks to come off his horse at any moment." She turned from the window and addressed Miles. "Do you know them, or are they more military strays come looking for work?"

As Miles uttered a "Good lord!" the Dowager Duchess gave a small cry of distress and flew from the room.

Miles turned to an inquisitive Lady Florence and a puzzled Eleanor. "I've only met him one time, but I think the man on the left is Major Leland Abernathy. The gentleman on the right is my half-brother, Lord Duncan."

Dear Reader,

I hope you enjoyed the sweet love story of Eleanor and Miles. If so, will you please leave a review with Amazon, Goodreads, or wherever you purchase your books? It does not have to be extensive, one or two lines will be fine.

Authors depend on reviews to spread the word and reviews do so much to help other readers, like you, find books that they can enjoy.

With many thanks,

Patricia

An Author's Quandary

The Usage of Words, Issues of Inheritance
&
Forms of Address

When setting out to write a historical novel, a number of challenges confronted me above and beyond simply getting the clothing and carriages correct. My first stumbling block was the very words themselves. Many of the words that I normally would use; chemise, bun (hair), bosoms, wink, climax, orgasm, gorgeous, foreplay, fiancée, pub, sex—and on and on, simply were not in use in 1814 or had a different definition entirely from the meaning we ascribe to them in present times. For example, "gorgeous" did not mean beautiful or handsome. It meant "extravagant or highly colorful" and was strictly applied to inanimate objects, *never* people. It was rather startling for me to discover that I could not use the word "bosoms" or "climax" because they didn't exist at the time of my story and to use them would be an anachronistic blunder. It was also curious to see words that I consider modern like "to come" (to indicate orgasm or ejaculation) or "dildo" (the type without batteries!) are, in fact, very old and have been in use for centuries. ("Come" originating around 1659 and "dildo" in 1593.)

So! Hi-ho, hi-ho, to the Oxford Dictionary I go. It was fascinating to see the origins of words and phrases but frustrating as I had to eliminate half of my vocabulary. Nevertheless, I have tried to the best of my ability to stay with the appropriate dress, social morays, and language of the time—or at least keep the anachronistic blunders to within the same decade. For example, indoor plumbing wasn't introduced to upper-income houses until the late 1800s; therefore, the wealthy estate house of Rutledge is still using chamber pots and having hot water brought up by maids. This story also adheres to the prevailing belief that "natural order" as established by the Creator, decrees the male has authority over the female in all things. Unapologetic sexism was the order of the day in the 1800s. A striking example of codified misogyny can be found in the fact that a husband could not be accused of marital rape as once a woman married, she ipso facto granted a blanket acceptance of all sexual intimacy between she and her husband.

And now I come to the second issue that tripped me up—forms of address for aristocrats and how aristocrats of the time addressed each other. The Regency society of 1814 was *very* formal. Unless you grew up with someone—knew them from childhood—you did not use a person's first name. *Ever*. It was considered immensely rude and lacking in respect. Being raised a southern belle, I can vouch for the fact that I was taught never to address another person who was older than me by their first name. *Ever*. It simply isn't "done" in better society. I'm still taken aback when total strangers (usually service personnel trying to be friendly) address me by my first name. The well-bred men and women of 1814 took it a degree further—even husbands and wives did not usually refer to each other by their first names.

In *A Husband For Hire*, Eleanor's father is properly announced as, The Right Honourable The Earl of Rutledge or simply, the Earl of Rutledge, and Eleanor's mother is The Right Honourable The Countess of Rutledge or Countess Rutledge. However, Rutledge is a *place* name and not a surname, therefore it is entirely appropriate for the Earl's wife to call him "Rutledge." Eleanor's family surname is Russell, therefore, Eleanor's name, as a single woman and daughter to an earl, is Lady Eleanor Constance Russell. Quite confusing. Wherever possible, I defaulted to "Madam" or "my lady".

Not using a person's first name presented a problem for me as my heroine's married name is properly Lady Miles Everleigh and she would be referred to as Lady Miles. Rather confusing to a modern reader when the heroine goes from Lady Eleanor Russell to Lady Miles Everleigh and her father is the Earl of Rutledge and her mother the Countess of Rutledge with nary a Russell in sight!

So…I took some liberties and had Miles occasionally refer to Eleanor by her first name and with the title that she was born with as the daughter of an earl. He calls her Lady Eleanor or Lady Miles and *very* rarely in moments of great intimacy, or when specifically requested, Eleanor. Upon occasion, a "my lady" or a "madam" will slip in. As the story progresses, you will see an occasional "dear" or "dearest." For people at the time, this would be an indication of *great* love or affection and an intimate acquaintance with the person addressed. For example, Miles first uses the word "dearest" to address his mother whom he loves dearly.

Another problem was the issue of the British rules of inheritance during the Regency period, and here I fudged rather significantly. In point of fact, Eleanor, as either a single or married woman, would never have inherited the entailed properties of Rutledge. She stood a much better *chance* of her *husband* being awarded the entailed properties because, lacking a male heir, her father, the Earl of Rutledge, could petition for a waiver or "Act of Lords" by "adopting" Eleanor's husband as his legal male heir (normal custom banned adopted children from inheriting) whereupon Miles would inherit the entailed properties *and* the title. As his wife, Eleanor would be totally dependent upon his administration of the estate. Barring a waiver such as that, Eleanor could petition for an exception to allow her firstborn son to inherit Rutledge. (Indeed, this is what she *thought* Elsington was filing on her behalf. He wasn't.) Her husband, Miles, would be trustee of the property and guardian of her child until such time as her firstborn son came of age. In this case, her son would not inherit the title of Earl unless it was conveyed by the Crown in a separate action.

Eleanor could inherit the personal or *freehold* properties of her father and administer them in her own name unless her father willed them to someone else—which he did.

Phew. I think I got that right.

There you have it, gentle reader. You can see some of the issues that writing historical romance brings with it, above and beyond getting the clothing and colloquialisms correct. To the extent that I thought the modern reader will understand, I have tried to stay true to the proper forms of address as existed in 1814. In some places, I have strayed from true accuracy and conformed to the modern norms so as not to confuse my reader.

I hope you enjoyed the sweet love story that is *A Husband For Hire*. I've made it as historically accurate as I knew how, but I'm sure I slipped up many times, sometimes intentionally, sometimes through ignorance. Book Two, *The Destitute Duke* (working title and subject to change) will follow with the story of Lord Duncan Everleigh and Lady Florence Lloyd-Smyth. There will also be a love interest for the Dowager Duchess of Chelsony— much to the consternation of the Everleigh men. Ned will also get his own story when the Everleighs have traveled some years into the future, and he has matured.

Warm regards,

Patricia A. Knight

In Praise of Older Women:

When Prinny's agent, Ludlow, meets with Miles and Eleanor, he asks Miles, if not for Eleanor's money, what could possibly compel a gentleman to marry a spinster so advanced in years. Miles returns that men marry older women for many excellent reasons and refers the agent to Benjamin Franklin's letter to a young friend wherein he extolled the virtues of taking a mature mistress. Here is the letter in its entirety as Benjamin Franklin wrote it in 1745.

Benjamin Franklin's

Letter To A Friend

June 25, 1745

My dear Friend,

I know of no Medicine fit to diminish the violent natural Inclinations you mention; and if I did, I think I should not communicate it to you. Marriage is the proper Remedy. It is the most natural State of Man, and therefore the State in which you are most likely to find solid

Happiness. Your Reasons against entering into it at present, appear to me not well-founded. The circumstantial Advantages you have in View by postponing it, are not only uncertain, but they are small in comparison with that of the Thing itself, the being *married and settled.* It is the Man and Woman united that make the compleat human Being. Separate, she wants his Force of Body and Strength of Reason; he, her Softness, Sensibility and acute Discernment. Together they are more likely to succeed in the World. A single Man has not nearly the Value he would have in that State of Union. He is an incomplete Animal. He resembles the odd Half of a Pair of Scissars. If you get a prudent healthy Wife, your Industry in your Profession, with her good Economy, will be a Fortune sufficient.

But if you will not take this Counsel, and persist in thinking a Commerce with the Sex inevitable, then I repeat my former Advice, that in all your Amours you should *prefer old Women to young ones.* You call this a Paradox, and demand my Reasons. They are these:

1. Because as they have more Knowledge of the World and their Minds are better stor'd with Observations, their Conversation is more improving and more lastingly agreable.

2. Because when Women cease to be handsome, they study to be good. To maintain their Influence over Men, they supply the Diminution of Beauty by an Augmentation of Utility. They learn to do a 1000 Services small and great, and are the most tender and useful of all Friends when you are sick. Thus they continue amiable. And hence there is hardly such a thing to be found as an old Woman who is not a good Woman.

3. Because there is no hazard of Children, which irregularly produc'd may be attended with much Inconvenience.

4. Because thro' more Experience, they are more prudent and discreet in conducting an Intrigue to prevent Suspicion. The Commerce with them is therefore safer with regard to your Reputation. And with regard to theirs, if the Affair should happen to be known, considerate People might be rather inclin'd to excuse an old Woman who would kindly take care of a young Man, form his Manners by her good Counsels, and prevent his ruining his Health and Fortune among mercenary Prostitutes.

5. Because in every Animal that walks upright, the Deficiency of the Fluids that fill the Muscles appears first in the highest Part: The Face first grows lank and wrinkled; then the Neck; then the Breast and Arms; the lower Parts continuing to the last as plump as ever: So that covering all above with a Basket, and regarding only what is below the Girdle, it is impossible of two Women to know an old from a young one. And as in the dark all Cats are grey, the Pleasure of corporal Enjoyment with an old Woman is at least equal, and frequently superior, every Knack being by Practice capable of Improvement.

6. Because the Sin is less. The debauching a Virgin may be her Ruin, and make her for Life unhappy.

7. Because the Compunction is less. The having made a young Girl *miserable* may give you frequent bitter Reflections; none of which can attend the making an old Woman *happy.*

8thly and Lastly They are *so grateful!!*

Thus much for my Paradox. But still I advise you to marry directly; being sincerely Your affectionate Friend.

For the Word Nerd & Others baffled by Regency terms:

English

"The problem with defending the purity of the English language is that English is about as pure as a cribhouse whore. We don't just borrow words; on occasion, English has pursued other languages down alleyways to beat them unconscious and rifle their pockets for new vocabulary."
James D. Nicoll

NOTE: The dates refer to when the word was first noticed in common usage, either spoken or written.

Ape leader
In the bible, a virgin who dies without marrying and producing children is sentenced to lead apes in hell. Therefore, a spinster in the Regency period was referred to in rather a scathing fashion as an "ape-leader," a reminder that a woman's worth was directly in proportion to her ability to bear.

Bite the dust
In ancient Greek, this was a favorite cliché of Homer. The phrases "bite the ground", "bite the sand", and/or "bite the dust" have been used in almost every English translation of the *Iliad* since 1697. "Lick the dust" is in the Bible.

Blink
Amazingly, this didn't mean "briefly close the eyes" until 1858. (To blink away tears is first recorded in 1905.) In Shakespeare's time the word meant "twinkle", and the original sense seems to

be the same word as "blench", to flinch or turn away. Cf. "see who blinks first" to describe a tense confrontation.

Blonde lace

Originally (about 1745) this extremely expensive delicate French lace (*dentelle blonde*) was indeed blonde in color, being made from unbleached silk. By 1800 the silk threads were almost always black or white, and the term was used for any fine silk lace woven with tiny hexagonal cells. These days it is usually called Chantilly lace.

PS — Blonde and blond are used almost interchangeably these days, particularly in the US, but technically

Bloody

All too many historical novelists seem to think this is a mild expletive — I can't think how many books I have read where Our Hero uses the word in front of Ye Gentle Heroine, and several where YGH says it herself when provoked. From about 1750 through the early 20th century this was *not* mild in Britain; it was a filthy obscenity, and a person with any sort of manners would no more have said "bloody" in mixed company than he or she would have said "fucking". As late as 1913, Shaw caused a minor riot when he had the semi-transformed Eliza Doolittle say "Walk! Not bloody likely!" in *Pygmalion*. Amusingly, when the play was made into the movie *My Fair Lady* fifty years later, the word had lost all its shock value, and Alan Jay Lerner had Eliza shout "Move your bloomin' arse!" to a horse at Ascot instead.

Bosoms (plural)

Not used as a euphemism for "breasts" ("Stop staring at my bosoms!" she said.) until 1959.

Bun

1894 as a bundle of hair at the nape of the neck. The older term was "chignon", which *does* mean "nape" in French. (The original meaning of "bun" seems to have been "rounded mass", leading to the bakery sense, the tail of the bunny rabbit, bunch, etc., but not bundle, which is a "bind" word.)

Bust

1819 as a euphemism for a woman's breasts. The sense of a sculpture consisting of head, shoulders, and chest is over a hundred years older in English. Bustline was not recorded until 1939, and busty until 1944.

Captain Sharp

A cheating bully, or one in a set of gamblers, whose office it to bully any pigeon, who, suspecting roguery, refuses to pay what he has lost.

Che sera sera

1558, in Marlowe's *Faustus*. (That version is Italian; the 1950's popular song changed it to French *Que sera sera*. Either way, it's "What will be will be".

Chemise

An old word for a shirt or smock. The current sense of "undergarment" dates from about 1840; it was a euphemism for the suddenly-vulgar "shift".

Cent per centers

Lenders who took advantage of their clients by lending at uxorious rates.

Climax

1918 as a noun meaning an orgasm. Not until 1975 as a verb "to achieve orgasm".

Come

In the sense "achieve sexual orgasm" or "ejaculate", this looks like modern vulgar slang, but it was first used with that meaning about 1650.

Corinthian

Not used in the sense of an elegant man about town until 1819. Corinthians replaced "dandies" and were in turn replaced by "swells". The earlier definition, to quote the *Dictionary of the Vulgar Tongue*, was "a frequenter of brothels; also an impudent brazen-faced fellow". All this goes back to the ancient reputation of Corinth for wealth and licentiousness.

Author's note: When used in Husband For Hire, the definition used is that of the somewhat later understanding of 1819, that of an elegant man about town.

Cudgel

A short, thick stick used as a weapon, e.g., a baton or nightstick, a club.

Dashed

1881 as a euphemism for "damned", perhaps from the practice of printing the word as d----d to avoid the censors. The exclamation "Dash it!" is recorded for 1800, though.

Dick

In the 19th century, it meant "riding whip"; the first slang use for "penis" isn't until 1890. (Both the latter sense and its synonym "dork" are probably from "dirk", dagger. Note those /R/s aren't pronounced in propuh British.)

Dildo

Despite the "look and feel" of being a 20th-century implement, it has meant "representation of a phallus" since 1593. The batteries are recent, though.

Disguised

Half-Drunk. Somewhat the worse for the over-consumption of drink. Tipsy

Double chin

1832.

Elope

The first unequivocal use to mean "run away with the intent of being married" is in 1813. Before that, it originally meant for a wife to desert her husband (a legal term), and to abscond or run away in general. Dickens mentions a valet eloping with all the valuables. To lope meant to escape long before it was generalized to simply "run".

Egalitarian

Relating to or believing in the principle that all people are equal and deserve equal rights and opportunities regardless of circumstances of birth. "Laborers deserve the same treatment as Lords."

Escheat

The reversion of property to the state, or (in feudal law) to a lord, on the owner's dying without legal heirs. Since the legal proceedings to transfer such property back to the Crown were necessarily involved and prolonged, a popular wit of the day referred to them as "peregrinations through escheat" or "wandering through the laws of reversion".

Farthing

A division of money. In 1814 the pound was divided into shillings and pennies. The pennies (or pence) were further divided:

2 farthings = 1 halfpenny (or "ha'penny")
2 halfpence = 1 penny
3 pence   = 1 thruppence
6 pence   = 1 sixpence (a "tanner")
12 pence   = 1 shilling (a "bob")
2 shillings = 1 florin (a "two bob bit")
2 shillings and a sixpence = 1 half crown
5 shillings = 1 crown
20 shillings = 1 pound

Fiancée

1853. The masculine fiancé appeared in 1864.

Foreplay

Although the practice itself might be of greater antiquity, the word was invented in 1929. It replaced "forepleasure", coined by Freud (*vorlust*) in 1910.

Fountain pen

1710 in English; even earlier in French.

Gorgeous

It now is a synonym of beautiful, but until the 20th century, the only meaning was showy or extremely colorful, and it was only used to describe inanimate objects — usually clothing but occasionally other showy things like a gorgeous sunset or carriage. It was never applied to people.

Jiffy

1785.

Kerfuffle

This looks like relatively modern slang for an agitated disturbance, but as kafuffle or curfuffle it goes back to 1583. The simple fuffle, to disorder, is even earlier.

Lingerie

1835 as "linen garment" in general; 1850 as women's underclothing.

Math/maths

Math is American and maths British as short forms of "mathematics" as a course of study. The former term was first recorded in 1847 as the explicit abbreviation "math."; it didn't lose the period and become a standalone word until almost 1900. The British form is found in 1911 as an abbreviation (maths.), which it lost in 1917. Both are therefore anachronistic for Regency or early Victorian times.

Merry widow

Although the phrase is famous because of Franz Lehár"s international sensation *Die Lustige Witwe* in 1905, it had been a cliché for hundreds of years. The first dictionary citation is in 1567, with the same sense of an amorous widow that it continued to have up to the present. Someone said that Shakespeare should have followed up *The Merry Wives of Windsor* with "The Merry Widows of Windsor". (The sense of a strapless corset with garters attached is from Lana Turner wearing one in the 1952 movie of the operetta.)

Mews

A group of stables, typically with rooms above, built around a yard or along an alley.

Molly house

Below is an 1800s illustration of a "molly."

Establishments for homosexuals in the 18th and 19th centuries. These establishments were typically coffee houses, taverns or simply private rooms where only male homosexuals met, frequently for sex. At the time of this story, homosexuality was a capital offense, i.e., if one were found guilty, you would be tried and hanged. Very little is written or known about "sapphic pleasure houses," or houses for female homosexuals although they certainly did exist. Surprisingly, while there are many records of men being put to death for the crime of buggery, sodomy or "unnatural intercourse", there is no record of any

Woman in England, Scotland, Ireland or Wales, being executed for the crime of lesbianism as it was not considered a crime.

On a side note: A modern swear word one frequently hears (particularly in the UK) is "bugger". It is the equivalent of our "fuck" although having the meaning of anal fucking. I have frequently heard this from the mouths of innocents and wondered if they realized what they were saying.

Mule

As a soft shoe or slipper, often made of velvet, 1565. (Both sexes could originally wear mules around the house, by the way — they were particularly recommended for men suffering from gout.)

Novels [popular]

Even though Jane Austen's novels and Walter Scott's *Waverly* stories of the Scottish border were indeed published during the 1811–1818 period of the Regency, *they were published anonymously* so nobody could curl up in the parlor with Miss Austen's new novel. The authorship of Austen's books was not known until after her death in 1818; *Northanger Abbey* and *Persuasion* were published posthumously, in fact. The earlier books were attributed to "A Lady of Quality". Scott was a well-known high-brow poet who didn't want the literary establishment to know he also wrote popular novels to make lots of money, and although some people suspected, he didn't come clean until 1827. After the first one, by "Anonymous", the rest were by "The Author of *Waverly*". ("Sir Walter Scott" was an anachronism until 1820 when he received a baronetcy for his poetry.)

Orgasm

1936 in the modern sense. Before that, it had to be qualified — sexual or venereal orgasm.

Peregrinations

Technically, peregrinations means a long, meandering journey. Used in Husband for Hire, it refers to the long legal convulsions that accrued when a titled estate reverted to the Crown.

Pub

This clipped version of "public house" for a tavern was recorded as underworld slang about 1860 but wasn't fully acceptable until 1890.

Sex

1929 as a synonym for "sexual intercourse", as in "have sex", "sex before marriage", "great sex", etc. Perhaps unsurprisingly, the first known use of the word in this sense was by D.H. Lawrence. Before that, the only noun usage was in phrases like "the female sex".

So-so

This synonym of "mediocre" or "passable" looks like 20th-century slang, but the first recorded use as an adverb was in 1530 and as an adjective (soso wine) in 1542. (In 1768, Fanny Burney described a disappointing party as "so so-so".)

"Too high in the instep"

A person overly impressed with his own consequence; pompous; arrogant; snobbish; pretentious

Traveling Chariot—also referred to as a "post-chaise" when fitted for more than two people

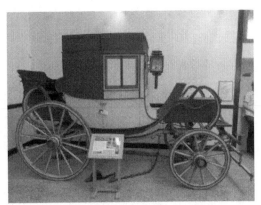

Travelling chariot, National Trust Carriage Museum, Arlington Court

Note the 19th-century illustration of a traveling chariot with passengers. It looks like the gentleman is leaning out the window of the chariot exhorting the postilions (the men in red coats riding the two horses on the left) to whip the team to greater effort. These vehicles were the "ultra-lights," the Ferraris, of their day. Very wealthy people such as Eleanor owned their own vehicle(s) along with teams of horses that were temporarily stabled at various posting inns along the routes. The less wealthy could hire one of these vehicles complete with the horses and postillions though the quality of the horses varied wildly depending upon the wealth of the owner of the posting house. The traveling chariots were commonly painted yellow. Below is a scene painted in 1881 by Samuel Waller (1850-1903) titled "Success". The scene is that of the survivor of a personal duel and his seconds assisting the rather shaken looking young man into his chariot. In the background you can see a figure huddling over another prone on the ground. (One assumes the doctor and loser of the duel?) The painting was presented in 1894 by Sir Henry Tate to the Tate Museum
http://www.tate.org.uk/art/work/NO1551
Note the two postillion riders and the optional elevated seat in the rear for grooms or extra passengers.

On Sex, Sex Toys & Naughty Books

Dildos, Godermiches, Consolateurs or Bijoux Indescets:

Dildos are ancient…one found made of stone dates back 26,000 years! Today they carry a titillating aura of the naughty and are certainly not available in your corner shop. Well, unless you live in New York or San Francisco. My home state, Texas, has an arcane law on the books that makes it illegal to own more than seven. Wow.

However, in the England of the late 1700s and early 1800s, dildos could be bought openly in London shops. The variety most commonly sold were made of leather over wood—sometimes with horse hair or sawdust stuffing—or simply polished wood. They came in a variety of sizes and varying degrees of realism. Some dildos were equipped with testicles and hair! And don't get me started on the hair. Women could buy hairpieces for their pubic areas. Apparently one of the treatments for syphilis made one's hair fall out and unlike today, being hairless "down there" was *not* considered desirable. So "merkins" were developed to disguise the lack. I have to wonder at how the prostitutes or their clients thought they could pull it off without being discovered?

The more exotic dildos were made of polished stone, sometimes precious, like jade or ivory. Here is an example from the late 1800's of a traveling set of dildos that recently sold at auction for £3,600.

"Lot Number: 340. Erotica. An extraordinary and exceptionally rare 'Travel Godermiche' being a pair of wooden phallus contained within a fitted kid leather covered Treen case with strap fleurs-de-lys decoration, one phallus 10 inches and with testicles and the other 11 inches and without testicles. The case, although having a re-lined interior appears to have age commensurate with those of the phallus and both are thought to date from the late 18th century and are probably French."

In addition to dildos, penis extenders and strap-ons (an entire chapter devoted to them in the Kama Sutra), ben-wa balls (originally used by men until women discovered them), anal plugs (though they were marketed as "dilators" and touted to be a cure for hemorrhoids and constipation),

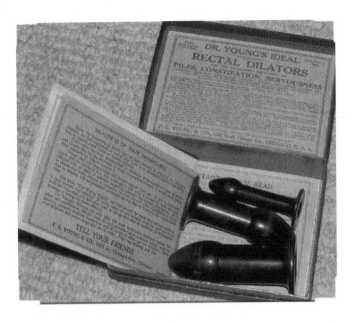

penis rings or cock rings (the Chinese thought them necessary for conception), and sex dolls (French sailors used them when women weren't available, and they were made of oiled cloth) were readily available in the 1800s. The various offerings to be found in the bookstore where Miles met Eleanor and Lady Florence would not have been out of the ordinary. The fact that Miles met her at Chesterton's would be viewed as uncommon.

As Eleanor comments on the night of her deflowering, she owes much to the ladies that came before her. They passed their frank, unabashed enjoyment of sex on to Miles and indirectly, the attitude that "good" women were capable of lust and enjoyed sexual intercourse just as much as men. For his day, he had a remarkably modern attitude about women and their ability to derive pleasure from physical intimacy, but then in 1814 where our story is set, the evangelicals and the moralists had yet to put the stranglehold on British mores they would achieve in 1837 (Queen Victoria) and after. London in 1814 was still under the influence of the much more liberal attitude toward all bodily functions (sex included) that had persisted from the 1700s on. An excellent example of some of the bawdy and outright pornographic prints that could be readily obtained during this period were those of Thomas Rowland:

https://commons.wikimedia.org/wiki/Thomas_Rowlandso n_erotic_engravings

In spite of what most historical romances would lead you to believe, the majority of "good" women from the mid-1800s on, were told nothing of sex—zero, zip, nada— and were not expected to enjoy it. For women, sex as a recreational pastime simply for pleasure was nonexistent. For a "proper" wife, sex was strictly for procreation and performed only in the missionary position. Contraception was considered immoral and in Great Britain was illegal. The condom was used to protect *men* from *disease*—not women from conception. If wives did enjoy conjugal relations, if they sought sexual relations from their husbands, many "proper" British males viewed them with disapproval and suspicion, seeing them as being "unnaturally" lustful, licentious and in need of moral correction while the same men happily kept multiple mistresses and frequented whorehouses to relieve their "natural" urges. No joke. This hypocritical behavior is still in evidence today with society's attitude toward women who have many sex partners versus men who have many sex partners. For the male, multiple lovers provide evidence of his virility and masculine prowess and society awards him a wink and a half-hearted shake of the finger. For a woman, such behavior brands her as promiscuous, a slut, a whore, and society sneers and berates her. Even today, it's permissible for a man to want sex for pleasure's sake because men "need" sex. Not so for women. A woman has to be married—or at least in a "committed" relationship for her desire for sexual gratification to be considered "appropriate". After all, women don't "need" sex. Yeah. Okay, off my soapbox.

The chastity belt was not a medieval invention. It was *Victorian*. Sex was *not* to be enjoyed outside of the marital bed and "good" women only "accommodated" their husbands to obtain children.

> *The first real chastity belts weren't created until the **1800s**, and they weren't for keeping women from straying sexually. The first chastity belts appear to have been crude devices designed to keep children from masturbating.*

> *Paul Joannides Psy.D.; Psychology Today*
> *PAK's emphasis

Eleanor knows only the most basic rudiments of sexual relations between a male and a female; a male puts his "breeding" organ into a female. That she has even this information is because she lives on a breeding farm and has seen a stallion with a mare. She couldn't have given you the anatomical names for the sexual parts of her *own* body and at the ripe age of thirty, had never seen a man with so much as his shirt off. While she has had an unconventional education in many areas, she is as ignorant as any woman of her time when it comes to matters pertaining to sex.

The Earl of Rutledge, the Countess of Rutledge and the Dowager Duchess of Chelsony, indeed all of Miles' patronesses, grew up in the bawdy and licentious Georgian period, a vastly different environment with a vastly different attitude toward women than that of the late Regency. If you are interested in some fascinating sexual romps, read some of the biographies of the more promiscuous men and women (especially the women!) of the Georgian era.

Happy reading!

Patricia

Thank you for reading *A Husband for Hire*. Reviews are a tremendous help for authors. If you enjoyed this book, writing a review would be a huge boon.

There will be at least 3 novels in the Heirs & Spares series, if you'd like to be notified when Patricia has a new release, or to be included in launch party events, join her Regency group at: http://eepurl.com/dcJVCn

About Patricia A. Knight

Patricia A. Knight is the pen name for an eternal romantic who lives in Dallas, Texas surrounded by her horses, dogs and the best man on the face of the earth – oh yeah, and the most enormous bullfrogs you will ever see. Word to the wise: don't swim in the pool after dark.

Patricia loves to hear from her readers and can be reached at:
http://www.patriciaaknight.com.

Other books by Patricia A. Knight:

<u>Verdantia Series</u>

Hers to Command

Hers to Choose

Hers to Cherish

Hers to Claim

Hers to Captivate

<u>Stand Alones</u>
Adam's Christmas Eve

Undertow

We often update our books when grammar errors are found, so please let us know if you've found one at: stephanie@trollriverpub.com

Other Great Books from Troll River Publications